Praise for Minot's Ledge

"In Minot's Ledge, David Allen returns to the world of New England boarding schools, a changing landscape he knows inside and out. In this archly observant, well-written story of a dedicated teacher fighting for his own relevance in a community that combines the sublime and the ridiculous, Allen entertains us with astute observations along with witty anecdotes. Allen's descriptions of teachers navigating a customer-service model of private school teaching while savoring moments of grace in the classroom are spot on."

JULIA BUCCI, Ph.D. English teacher,
DANA HALL SCHOOL

"The world of boarding schools is easy to get wrong. David Allen gets it right. Minot's Ledge is a fun and funny romp set in this world familiar to some of us. The buildings, characters, and zeitgeist ring both familiar and true. The best reason for the continued existence of such institutions is the fact that they provide a setting for David Allen's enjoyable novels. Clearly, I should have listened to my teachers more."

SEAN DRISCOLL, teacher,
SOUTH KENT SCHOOL, alumnus

"Allen captures the creeping ennui and philosophical contradictions of boarding school life. As society and the families that send children to them have morphed so much since such institutions were founded, it is reasonable to ask the question: what exactly are these schools trying to accomplish today?"

CASWELL NILSEN, teacher,
THE STONY BROOK SCHOOL and CHATHAM HALL

"Very relatable, especially the passages about dorm life. Some things at schools have changed, but some haven't – like fire alarms at ridiculous hours, and returning to campus late from a game, usually the night before a quiz. Can't believe I miss such stuff."

MELISSA FITZGERALD
NORTHFIELD MOUNT HERMON, alumna

Also by David Story Allen

Off Tom Nevers

Minot's Ledge

Minot's Ledge

David Story Allen

WEST ESSEX PRESS – INTERLOCHEN, MICHIGAN

MINOT'S LEDGE Copyright © 2023 by David Story Allen
Cover Art Copyright © 2023 by David Story Allen

All rights reserved. Printed in the United States of America. No part of this book may be reproduced or transmitted in any manner whatsoever without written permission from the author except for the inclusion of brief quotations embodied in critical articles or reviews.

This book is a work of fiction. Names, characters, businesses, organizations, places, events and incidents either are the product of the author's imagination or are used fictitiously. Any resemblance to persons, living or dead, events, or locales is entirely coincidental.

For information contact:
West Essex Press
9900 Diamond Park Rd.
Interlochen, Michigan 49643

ISBN 979-8-857-74409-3

First Edition: November 2023

10 9 8 7 6 5 4 3 2 1

Cover photo by Richard Arlington Martin Allen
Author photo by Holly Allen

Dedication

For Baxter,
the disapproving muse.

All this pitting of sex against sex, of quality against quality; all this claiming of superiority and imputing inferiority belong to the private school stage of human existence where there are sides, and it is necessary for one side to beat another side.

Virginia Woolf
A Room of One's Own

Sept 1

GETTING AN ACADEMIC SABBATICAL for a year is a bit like registering for a half marathon, in that the notion seems like great fun until you actually have to do something about it. When I submitted a proposal to dive deeply into southern literature and culture to enhance the school's curriculum, it seemed a reach to think I'd get it. You're eligible for a sabbatical after six years at Griswold, so after my seventh, I applied for one, but didn't hold my breath. Some who'd been at the school longer also wrote proposals, and it wasn't clear to me that the English Department wanted a more in-depth look at the works of Eudora Welty, William Faulkner or Tennessee Williams.

"More on lit about grits, eh?" Earl Blackabby half-chuckled when we discussed my idea. "I suppose if you mention southern gothic, you could get some takers. Kids might think 'gothic' has a tie-in with some video game, or that you'll read graphic novels. Hey, you could try that as a hook."

Earl was tapped to become chair of the English Department when the person who hired him two years earlier retired. There were whispers that our Head of School, Barclay Sears, would find this least experienced teacher in our midst to be quite malleable in terms of embracing his ideas and policies. A month after Earl was hired, nobody could quite recall where he'd taught or been educated, but as the Head made him chair by fiat as opposed to traditional channels, it was clear he had Barclay's support, so was not to be crossed. On a snowy afternoon a year and half earlier in Earl's office, I made my case for the sabbatical.

"The pendulum has swung so far away from American lit that's been part of the canon for decades, it just seems that we need to expose kids to some authors before they're entirely forgotten."

Behind an immaculate desk he didn't appear to have much need for, Earl tilted back, his flannel shirt and dark, tussled mop suggesting undergrad TA more than boarding school department head. His distant gaze betrayed nothing, so I pressed on. "I'm not just trying to make a last stand for dead, white males - there's Zora Neal Hurston, Richard Wright and Carson McCullers...lots of voices that we as a department never get to anymore, and a course on the region could include a look at this whole red state thing."

That got his attention. He agreed to submit it to the committee, and six months later I was mapping a trip down I-95, into the Glades, up through the bayous and the backroads of Flannery O'Connor's and Harper Lee's stomping grounds, and to the building in New Orleans where Tennessee Williams choked to death on a bottle cap. When I returned up north in June, I told myself I'd organize all my notes for a new elective this year, but with a fresh set of sails for the boat and people to catch up with, somehow I didn't get around to it. In August, an email spelled out what I'd been putting off.

To: Ben Minot
From: Fred Talleyrand
Re: Sabbatical Report

Ben -

Welcome back! While we've never met, I've heard great things about you and am looking forward to seeing you back on campus. As Dean of Curriculum, I'm assisting teachers in their framing of content and research to help optimize it for learning purposes. To that end, in addition to your research presentation to the full faculty on the fruits of your sabbatical in November, there's a chronicling exercise people returning from any kind of professional development are being asked to be part of. It involves tracing the arc of your work in the wake of this experience and slotting your reflections under one or more of three headings in an evolving document. The categories are 1) Enhanced Content, 2) Educational Practices and Implementation and 3) Professional Relationships. Ideally your reflections would all come under such headings - EC, EPI or PR - which will help you and us to put all of your research and work in context. Ideally you will make weekly entries into this document so that we can also assess the validity of your undertaking.

We can chat about this more when you arrive on campus - here's to a great year.

Yours -
Fred Talleyrand
Dean for Curriculum

Two of the reasons teaching is fun are the kids and the content. For me, the moments when they truly grasp a concept for the first time or start to develop a thoughtful opinion are like touching the bases on a home run trot. Then there's the content; what other job is there that involves reading great books with other people? One reality of the work that sends me grinding my teeth is when administrators micromanage matters in the classrooms where they no longer toil. Fred Talleyrand was hired the summer before I went south, so we indeed had no history. Why an allegedly accomplished

French teacher with degrees from Princeton and BU would give up working with the language and the free annual trips to Paris to run meetings on curriculum mapping was a mystery to me. I'll withhold judgment on him for now, and be thankful that I had the experience down south that I now need to recount - and that I'm no longer there, as it's hurricane season.

***

I'm not sure where this would fit into one of Fred's headings, which I'll figure out when I'm done with this project, but long after dark tonight I rolled back onto campus. The black lamps atop the school gate posts had been painted recently, and I couldn't decide if this was a good thing or not. Black and glossy says 'well-maintained,' but weathered and worn says *old and venerable,* traits which every New England school hopes people will associate with it. Griswold is still a third tier school, but the granite pillars at the entrance were stoic efforts to hint at a timelessness that would appeal to anyone who bothered to notice them.

Winding up the elm-lined drive close to midnight, I wondered how the school had decompressed from the previous academic year. Either a death during a chapel service or the threat of terrorism emanating from a student's attendance at the school would make for an odyssey that nobody would like to read about in the alumni magazine. Both in the same year, and a collapsed roof on the hockey rink in the middle of winter term made for a year that, while I was glad to miss in some respects, would also have been one to remember.

Late August is like a long, extended sunset for educators. Emails regarding the new school year become more frequent, and mailers from travel firms arrive, suggesting amazing student trips one should organize. Calendars are checked to see whether they'll accommodate one last weekend by the water or at least with no alarm clocks. After a year away, I honestly felt a bit selfish for wishing to extend the failing days of summer, but perhaps it was exactly being out of the game so long that made getting back into it so hard. Late at night I didn't expect to see anyone, but of course there's campus security.

"Benjamin Minot, as I live and breathe!" Charlie, the wizened security officer whose looks always remind me of a lighthouse keeper, recognized my red Volvo with the lobster trap on the ski rack. "Thought you were on that airliner, the one from Indonesia that disappeared."

He rested his hands on his hips, then shined his flashlight my way. "You look good."

"Thanks. Malaysian," I shook his hand.

"Eh?" He shook the offering warmly.

"It was a Malaysian airliner, the one that disappeared." I didn't add that the crash was six years ago in 2014.

"Oh. Fine."

Glad he thought I didn't look like crap after a year away from the cross country course. Per the bathroom scale on the island, I'm carrying ten more pounds than I weighed in college.

"Been gettin' some rays?" He pointed to my sunburn and yellowish buzz cut.

"Nah - just working outside." This was a lie, but certainly a white one.

"Where y' been?" Charlie leaned on the driver's door with his forearms over the window slot.

"Sabbatical. All last year. Back for the fall."

"*Sabbatical,*" Charlie feigned being slighted. "*We* don't get those."

"You also don't get to grade papers that kids don't want to write or get to examine them to uncover their plagiarized content."

"True." Charlie nodded, "So where'd 'y go?"

"South. Way south. Studied some writers from down there. Gonna offer a course on them in the spring."

"Good f' you. Back in your old place? Wallace?"

" 'Less they tore it down last week to make room for the new field house."

"Don't hold your breath on that," Charlie shook his head, "Some problem came up with the major donor. Don't ask me the details."

"Really?" I was a bit surprised but not devastated. Construction during a school year is always disruptive.

"Don't look for any email about a groundbreaking. So, where you coming from now? The south?"

"The Cape. Squeezing the last few minutes of summer before the pre-school meetings, which start in seven hours." Actually, I'd been on Nantucket, but 'the Cape' sounded less interesting, and I did not want to be interesting at this hour. "Probably ought to get some sleep," which he took as a cue and waved me on. Wallace is a weathered-shingle cape with two faculty apartments and a pottery studio. The art teacher lives eight miles away in Boston with her husband and an unruly eight-year old son, so I have the place to myself with no adjoining neighbor. In a serendipitous turn of events, last year's sabbatical replacement for the Japanese teacher was a distant cousin of mine who I first met during a summer in Osaka in 2010. Her background and my recommendation made it happen, and that she stayed at the house while I was away assured that it would be just as I left it, except spotless. I made it a point to avoid campus for the year away, so once inside the darkened rooms, I moved about a bit slower than I might have. Opening windows and turning on lamps, it was all silently familiar: nautical prints, shabby-genteel furniture, a framed poster from the Head of the Charles, the fall rowing regatta in Boston, and the smiling photos of a honeymoon in Paris and hiking trip to Alaska.

Minot's Ledge

As promised, my cousin left some Blue Moon in the fridge, so I poured one with a big head to force the air out of it and slumped into an Adirondack chair outside the front door. From somewhere in the night, a breeze stirred weeping willows in the school quad a bit, but things were otherwise still and quiet. Enough light filtered through the trees to make out the dark shapes of the familiar buildings. In some cases, with the exception of new storm windows and some fresh paint, many looked much as they had fifty or a hundred years earlier. Like many New England boarding schools, Griswold was founded in the 1800s, amidst the mad scramble to do so before the new century in order to confer instant venerability upon each institution that broke ground before 1900. The Georgian brick structures surrounding the campus green are not quite as gothic as some of the church schools that we play in sports, yet there is a constancy about the place; all seems quite perpetual.

An ancient elm's leaves dangled in front of the science building, seemingly spent from being blown about in the daylight. I tried to make sense of the news I'd heard of the school while away. Peter Burnham of the History Department kept me up to speed with life on campus during the year: a dorm caught fire on Parents' Weekend, a distinguished alum died as a result of a visit to school, the roof of the rink collapsed, and a student from Kuwait had left Griswold, yet his father made a generous gift to the school all the same. Any one of those events would make for school news that would grow to apocryphal proportions over time. Peter also suggested that all was not well with the Head of School, at least on the home front. This last matter could make for some interesting faculty receptions, for Mrs. Sears was known to become "overserved" at such affairs. After a few sips of Moon, I realized that I was sitting outside with a beer for no reason other than that I could. I poured the rest into the hydrangea by my door, and went to bed.

Sept 2

THE CAMPUS OF A boarding school on a late summer morning before students arrive is truly a sanguine place. The athletic fields are trimmed and ready for practices, peeling paint is touched up, and on this particular morning, the rising sun caused the dew on the manicured lawns to glisten before it burned it off. Sipping French Roast from a WBUR mug, I mulled my re-entry into the Griswold universe. We were expected in the Bernau Room by nine to hear all the "must-knows" for the new school year. As faculty meetings are a bane of the run-up to the academic year, I got some strong brew in me at home so I could cloister myself in the back and not venture to the continental breakfast table. There, one faces the prospect of warm water with brown food coloring that passes for school coffee. I'm not anti-social, but simply didn't want to answer the same questions thirty times about my year away, nor did I feel obliged to chuckle at prompts such as, "You came back? *Why?*" Nevertheless, a dozen or so colleagues came by my perch to say, "hi," and sprinkled their greetings with comments as they patted my pink-red upper arm. "Don't they have sunblock down south?"

"Looks like they made a *real* redneck out of you." Over someone's shoulder I spotted Peter Burnham. He was nodding at the emphatic points being made by my boss, Earl Blackabby. Shorter than Burnsy's six-foot frame, Earl lives in plaid shirts, although I don't think he owns more than four of them. The meeting was a garden variety *welcome back / here are some changes to know about / this year will be the best ever* update and pep talk. No particular details from it stick in my mind, but I suppose admins have to grab the mantle now and again; show the flag as my cousin in the navy likes to say.

Sept 4

THIS BEING THE DAY before kids arrive, a few of us dedicated coffee fiends and fans of The New York Times were fine-tuning the teachers' lounge, the summer having seen it become a storage space for student artwork unclaimed in June. Burnsy was rummaging through a cabinet for coffee filters. Ralph Brady was tinkering with a chair from Ikea, a grateful parent having sent several for this room last spring, and I was getting the printer to recognize my laptop after being away. Peter wanted to hear about any discussions I'd had last year regarding 'the War of Northern Aggression.' One of only three faculty of color, for some reason, Ralph seems to find us better company than his science department colleagues, or at least he has meals with us more than he does them. This might be because most of them have toddlers and grade school children, and seem incapable of discussing anything else at lunch, or in any other setting.

"Any reason we can't get a Keurig for this room?" Peter was opening coffee cans with various quantities in them.

"Fine with me," I shrugged. "I'm down to one cup a day anyway, but I'll kick in."

"*You?*" Ralph looked up from his assembling project, "Mr. Maxwell House? Since when?"

"Driving around all last year, I didn't find as many good coffee spots down there as I'd hoped. Sorta got out of the habit."

"You mean you couldn't find any Charbucks in the bayou?" Burnsy threw out, using his term for a chain I like but which he thinks burns their brew.

"Yeah," I admitted, "Thelma's Diner in Biloxi was as close as I came."

"How *was* it there?" Ralph looked at me thoughtfully.

" 'Bout what you'd expect. You see the roots of a lot of literature still alive and well. A lot of it is like Pennsylvania without the mountains."

"Pennsyl - v*ania?*" Ralph wrinkled his brow.

"You know," Peter smirked, "Philly in the east, Pittsburgh in the west, Alabama in the middle."

Ralph chuckled, and wondered if the Keystone State was truly a site for a reshoot of "Deliverance."

"Yeah," I nodded, "Pennsyl-tucky is alive and well. Never seen so many confederate flags as when I visited Mercersburg…'til I went to the real confederacy, anyway."

"Really? Pennsylvania?" Ralph was incredulous. "It's in the north, f'crying out loud."

"So is Michigan," sputtered Peter, "and in the 1920s, Detroit had a mayor who was in the Klan, so forget geography. Look at…"

"What the hell is this?" I spotted a memo beside a mouse pad with the header TO FACULTY and STAFF and read the subject line aloud. "No Tiers, No Ties, No Tears. What the…"

Ralph and Peter eyed each other with a mix of dread and juicy anticipation. Finally Burnsy spoke.

"That's the…suggestion, from Fred Talleyrand, assisted by your able department chair slash ass-kissing jellyfish, Earl Blackabby." Peter leaned back onto a butcher block table, and tipped his hand toward Ralph for him to pick it up there. Ralph perched himself on the base of a chair, the only part of the Ikea project he'd managed to assemble so far, and launched into what he offered as a tired explanation.

"That's...the new *theme* this year. When Talleyrand came on board last year, he spent the whole first term schmoozing with kids, acting like their pal, to the point that he actually creeped a few kids out. So at the first faculty meeting after spring break, he announces this new *initiative* for this year, 'No tiers, no ties, no tears.' Scrapping the AP courses, encouraging faculty to adopt a more student-friendly dress code, and suggesting that this would be better for students' mental health: *no tears.*"

I glanced at Peter, thinking he'd start smirking at what must have been some April Fool's joke. One year our Head of School got into the spirit of things and on April 1st sent out an email blast announcing that the Board of Trustees had approved the adoption of Saturday classes starting in two weeks. A few folks who didn't check the calendar or were simply given to panicking by nature, flipped out at breakfast, which was quite entertaining.

"You *are* joking," I pleaded.

Peter shook his head like a mechanic who'd been asked if changing gasoline brands would save a car's water pump.

"We had this guy in for a workshop one morning," Ralph sat up a bit straighter, "Allan someone. Spent two plus hours ranting about how grades in schools were bad for kids. Then some psychologist told us about all the damage we do to kids by slotting them into AP and Honors courses, and giving them and wearing "signals of authority." Ralph made quotation marks with his fingers to indicate what he thought of the notion. "She, the workshop presenter, pulled up pictures of lots of guys in formal dress, and stats about teenage anxiety. One of 'em suggested we let kids call us by our first names. Basically we were told to lighten up."

"Lighten up?" I squinted at him. "From providing the education that their parents are paying for? Kids are *already* on a bunch of drugs to deal with, heck, anxiety, all kinds of stuff, and *then* there's the drugs they buy on their own. We want kids to do well, right? We don't have tough courses to torture them; it's to help them, get them ready for what's next. My AP kids two years ago were great. So now we're told to scrap good classes and how to dress?"

"Not just yet," Peter stood up and resumed his coffee can consolidation. "Kids were admitted here because we *have* APs, so we have to keep them for a few years, but it was *suggested* that male teachers consider a more casual Friday attitude in their dress."

"And this will cut down on tears? I don't recall seeing kids bawling outside my classroom. Were you guys giving kids the lash while I was gone? What *tears,* f'Godsake?"

"C'mon, Ben," Ralph turned back to his chair assembly, "You know that there are kids out there now who freak out when they get an 82 on a test, They..."

"Melt down when papers they spent two hours on earn them a B," Peter tossed his head skyward, "even though it would have earned a C- ten years earlier, but doing that today might send the kid on an Emotional/Medical leave, and require a meeting with the parents. You haven't forgotten the rule about emails home when a kid's average drops below a C, right? You, Benjamin C. Minot, aka Benjamin C Minus."

Ralph tossed his head back and laughed at this moniker from a few years ago when grades in my classes alone were said to have kept a dozen kids off the honor roll. I nodded, but hadn't thought about that for over a year. "Where does this guy Talleyrand get off?"

"He's a Dean of Curriculum," Ralph chuckled, "He *doesn't* get off. He's on the gravy train for the long haul. And I counted yesterday," he continued, "We still have a few more teachers than deans and other administrators, but they're gaining on us."

"But we have Scott. He's Dean of Academics, right?"

"But not *curriculum,*" Peter offered, waving a cautionary finger.

"What's the difference?" I squinted, baffled.

"About $140,000 more out of the operating budget," Ralph tossed out casually. "That's what his salary is supposed to be, anyway." I mulled all this for a bit, then scanned the room. I'm back here, and it's September. Nothing to do or even say about this now. I tapped a few keys on my laptop, and out came some Charlie Parker to help us press on.

Sept 5

AS IF IT WOULD not dare to do otherwise, student arrival day broke clear and calm. Lawns and playing fields were manicured, sawhorses sporting signs that steered families toward "Registration" or "Bookstore" had landed in place overnight, and most school personnel looked pretty polished. Some international students had arrived earlier, and were provided with a list of area hotels. A few of these also depart before breaks start. Their parents book plane tickets based on fares, not the last day of finals.

"Geez Louise," Howard Bagwell sputtered at lunch one day after half of an ESL class he was covering for a colleague had failed to appear two days before a vacation. "The school calendar is a mere suggestion to these kids."

"To their families is more like it." Schyler van Wyck corrected him, "They're the ones who buy the tickets." Schy is an English Department colleague who seems to glide through the year with a presence that is something between a TV reporter posted in the Middle East and a surfer; never seems ruffled and is perpetually tanned. Bagwell - 'Bags' to anyone who's been here a few years - rolled his eyes at this pedantic clarification. A whiskered and corduroy blazered institution north of sixty in the languages department, he didn't appreciate the hairsplitting from Schy, who could pass for an Abercrombie & Fitch salesperson.

"My point *is*," Bags stabbed at his salad, "they spend all that money to send their kid here from China or Korea and then skip exams so they can save a few hundred bucks with a midweek flight."

I'd encountered this issue the year prior to my sabbatical. On January 3rd I emailed all the students in my African American Literature class who had left early and skipped the final. I alerted them to report to my classroom on the following Monday for the make-up exam. The questioning of their analysis of the works they'd read by Hughes, Baldwin, Hurston, Wright, Ellison *et al* was admittedly more challenging than the final given before the break. Most of the students sitting for the make-up also missed the review session in December. As such, asking the kids in early January to recall the content and passages from works they'd read in the fall was a bridge too far for many. When marks were submitted, a few students complained about how the exam sank their final grades a bit, or a lot. I was matter of fact about it in the office of the Academic Dean where the issue was addressed.

"Of *course* the make-up exam was different from the original." I tipped my hand skyward in a *what-would-you-expect* sort of way while explaining myself in Scott Paone's office. A few parents had complained after their children whined about how hard the new exam was. "The kids set to take the new test would be besieging the kids who took the first one with questions about what was on it. I *have* to tweak it." I began scratching at a spot on my tie as Scott drummed fingers on his desk, pursing his lips.

"Tweak, sure, but I'm looking at both versions here, and the make-up is honestly…more…*thorough*…"

"And," I kept at the spot on my tie without looking up, "that's a bad thing?"

"No," Scott tipped his head left and right, fishing for a better word, "not bad, but…these questions are on another level."

"Same level Scott – just coming at the content differently. Look," I sat up a bit, and bored in, "I'm not a sphynx. My assessments are pretty straightforward. But once I've posed the most straightforward questions on matters, the second round of them is going to be reworded. I'm not going to ask the same thing twice - at least not the same way."

"Okay, but…"

"And by the way: how is it that some kids *know* that their make-up tests were different from the original?"

Scott gave a *who knows* shrug.

"Obviously someone with a recollection of the original essay questions was in touch. Otherwise, how would any difference be known?" I leaned forward to round third base. "Folks at the SAT don't like it when questions and content are conveyed to others. They call it a *breach of the integrity of the assessment process*." Can't recall where I read that phrase, but glad I did. Scott has been an administrator for more than a decade, so the last time he experienced what really goes on in a classroom was when someone named Bush was in the White House. Since then, as a dean, he'd had as much to do with teaching young people as a Yankees' vice-president has to do with turning a double play against the Red Sox. But having an office, he raised a finger to convey an objection, which I cut off at the pass.

"And by the way, does the fact that these kids basically flipped the bird to the school's schedule, which prompted all this, matter? I can't be the only teacher who has to create make-up tests because families don't care what our schedule is." Ultimately, I prevailed. At the Blackburn School in Michigan, a college classmate of mine who was teaching there quit mid-year once it was learned that her department head had changed some grades and comments after she had submitted them. My classmate was a Gamble, as in *Procter and*, so bailing mid-year wouldn't have landed her on food stamps in the name of principle. Dividend-wise, the Minots are not Gambles, but with nobody but myself to support, it was still a risk to press the matter with Scott. Pulling out the school calendar card along with the plagiarism issue, I added that kids shouldn't dictate what exams and grades they get.

"I'll…have another look at all this," Scott shuffled the papers on his desk in a way that said that the meeting was over. One of the takeaways he'd perhaps gleaned from the encounter was that I viewed a private school as something other than a customer service endeavor in which people got what they wanted. In my world, people got what they had earned, or deserved. A very quaint notion, as it turns out.

***

In the course of student arrivals, I manned the Student Activities table, where returning students nudged passersby to consider the Chess Club, the LGBTQIA Alliance or the Amnesty International chapter at Griswold. After a morning of tapping all the names they got for this or that club into a spreadsheet, I repaired to my classroom to see how it had weathered my absence. Within the English wing of the humanities building, room 204 was intact. Images of Thoreau, Whitman, Morrison and Cather still hung over the center whiteboard, and stacks of dog-eared paperbacks were piled up against the wainscoting. Laptop in hand, I sat at an oak desk older than the nation of Panama and printed out syllabi for the courses I'd be teaching this fall: "Short Stories: Theirs and Yours," and "Freshman English."

Sept 8

THE FIRST DAY OF classes is such a clean slate that it seems to inspire optimism in even the most jaded educator. As the blue and yellow September morning burned the dew off the playing fields and the campus green, even Howard Bagwell stepped out of his faculty apartment and took up a gait with a spring in his step. His tweed blazer and Oliver Wendell Holmes mustache told all: New England schools were where he was most at home, and for more than a quarter-century, specifically Griswold. Some of the changes over these years haven't set well with him. Students spill out of the dining hall, faces glued to their phones, which sends his eyes rolling.

"If you lit a kid's backpack on fire," he muttered at lunch one day, "he'd let himself get third degree burns before he stopped scrolling through everything to roll on the ground."

"Then, he wouldn't let the ambulance pull out until they gave him back his phone while attaching IVs to keep him alive." Schyler van Wyck chimed in. Schy has been known to finger his own device during lunch and faculty meetings, but as all at the table that day concurred, nobody bothered to point this out. My frosh English sections were flummoxed at expectations in class today. Ninth graders - 'freshmen' had been deemed too sexist a term years earlier, but 'frosh' seems to have evaded the woke radar - bring a willingness to discover and think new things that makes teaching them fun. Many, however, eyed each other in confusion when reading my syllabus. Requirements of "MLA format," and pounding home the "Late Work Policy," which is *after a three-day window, don't bother* — left some silent, but not all.

"So, for instance," an apple-cheeked boy in an oversized rugby shirt raised his hand and continued, "after four days, we get no credit if we turn something in?"

"Well, unless there's a really good reason for the late work - an illness or a family matter, for instance. Yes." I nodded with a hint of a smile, suggesting approval at the boy's comprehension.

"Why can't you just..." Rugby was searching for words, "you know, mark it down a grade for each day it's late instead?"

This was familiar ground, but I affected to chew on the idea as if it was the first time it had been suggested, then I raised a finger. "What if the original work only earns a C for a grade? Three days late, then he or she or they gets it marked down. What might have been an initial grade of a C, is now an F. Does this *help* you?"

"But what if it's an A?" a freshman girl in a purple bob cut wondered.

"Well, you'd still be down to a D as a result."

"So what should we do?" Rugby wondered.

"*Do* it," I flattened my tie and twirled a pen between two fingers with the other hand, "*on time.*" The subsequent silence suggested that these fourteen and fifteen-year-olds had never heard such an imperative before. I'm not channeling some draconian schoolmaster out of Dickens, but am trying to get them in the habit of being conscious of deadlines and due dates. Being aware of such things when they start registering for the SAT and submitting financial aid forms will serve them well.

"Isn't your nickname," one student ventured ever so gently, "Mr. D Minus?"

Minot's Ledge

A few others traded on-edge glances, and I couldn't resist a chuckle.

"No, don't be silly." I waved off the notion. "My middle initial is C, so it's Mr. *C* Minus."

"Is...that because you give a lot of those for grades?" Rugby wondered.

"I don't 'give' grades - students *earn* them. And I am sure that all of you will earn grades higher than that."

"My brother went here," The purple bob cut offered. "He's in college now, but he had you for a teacher."

"What a shame he peaked so young." I shook my head.

"What?" She twisted her face, and I explained that it was just a joke. I didn't want to know more about her brother, as there's always the chance that you'll superimpose your experience with the elder sibling upon a younger one.

"Are you, like, from Scituate?" another student asked. I knew why, and could honestly shake my head in response.

"I've lived in lots of places, but never there," I smiled.

"There's a lighthouse offshore there," she went on. "Minot's Light."

"I've heard that, but...that would be quite a commute for me every day." She gave a thin-lipped smile, which I returned. No doubt way back in the genealogy tree, there's probably some connection, but it's not something to play up, especially with an employer. Dropping hints that you were of old Yankee stock might have been helpful with ingratiating yourself to schools like this generations ago, but not now. These days, schools have offices devoted to diversity on campus. This is actually overdue, but it also means that there's nothing to be gained by mentioning that a dangerous underwater ledge south of Boston Harbor shares your family name, even if you don't know why. Switching gears, I asked students to dig out their anthologies and we turned to "The Lottery," Shirley Jackson's dystopian story of a small town. When I asked for volunteers to read whole paragraphs, lots of hands went up - a good sign on the first day.

Sept 11

UNLIKE NEW YORK, THE Pentagon and Shanksville, most boarding schools do not take to annually commemorating the acts of terror a number of Septembers ago. Doing so would perhaps have never occurred to anyone at Griswold either, were it not for a Byzantine chain of events.

By July of 2001, the head of Dining Services at the school had been casting about for a while in search of somewhere to apply his upgraded culinary skills, courtesy of several months at the Cordon Bleu School the previous summer. He'd lingered here out of gratitude for Griswold giving him some time off to study in London, agreeing to stick around for at least a year afterward. With the debt settled, he'd wrangled an interview at the Yale Club in New York, albeit in late August. Taking a new position at that point on the calendar would perhaps put the school in a bind, but business is business. On the appointed day, he appeared at 50 Vanderbilt Avenue in Manhattan. Inside, he learned that the person with whom he was set to meet had called in that morning to say that a family matter had come up, so the interview would have to be rescheduled. In a Griswold tie, looking like he'd just had his car stolen, the head cook was leaning against a street sign on West 44th when a well-groomed executive type tapped his shoulder. The fellow was the parent of a Griswold student who recognized him from the dining hall. When visiting his daughter for Parents' Weekend the previous fall, he'd stuck his head in the kitchen to inquire about the chance of a slight variation in a small serving of the day's fare to accommodate his wife's food allergy. When the head cook obliged, he was told, "You're a saint – I won't forget this." Good to his word, there in front of the Yale Club, he listened to the sullen chef's tale and mentioned that his firm had offices in the World Trade Center and that he knew someone at Windows on the World, the restaurant atop Building One, and would be happy to speak to her about a position there. A little more than a week later, the call came, inviting him to come to their executive offices at 8:30 in the North Tower. While this was before I started here, learning that a former employee had perished that morning apparently floored everyone at Griswold. In addition to renaming the main dining space for him, every 9/11, remembrances of the fellow by anyone who cared to speak earned a few minutes at the all-school meeting closest to the date. Gradually, this exercise came to include the mention of any family, extended family or acquaintances who perished that day. I've always skipped the event. I hate the day, and all the bell-ringing they do in New York on it. Never understood this American need to commemorate acts of destruction. It probably makes the architects of it feel good to see people clench their jaws and wipe away tears. Admittedly, I shed a few over my loss that day, sometimes at the oddest prompts, but I don't dwell on it in public for all the cable channels. I'd rather remember a life, not the end of it. Does anybody think that the Kennedys all get together on November 22nd and recount Dallas *en famille*?

    I had the first block free this morning, so took the liberty of skipping the all-school meeting and went to my room to prep. Frosh Lit's first readings have been selected to highlight individuals battling various personal challenges, the hope being that lessons from the works would help students negotiate the speed bumps that come with living away at school at the age of fourteen. I'd just finished putting some discussion questions for the book, *Death Be Not Proud* on Google classroom when I heard the sounds of students fresh from the meeting drifting up the stairwell. In September, freshmen at boarding school still have a sanguine way about them. Their clothes still tend to be what their parents bought for them in August, they walk quickly, and many are still wide-eyed, discovering something new about their new life here every day. Returning students, especially juniors, often affect a certain *weltschmerz*, as if all endeavors are either tiresome or unnecessary. Seniors tend to be more buoyant, thinking past their common app essays to the acceptances they hope they'll be able to boast about in the spring. Many sophomores seem simply like taller freshmen. Eyeing the dozen or so students before me, I warmed things up while taking attendance on-line.

"So, how, after one week, are you frosh all finding Griswold…or haven't you found it yet?"

"Frosh?" A freckled boy in Harry Potter specs twisted his face at the term.

"It is," a pale, pony-tailed blonde didn't quite suppress her disbelief at having to explain the term, "a non-binary way to say 'freshmen.'"

"Non-binary?" Harry was only more confused.

The out-of-patience blonde gave up an audible sigh, accompanied by Olympic-level eye rolling. "Not grounded in the traditional male-female only tradition."

Harry and a few others exchanged glances, a la *We're gonna deal with her all year?*

"She's right," I nodded, "but the term is still a bit more Griswold than 'ninth graders'."

From around the room, students offered thoughts on the lights out rule, faculty dogs and food.

"Why does the school still serve slaughtered animals to us?" one girl, who couldn't be bothered to look up, wondered. I let others provide answers, and checked the menu online - Philly Cheese Steak for lunch.

Sept 12

I HAD JUST FLOPPED onto my couch after watching Westgate's varsity girls thrash our soccer squad, prior to which I'd done two loops on the cross country course. Thus I had just enough energy to watch the afternoon's shadows creep glacially across my braided rug when there was an emphatic pounding on my door. The urgency of it suggested that I had just been poisoned or that the president had been shot. It was Ralph, whose sweat and demeanor were immediately unnerving.

"Y'seen Burnsy?"

"N-n-n-o-o-o-o-o. I was at the girls' soc..."

"He's not in his apartment." He caught his breath, "Ideas?"

I shrugged, clueless. "What's the big—"

"His boat is loose," he was still huffing and puffing as he spoke, "Off its mooring. Couple 'a kids on it."

As his words sank in, I conjured up an image of something between Huck Finn and Hitchcock's "Lifeboat."

"So, how are they," I thought out loud, "Are they sailing it?"

"You can sail, right?" and with that, his phone rang. He nodded as he listened, then shoved it back into his pocket. "Gotta go," and he was off. Between rowing and sailing, I probably have more experience on the water than perhaps anyone at the school except

Peter. Thus, it felt like being told that your neighbor's house was on fire and recalling that you have a pond in your backyard as a water supply. For many things nautical, rope is useful, so I grabbed a coil of it from my mud room and headed down to the river.

Fall afternoons on campus often look like the postcards you see in Vermont general stores, yet jogging down to the boathouse on such a day, given the circumstances, Norman Rockwell wasn't coming to mind. The cloudless, failing sky came down to meet the hills on the opposite bank of the Tuxumet River, yet teenagers were adrift on it, and it's two hundred feet wide in some parts. Having helped Peter with a bit of interior fiber glassing and actually stepping the mast on land and dropping it just to check the stays a few weeks earlier, I distinctly recall that the boat was lacking certain basics: telltales, which are threads that convey the wind's direction, were one, and life vests were another. As he wasn't planning on sailing it here, who cared?

One of the perks of living at a school is being able to park or store on campus the odd acquisition, which might not fit into the average garage or belong in the front yard of a certain overly snobbish suburb. A few years ago when he retired, a taciturn science teacher finally removed his tiger skin rug – head and all – from his dorm apartment. Earlier, a student and advisee of his announced a previously undiagnosed allergy to Bengal Tiger skins, making it impossible for her to enjoy dinners in his faculty apartment.

"Really? *Really?*" My former colleague was incredulous. "Have you ever *heard* of anyone being allergic to *Bengal Tiger skins?*" He was on his feet at a residential life meeting, palms up in disbelief. "That's like saying you have a phobia about watching Belgian silent movies – how does a teenager *know* this?" His frustration may well have stemmed from the subtext to it all – a number of students and at least two faculty took great ethical exception to the mere existence of an animal skin on campus. It didn't help that the owner was said to have mentioned at one point that the unfortunate feline was originally shot by Ernest Hemingway. Tethering this trophy to a white male writer came back to bite him even more, if that was possible. The rug is said to remain in an unused room in the science building, which the retired teacher supposedly visits now and again with a good book to read and a travel mug containing something other than coffee.

Griswold's Lower Fields run down to the Tuxamet, which eventually flows into the Charles as it winds toward Boston. The Tux is so brown that sometimes after rowing races, the winning crews refrain from tossing their coxswains off the dock, which is the traditional celebration of a victory. Farmers on the other side of the river are said to grumble that its water is "too thick to drink and too thin to plow." Such a river is not commonly a place to sail, but mooring a small sailboat just downstream from the boathouse held some logic for Peter. For nine months of the year, Burnsy can't get to Nantucket to grab some wind, so settles for bringing an armload of student papers to his 15' Sailcraft and wielding his red pen as he reclines on a bag of sails, letting the current toss him about on his mooring. He bought the toy before I left for the South, and even though I helped him with the odd task on it, apparently it still needs some work. A few bends farther downstream is a drop of perhaps thirty feet. As a crumbling water wheel there suggests, the stretch provided some nice industrial power a century and a half earlier. This is usually a quite unremarkable point, save that at the moment, two Griswold students, neither of whom might have any nautical skills, chose to liberate Burnsy's boat from its mooring, and were at the mercy of the current. Just as I reached a point along the river where some trails converged, I ran into two guys from campus security lugging more ropes as well as some life jackets from the boathouse. Their two-way radios were squawking away in that unintelligible way such devices tend to.

"Waddayu guys know?" I asked as we became a running gang of three.

"Know the current is faster now than it was this morning," one of them managed under the gear. "The dam at Fitzwilliam had a release at noon." The Fitz Dam is ten miles upstream. After a bit we came upon a clearing that was jammed with EMTs and firemen suited up and pointing downstream while talking into their radios. Out of breath, I was hunched over, but perhaps a school sweatshirt gave me away, and one of the EMTs in size sixty overalls came my way.

"How did these kids get a boat out? I didn't know you had a sailing team." He was fingering an iPad that had a map on it, occasionally looking at me, not making a great effort to convey some contempt at our apparent lack of student supervision.

"We don't," I rolled my eyes, "but kids will…"

"Waddayu know about them? They on drugs? Booze? This some kind of a joyride?"

"What? No. I don't know. All I know is that there are two of 'em."

This was not the first time that I'd heard a local person voice a sense that lots of our kids were spoiled miscreants or perhaps on waiting lists for Betty Ford.

"Well," he huffed, "they passed here two minutes ago and wouldn't even acknowledge us - or more importantly, reach for the line we shot their way. Just sat there, taking pictures of us, or…doing something with their phones." His skyward roll of the eyes told all.

"So…" one of the school's security guards jumped in, "what's next?

"Next we let the engine company at Route 2 catch 'em. You got these kids' phone numbers? Can you tell 'em to grab the lines we throw them?"

"I'll call Paone," one of the security guards fished his phone out, "Get their numbers."

"Well, cross your fingers," I muttered.

"Why? Why izzat a bad idea?" The fireman pulled a face.

"You don't have kids, do you?" I cocked my head, "They use their phones for everything but talking. They'll answer them about ten years from next Tuesday."

"Hope they'll answer them before they get to Stoddard." another firefighter offered to no one in particular.

"Why?" I wondered, "What's there?"

He squared up and looked at me with a deadpan. "They don't call it Stoddard Falls for nothing."

Although perhaps useless, running downstream seemed the thing to do. The blue and yellow glow of the hour of the day made it all seem surreal; this was the kind of day photographers like to get catalog shots on campus. They go for a definite scene: the white kid in Bermuda shorts, the blonde girl in a field hockey uniform, the black kid with a chemistry book and the Asian holding a lacrosse stick, all ideally sitting on the library steps, laughing at the funniest clean joke ever told. A friend of mine who puts such images together at another school calls it *the box of crayons* shot. I texted Peter to see if he'd left paddles in the boat since I'd seen it, and he called me back to say, "no." He was driving toward Stoddard, his voice a mix of anger and guilt.

"Christ. Never saw this coming," he muttered, "I don't even lock my apartment, f'Chrissakes. Since when is this a weekend activity?"

"Since they're not required to play a fall sport," I told him. Gone are the days when all kids played something every term, even if it was fourth level intramural soccer, aka Dweeb Soccer. Activities such as yearbook and the school paper now count the same, so kids are busy after three PM, but these non-team groups don't meet on weekends, providing time for stupid diversions like this.

"Wait a minute," I asked him, "Are you near the bridge, the one by the Getty station?"

"Almost. Why?"

"I've run past it. Pretty low. Is your mast still in the crutch?"

"Hope so. Was last week." When not being sailed, some boats will have their mast dropped and laid into a crutch on which it rests off the stern.

"Okay. Come back and meet me. Know that big red barn with the tipping silo?"

"Why?"

"I have an idea. Just *do* it, alright?" Over the phone I could hear him downshifting and changing direction. "You have any rope in the car?"

"Maybe."

"See you in a few. I'll run up to the barn."

There must be some law in every New England town mandating that there be an abandoned railroad bridge spanning a murky river running under it. Gates on them with signs saying NO TRESPASSING might as well announce 'Welcome Teenagers With Beer.' Once Peter picked me up at the barn, we drove to one end of the bridge in seconds and parked by the ghostly depot which perhaps hadn't been used since I was born. Maybe my father too. We grabbed the rope from his trunk and jogged to the middle of the span, which kept bringing to mind that movie, "Stand By Me." Peter was pretty stoic, like a character in a film who'd been told to meet someone at a hospital emergency room with no explanation why. His *whatever* shock of hair, paint-stained sweatshirt and two-day stubble suggested more school maintenance staff than History Department Chair. Scott Paone had sent me the kids' phone numbers, so I started texting them about the falls downstream. Found a photo of the Turners Falls Dam on the Connecticut in western Mass and attached it for effect, adding, "**Guys - PLEASE follow instructions! This is getting dicey. Instructions in my next text.**" Then I tried to lighten the mood for them. "**You don't want your roommates to suddenly have single rooms, do you?**"

Squinting at the bend upstream, Peter managed a question, "What's your plan?"

"If we can get them to step the mast, this bridge is low enough that it'll get snagged on it, but if not, we throw them this line and get them to tie it to the eyelet on the bow."

"Hmmm. Gotta plan B? I took the eyelet out last month. Haven't replaced it yet. That's why it was on my trailer."

"Fuck! Fuck it all!!" It wasn't his fault. Hell, it's his boat, but that *was* plan B.

"Well, why the hell would I rush to replace it now? It's fucking October! Didn't think we'd have to play "Baywatch" for a couple of kids."

"No, no. I get it." I waved off the notion that I was being critical. " 'Course not. Just kind of…limits what we…" Then I got a text from one of the kids, sounding like he got the point of my message. I showed it to Peter and gave him the phone as the boat began to appear around the bend, drifting peacefully, its bow pointing one way then another, carrying two teenagers huddled over a phone. "Can you walk them through stepping the mast?"

"I can tell them how," his thumbs were at it, "but whether they can do it is another thing. Let's face it - these kids aren't the Lord's best work if this is their idea of a fun Saturday. But, hell - last thing I'd want to do is have a parent get a call with some awful news."

The boat was still perhaps a hundred yards upstream with the kids now trying to handle the aluminum mast which was laying bow to stern. The mast was lifted off the crutch at the stern and slid back a bit. The pirates were shouldering it while checking their phones as Peter tapped away, and eventually they got the foot of it affixed to the base on top of the boat's cuddy. Raising it was another matter, as it requires walking toward the bow while pushing it higher, creating the image of a clock's second hand working its way from nine to twelve, or the raising of the flag on Iwo Jima.

The trouble they had physically working together on this made it clear that we need more weight training at the school.

"Christ, c'mon guys." Peter was shaking his head as he tapped. By now, the boat was close enough that they could hear us, so he started shouting instructions to them.

"Keep the mast in the base! Work *together!* You've got to walk it up *slowly!*"

"If these kids had been on Mt. Surabachi, there'd be one less monument in DC," I offered, and that forced a chuckle out of Peter, as I knew he was big on the war in the Pacific, and had a grandfather who'd been on Iwo Jima. Fifty feet upstream, they had it in place, upright, and smiled at us with thumbs up. By now the volunteer firemen had their pram with an outboard down to the shore, and were launching it. The boys glided toward the bridge about twenty feet away from where we were at the railing, and just as we got there, the mast hitting the bridge sent it smashing back down into the boat.

"Fuck! For *fuck's* sake!" Peter pounded the railing. Looking toward the shore, we could see that the town's boat was drifting into the current, but one of the firemen was still pulling frantically at the outboard's start cord, so it just drifted. We ran across the trestle to the downstream side of the bridge and I tossed a coil of rope over the side. The end of it went under the surface, and Peter began barking directions to under the bridge as to what they should do with the rope. As the bow appeared underneath, some frantic arms reached for the line and Peter walked them step by step on threading it through the cleat, a device on each side made for ropes to control the jib. Once they did that and tied a pretty unnautical knot at their end, Peter began towing it to shore from twenty feet up. The silence was eventually broken by sheepish "thank yous" from below. The EMT got the outboard started, and met up with Peter's boat, grabbed the rope near the waterline and pulled it the rest of the way to the riverbank. A few others waded in to catch it so the EMT's motor wouldn't get stuck in a shallow spot. On land, the EMTs and two school nurses tended to the students who seemed perfectly fine save for an inability to look Peter or me in the eye. We moved among the volunteer fire folks and thanked them for their efforts as they packed up their vehicles. We hauled his craft up on the river bank and surveyed its condition, chatting about how a boat can be replaced but people can't, and with that we exchanged glances that needed no words: *this could have been a lot worse.* One local fireman, against the wishes of his supervisor, strolled over to the students and nurses. His greasy shirt and oil-blackened hands hinted that this guy wasn't afraid to do whatever he had to do in order to do something well, even if it included getting wet. Hands on hips with some grime on his face and tousled black hair, he could have just walked out of the caved-in coal mine, but actually he'd devoted part of a Saturday afternoon to a river rescue when asked to do so.

"Y'know? It's good that you're safe," he varied his glare from one boy to the other and back, "but this was *really* avoidable. *Really freaking* avoidable"

"Don," an EMT raised a cautionary finger.

"No," Don turned back to him, "I don't care. I'm a *volunteer*. I don't need this. I need my *job,* which I *didn't go to* today so I could watch my kid play soccer, which I *didn't get to do* because I got a call to come to this little picnic." Then he came back to the boys. "You kids have some nice facilities at your school. Lots 'a fields, a gym, a pool. So what are you doing on a Saturday afternoon? Joyriding in a boat y' don't even know how 'ta sail. 'Zat what they teach you there? For how much a year?" He looked at Peter and me for an answer, and all I could muster was a nod. He huffed and went on. "Well, take a suggestion? Stick to the soccer fields. My kids are seven and ten, go to the local public school, and one 'o 'em is on the spectrum, but *they* know better than to not try a dumb stunt like this." He shook his head as he turned to pack up the EMS truck, and Peter and I talked about getting his trailer down here for the boat. Scott appeared, huddled with the nurses for a minute to get brought up to speed, and called out to us.

"I should close this loop with the EMTs here. Could you guys give these boys a ride back to school?"

I could see Peter's eyes widen at the suggestion, and tapped his arm before he could speak.

"We really need to secure the boat," I explained, "and get it back too. Afraid we'll be here for a bit." Scott nodded slightly, perhaps realizing that this was a ludicrous ask, of Peter anyway. As glad as we were that the boys were safe, it was quite avoidable. From words we'd had a bit earlier, I knew Peter wasn't concerned about any damage to his boat, but rather that it might have contributed to a tragedy, and this left him shaken. We waited until all were gone, secured the mast on the crutch, and headed back to campus for his trailer. Once loaded, we hauled it back to school, using very unprofessional language all the way.

Sept 14

DORM DUTY ALWAYS LOOMS worse than it is. Parking yourself in a common area for three and a half hours is actually kind of a study hall for me - just about all I can do is grade papers or read, which are useful and fun respectively. It's the being tethered near students that seems restrictive - no late evening run or glass of wine before dinner in my digs. The main idea is to be seen so as to impose quiet for a few hours and to check rooms later on at lights out. This concluding task is a rather silly notion these days. With phones that can act as internet hotspots, to expect anybody but a few frosh to head off to the land of Nod at 10:30 or 11 PM is foolish. Even for those who are on a team, practices are now limited to ninety minutes, so unlike a generation or two ago, they're no longer being run ragged enough in the afternoons to have them drop off to sleep when we'd like them to. Apparently, however, the dance troupe does overtime.

About nine PM a first-year junior came to my desk in the center lounge with a request. I don't have her in class, but the nights I've been on duty, she's worn this Philadelphia Eagles jersey, and on the dorm roll her name is actually Millicent, so I call her Millie from Philly.

"Mr. Minot," she held up a fattened envelope, "can I pop this?"

I looked at the packet of Magic Pop in her hand, and then at my watch, just to affect that I was considering her request.

"It's nine. Not 'sposed to use the kitchen during study hall."

"But I'm *starved,*" she winced, rubbing her stomach for more effect.

"Dinner just ended two and a half hours ago. How can you be starved?"

"I'm with the dance troupe," she raised her arms and began to twirl. "We ran late today. There's a recital on Saturday. You should come. So Miss What's-her-name, she knows there are lots of day students in the troupe, so since they can drive home and have dinner later, she keeps us late. By the time we got done, all that was left at dinner was the salad bar and some egg rolls." She was on her toes now, twirling, perhaps for practice, or effect.

"Well, why are you just deciding now that---"

"And they also had pasta. Again. I hate pasta."

At this point, it was clear that my grandmother's Depends hold water better than her story of being on the verge of a Donner party diet. Where to go with this? *That popcorn isn't really a meal and won't fill her up? That rules are rules?* It being early in the school year, against my better judgment, I opted for some goodwill.

"So: if you don't ask me this again all year, and don't tell anyone I said it was okay, *and* you eat it in the kitchen. Just this once, okay?"

"Th-a-a-a-a-n-k you," she pirouetted gleefully towards the kitchen and was gone. This seemed like a good time to go walkabout. Making rounds, I always announce, "Man on the floor." Nudging doors that aren't already open to a ninety-degree angle can be perilous, but with so many faces glued to screens and earbuds in, I often go unnoticed. Hard to know if there's actually any studying going on during study hall these days; is a pack of giggling students socializing or are they in a French III chatroom? Is a student watching "Mulan" as part of a unit on Asian stereotypes or is she putting off homework? Half the time these aren't matters I'm inspired to investigate – you have to pick your battles. On the third floor I knocked on Millie's closed door to remind her roommate to leave it open. Nothing. My third round of knocking was more emphatic, and still no response. so I turned the knob to enter. As I did, a piercing siren like a car alarm filled the air.

Fire drills are scheduled to let us practice getting out safely, and to help with this, Campus Safety lets faculty and staff know when they're coming, so that the family with a new baby or anyone else not pining to stand in a parking lot at nine in the evening can plan to be elsewhere. As no advance word was provided, it suddenly occurred to me that this wasn't a drill.

Naomi Zhang, Millie's roommate, flung the door open and seemed startled to find me there, perhaps because of the earbuds she had in, and thus didn't hear the audio eruption all about us. In a tank top and shorts with some kind of cosmetic mask smeared on her face, her look switched from surprise to embarrassment to anger in as many seconds. She scanned the hallway, spat out frustration in Mandarin and rolled her eyes when I pointed to the stairwell door. Amidst the alarm and strobe light blasting from the red box in the hallway, I bellowed for all to head to the drop off lot in front of the building. Any interruption of study hall is usually quite welcome, so as twenty-eight girls emerged from their rooms, reactions ranged from nonchalant to buoyant.

"Maybe she'll cancel the Spanish quiz tomorrow if we all tell her we couldn't study because of this," was one hopeful thought I heard on the way outside. In center lounge I grabbed the sign out list so that I wouldn't be looking for any who were at the library, and working its way into the mix of high school perfume, Tide - the detergent of choice - and eau de dorm, a distinctly out of place scent was clear. As the last of the girls exited the lounge, it came to me: burnt popcorn. Across the room in the kitchen area, I saw the faintest smoky haze clinging to the ceiling.

"Millie!! Judas *Priest!*" I couldn't believe it. Admittedly, the kitchen microwave might be older than some of the dorm's residents, but still. Inside it was a burst bag of Magic Pop that was slowly being devoured by a small but patient flame. Next to this was what may have once been a burrito wrapped in tin foil - *tin foil.* Apparently popcorn was just the first course. Hopefully the alarm drowned out my occasional profanity as I unplugged the microwave, opened the windows and wrestled with the pin to the fire extinguisher, which made short work of the well-done fare. It's probably by design that fire alarms are annoying, but once it's clear the danger has passed, they're downright maddening. Heading out through the lounge I literally bumped into Millie in a bathrobe, hair dripping wet.

"What...*why are you still in here?!*" For those three seconds I'm confident my voice had the better of the alarm.

"I was in the shower."

"Did you *hear* that??" Clearly my tone and Ozzy Osbourne eyes unnerved her. Good.

"I figured it was...y'know, a dri---" Just then Campus Safety came through the door and headed for the alarm unit on the wall. Over the din I could hear the siren of an approaching fire engine. I pointed to the door for this walking Darwin Award clad in a terry cloth robe to head outside, and I followed her to take attendance. In ten minutes, the scene was "secure," and as they departed, the Safety officer and local fire captain eyed the gaggle in the lot outside with a mixture of humor and unspoken eye rolling. While we headed back inside, I heard Millie tell someone that she didn't realize she'd set the microwave timer for so long.

"How'd you get permission to make it during study hall anyway?" someone asked. This would be a fun dorm report to write. *Trying to engender some goodwill with a student resulted in a practice call for our local fire department when...Goodwill is overrated.*

The cherry on top was when an hour later, an obviously very clean Millie came downstairs and crept my way to sheepishly ask if she could visit the other girls' dorm to make a snack with a friend. I'm not making this up. She explained the request by noting that she never got to eat her popcorn.

"Or, the burrito, right?" She nodded. "Has anyone ever mentioned, or have you ever noticed why you never see people put tin foil in a microwave?" She shook her head while scowling to confirm her answer.

"But that's what I *saved it* in?" Life is hard. It's harder when you think popcorn is a food group or an adequate meal. I was actually a bit ashamed at how good it felt to deny her request.

"But I want something to eat," She stomped a flip-flopped foot for effect.

"And people in hell want ice." She didn't know quite what to do with that, but in spite of herself, she figured out that this was the end of the discussion. Huffing at this defeat, she turned and headed back upstairs, shoulders hitched, thumbs announcing her disappointment to the world on her phone.

Sept 19

DUTY THIS PAST WEEKEND meant chaperoning a student trip off campus Saturday. Someone had already signed up for the whale watch in Boston Harbor, so I settled for driving a minibus to Cambridge and letting our kids loose on Harvard Square for the afternoon.
"What are we 'sposed to do there for three hours?" came one voice from the back of the bus.
   "W-w-w-e-e-e-e-l-l," I was looking frantically for a parking space, "you signed up for the trip – what did you have in mind?" In the mirror overhead that showed the students, I saw kids turn to one another; apparently nobody had anything in mind beyond simply getting off campus for an afternoon. A couple of pony-tailed girls with braces sitting up front were finding something hysterical on their phones while in the back, a group of freshman boys were conspiring across the aisle to make the most of this independence.   Frosh are great. They're such a small group – no more than eighty or so in the whole class – that they bond pretty quickly without regard to class, color or size. There were a couple of sophomore boys there too. Behind the giggling girls were two rows of boys - three white kids, a Black student and two East Asians, all snickering in hushed tones about something that the girls probably

couldn't have cared less about. Maturity levels tend to inform the romantic interest food chain. This dictates that the only boys frosh girls might be interested in are juniors or seniors. Finding a parking spot near the law school, I gathered the students outside the bus before loosing them on the streets. Parts of Harvard Square look as they did when either of the Roosevelts were here. Windows in red brick dorms stare out over black wrought iron fences and gates. Across Mass. Ave. a large common is sprinkled with dog walkers, stroller pushers and a few airborne frisbees. Beside a Unitarian church is a cemetery that is older than the United States. Southward toward the river is the center of things, where Mass Ave. bends our way, toward the law school, after running through Boston, across the Charles and through MIT. This is where the students would probably go carousing. Typical college fare is all about, including the odd sidewalk musician and panhandler. At the center of the square, which is actually more of a triangle, is the Harvard Cooperative Society - the Coop. It was a pretty mild day, but the morning sun had given way to a milky sky overhead.

"So," I jabbed a finger over their heads, "the square is *that* way. So's the university, and some divinity schools. You can get all kinds of healthy and unhealthy food all around, and wander the Yard if you want."

"Did you go here?" one girl asked.

"Not for my undergrad work, but I hear it's a good school." A few eyed each other at my ignorance, as they had yet to develop sarcasm detectors. "Everyone pair up with at least one other person. Everyone got phones?" This is like asking them if they have noses. I gave them my number to call in a pinch and said to be back at the bus at 4:20, figuring they'd be there by 4:30. Never say 4:15 to a group that might involve some non-native English speakers. I made this mistake two years ago and a boy from Seoul *thought* he'd heard 4:50, the result being that the dining hall staff had to wait dinner for us.

"What are *you* gonna do?" a sophomore boy asked?

I held up a three-ring binder, "I'll be grading these in the café on the second floor of the Coop. I've got a lot to read, so don't get arrested or play in traffic." As a gaggle, we strolled towards the square with pairs and groups of three peeling off here and there, my words following them again as they did. The Coop was once the college's bookstore, but today seems devoted to offering *New York Times* best-sellers and books by Harvard profs as well as everything from Christmas ornaments to dog leashes with VE RI TAS emblazoned on them. Atop a staircase flanked with images of TR and Kennedy, a café seemed a good place to grade papers over caffeine for a few hours, but adolescence took a hand. After perhaps a half hour, the two sophomore boys from the bus came up the stairs, scanned the area, and rushed my table, breathless.

"Mr. Minot – y' gotta come."

"And...why is that?"

"Jerry," the other one managed, "Jerome. They caught him."

"Jerome. From the bus," I put my pen down, "Caught him *what?*"

They eyed each other perhaps hoping that the other one would respond. The taller one spilled.

"We were in the other part of this place. Not books. Sweatshirts, swag, that kind of stuff, and suddenly this guy grabbed his collar. Asked him to go with him. We kind of followed, and asked what it was about."

Absorbing all this, I pointed to the chairs on the other side of my table with a glare that told them to sit.

"And?"

"He," the smaller one had eyes like saucers as he spoke, "the store guard or whatever, said that there was something in Jerome's pocket that shouldn't be there, and hauled him into some room where we couldn't go."

"So…he was saying Jerome took something without paying for it?" I asked.

They looked at each other, and shrugged. "I guess." "Yeah."

"You *guess* or you *know?* Either he was accused of shoplifting or he wasn't? Which is it?"

"Well…yeah" they agreed. Cheeks still flushed from the run, again they looked at each other, both holding their breath. "But," the shorter one thinned his lips with a pregnant pause.

"Shut up dipwad." His taller partner backhanded his chest.

"Easy pal." At this point I stood, and went all "Law & Order" on them, "Think carefully about how you answer this: why do *you,*" I pointed to one boy, then the other, "want *him* to shut up?"

After ten seconds that must have seemed like an hour to them, the taller one came out with it. "We were with him…but, then we weren't. And…it was kind if a dare."

The boys led me to the store's Security offices, where my explanation admitted me to a windowless room. There behind a desk, a Coop Security officer who'd never met a doughnut he didn't like was reclined to the point that his girth was stretching his white shirt, making his Harvard Security badge seem quite small. On the other side of his desk sat Jerome, a jeans and hoodie-clad freshman who perhaps weighed ninety pounds wet. His face brightened a bit when he saw me, then quickly retreated to a recognition of reality: he was a teenager who'd been hauled in by an authority figure on a shoplifting charge in a store at the nation's oldest university, and he was black.

"Sir, my name is Ben Minot and I'm responsible for this young man," I gestured to and smiled at Jerome, who was probably not constipated at that moment, "I gather…could you bring me up to speed on things?"

"The Coop has a policy," he sat up towards his desk a bit, "of having people pay for merchandise prior to leaving the store with it. This young man you're responsible for…" he eyed Jerome for a few seconds while choosing his words, "He seemed quite unaccustomed to such a policy." With that he fished out of a desk drawer and placed on his blotter a crimson bottle opener with VE RI TAS on the handle. "Was seen stuffing this into his pocket by a sales associate."

Without being asked to, I took a seat beside Jerome and asked him if this was true. While he probably hadn't had six cups of coffee and been refused a bathroom, by the way his knee was bouncing you'd have thought as much. He kept looking straight ahead, really at nothing. I wasn't familiar with his background prior to Griswold nor how much he knew about how figures of authority and the justice system have been known to treat young men of color. I figured he'd picked up on a few things, such as maybe Freddie Gray, Tamir Rice, maybe not Emmett Till. Not a good situation for anyone, but unless you've been living under a rock, you'd know that store cop or not, in today's America, as my students would say, "sucks to be him."

"Jerome," I leaned his way, "this would be a good time to say whatever...should be said, especially if someone else is going to say it later."

His lower lip quivered a bit, but that was it. I turned to the Coop officer. "I'm told...by some equally young store patrons that---"

"Patrons *patron*ize a store," he corrected me, "they don't steal from it." A pedantic store cop – wonderful.

"Indeed, that's true. I'm told that they, in a case of really bad judgment, which will come back to haunt them I assure you, dared Jerome here to...do whatever he's alleged to have done. Boys can often be..." Didn't know how to finish that exactly, but that was all I had.

"Stupid?" the store cop raised his eyebrows seeking agreement, "That's f' sure. Got four of them myself. But none of 'em ever sought a five-finger discount from a store."

I suppressed the urge to say *not that you* know *of* here, realizing that it wouldn't help Jerome to do so.

Minot's Ledge

"What's your relationship to this young man?" He began tapping on a keyboard which probably dropped Jerome's heart even more than mine. After ten minutes, the typing was done, but it was clear in the course of it that Sergeant Crimson found it curious that a student at an expensive private school would be shoplifting a seven-dollar bottle opener. Jerome's picture was taken and a form signed that recounted events – save the dare suggestion – and it was explained that Jerome was banned from the Coop for five years and that his photo would be posted in a room elsewhere in the store. He was told to sign a document, and being *in loco parentis*, so was I. As this was a first for me, I had no road map as to how to respond otherwise.

On the ride back to school, I shot the occasional glare at the two students whose cowering looks suggested that there was more to the story of the disappearing bottle opener. Had they dared him to grab it? As some guy named Hamilton might suggest, accepting dares can have consequences bigger than having to shop at a different store for a while. Having jumped forty feet into a rain-filled granite quarry in Rockport and downed a pint of tequila at two points in my life, I can't claim to be immune from the stupidity of accepting dares.

Less than a month into the school year, I knew my students' names, but not those I didn't have in class. Thus I knew little more about Jerome than I did Officer Crimson. Not a lot of families will commit to sending their children away for high school, especially not a fourteen year-old. A few situations result in this: 1) families are rolling in money but can't be bothered to parent, 2) mom and dad are convinced they have a prodigy who won't be challenged at the local school, 3) parents believe they've spawned an accomplished and obsessive hockey or squash player who needs grooming for some Ivy squad or the NHL, or 4) Billy or Betsie is a legacy, going to where mom or dad went, and mom or dad has subsequently done well and can splurge on what can be had for free in their local community. Rear window stickers for bragging purposes optional. After parking back on campus, I had Jerome stand outside it while I dealt with the two sophomores in a pretty empty minibus.

"Is there anything more about this episode at the Coop you wanna tell me?" After eyeing each other, they shook their heads. "Reason I ask is, it just feels…I dunno, like, it's kind of random. I mean…a *bottle opener?*"

They shuffled their feet a bit, and mentioned how as he's a freshman, they don't know Jerome that well.

"Well, just please keep this to yourselves, alright? I *hope* you haven't texted people about it, but, that may be naive on my part. If for some reason you haven't, please don't, okay?" They nodded, and left the bus as if it was about to combust.

Outside, Jerome was scanning the scene before him, a bucolic menagerie of brick buildings with ivy climbing them, soccer nets bookending manicured fields and a dining hall with well-stocked lines and a huge salad bar. While Griswold was more diverse earlier than many church schools, there was still a good chance that a student of color you'd find on campus in the 1960s was a fac brat or more likely the child of a dining hall worker. However far Jerome was from those days, this afternoon's developments conjured up a stink that my quarry-jumping escapade never did. His silent gaze across campus seemed to be asking *Is this really my world, or is it just a tease?*

"I'll speak to someone at dinner, and I'll let you know what's next." He shrugged and looked away. "What the Coop cop said - is that accurate?"

He cocked his head back my way and gazed vaguely at something over my shoulder.

" 'Zit matter? I mean…really?"

"Yeah, it does, because when other students---"

"Really? *Really?* What you..." and without finishing the thought, he turned to head back to his dorm. As I watched him, it struck me that this would be a good time to not leave him to his own devices. I kept him in the dorm lounge while I called the weekend dean, filled her in while he flipped through channels on the lounge TV, then left it to her and returned the bus key.

Sept 21

NO GOOD DEED GOES unpunished. Today I subbed for one period to cover for Mary Carpenter, my favorite colleague. The only woman in the department, I'm sure it would annoy some colleagues to hear me refer to her as a lady, which she genuinely is, instead of a woman. A long Kate Hepburn-type from Maine, she seems to have read any book you care to mention, and many I could not. Her fair isle sweaters and faux pearls, as she insists on telling us they are, suggest a girls' school two generations ago. In all my years at Griswold, I've never heard her say an untoward word about anyone. Even when someone in one of her classes is drowning in spite of her best efforts, she'd allow, "He's not doing as well as I'd like to report..." She had a meeting with Fred today about some students who wanted to switch to her honors section, so asked me to cover her class during my prep period.

"It's just a test I have planned," she explained over breakfast, "but there are some international students who, if they don't truly do well, I'll perhaps recommend them for the transitional class." Administering someone else's test allows you to camp out in another room and get grading done, so it's actually a useful way to spend a prep period. She's also Jerome's advisor, so the business at the Coop will no doubt come up in the meeting as well.

Mary's test was on literary terms – metaphors, euphemisms – just to see that everyone was a good fit for the class, or perhaps better suited to an easier offering. It's good to get a baseline for where everyone is early in the year, especially before the add/drop deadline next week. As I always do, I have students place their phones on a side table in the room.

"Do you really think we'd cheat, Mr. Minot?" someone whined. "That's kind of insulting."

" 'Course not. I know you won't cheat. You don't have your phones."

"But you're kind of saying…that you don't trust us." another offered.

"Don't look at it that way," I sat on top of the desk and put the tests behind me. "Are banks locked at night?"

They wrinkled their brows, wondering where this came from. After a few seconds, I remembered that as far as they knew, 'bank' means ATM, so I reframed the question and on my computer, pulled up some images of a Chase branch nearby, and a bank vault, and projected them on the whiteboard.

"So: think this place is locked at night?"

" 'Course it is," a few offered.

"Why?" I asked.

"There's money in it."

"So, knowing there's money in it, if you could somehow get in there and grab some, would you?"

The students eyed each other silently, perhaps wondering if this was some trick physics problem.

"Sure," came from the back of the room. "My dad says banks are insured, so even if they lose money, they're okay."

"Fine. Anyone else game?" I tilted back, hands clasped on my knee, like a Dickies ad with Pat Boone from the 1950s.

"If you thought you could get away with it, if it wasn't locked or monitored or anything. Candy from a baby. Easy money. Would you?" I raised my hand to nudge any takers; the only one was the FDIC expert in the back.

"Right. You wouldn't. Most of you anyway. One of you might." I stood up from the desk and waved to Willie Sutton in the back, "See you on visiting day. Here's the point: most people won't rob banks – but a few might, so banks lock the money in vaults and lock their doors and have alarms for the few people who might try it. Same at school."

I began erasing the whiteboard, realizing that there were notes from Mary's review session for the test on it. An audible sigh suggested they'd hoped I wouldn't notice. "Most students aren't going to cheat on a test, but one or two might, and we don't know who they'll be."

"It'll probably be Josh," someone threw out, and that broke everybody up, prompting Josh to silently mouth something nasty to the commentator. It also demonstrated that someone was a good judge of character. I'd heard his humor in the dining hall, and if I had a daughter, I would not allow her to go out with Josh.

"Point is, ninety percent of the rules in school - in life, really are there because of the ten percent of people who did certain things before we wrote these rules down. They're not a comment on everyone, but it's the fairest way to keep everybody in line, even though most of you would be in line anyway."

Silence. That took care of that. Onward, Students were nudged to space themselves apart and I handed out the test, asking them to bring it up and grab a Capote story on Mary's desk when done. Always have something for students who finish before others to busy themselves with.

If orange is the new black, water is the new coffee. Perhaps not new, but pretty ubiquitous in classes, especially since coaches and health teachers push drinking it. The plastic involved in all the bottles is criminal, but I don't get too Greenpeace about it usually.

Today in one corner, Eric Zhang was nursing his water while scribbling down answers. He was especially focused, his face buried as he scratched away. A few kids brought their tests up and took "Miriam," Capote's tale which I've always thought to be a ghost story. Of the few stragglers, Eric was one, and eventually I noticed him just gazing at his water. "Eric" is his nom de plume, his actual name being Bohong. Dad is some big deal at Sinochem, a ginormous firm headquartered in Beijing, and word was that he felt strongly that his son should not have to spin his wheels in ESL courses, but should instead be placed in mainstream classes. As it has yet to be clear to Mary that "Eric" can spell "mainstream," here he was. Over spring break last year, Mr. Zhang invited ten faculty to his compound in northeast China, and paid for them to get there. He also is said to have written a check to finish repairs on the hockey rink's roof that collapsed last winter. Must be nice.

It took perhaps half a minute for me to realize that Eric's bottle was lacking a familiar Dasani or Poland Springs label. Creeping up to look over his shoulder, I encountered a new one. Sensing my shadow, he whirled around, fixed a terrified glare on me, and reached for his water bottle, which I got a good look at before he wrapped a hand around the label.

"I...have more time, yes?"

"You still have time Eric," I whispered, "but let me recycle that bottle for you," and as I reached for it, he clenched it like the last vial of snake bite medicine in Death Valley. I tipped my head a bit, asking if he really wanted to fight me on this. It seemed he did. I leaned in a bit.

"You'll be happier later, if you don't fight me on this now."

The bottle slipped from what looked like a claw at that point. I took hold of it and returned to my desk. It was impossible to know how much other students knew about what was up, but owing to campus life, they all would soon enough.

The room cleared at the end of the period, and I actually had to call after Eric to get him to stay back..

"You're a thirsty guy," I threw out as he slinked toward my desk. He avoided eye contact, as though there was actually something new elsewhere in the room to look at. I placed his plastic bottle on the blotter and leaned back in Mary's chair.

"Congratulations: first time I've seen this one." His clear water bottle had no original label on it, and certainly no water. It had been sliced down the side and pieced back together again, but between these steps, a small cheat sheet of terms and definitions had been taped facing inward to where the label would be. Nobody's going to deny a student water in class. There's little to say in such situations, especially when the evidence is plain as day. He didn't try to deny the obvious.

"What is now?" I figured he meant "Now what?" His backpack was slung over one shoulder, his hoodie and t-shirt being a uniform that perhaps a third of the boys here prefer daily. His big, dark eyes conveyed a mix of annoyance and dread, but not the terror that I'd have felt in such a situation years earlier.

"Well, I'll be handing this over to Mr. Paone, and I expect he'll want to meet with us, and there could be a Disciplinary Board convened, or not, but that's his call."

"I was just..," he offered a helpless, palms up plea, "I have...chemistry lab report due this week. I had to study late. Into after the study hall. I did not have..." and he looked away as he ran out of words. The choppy English actually inspired a bit of empathy in me, but it's Mary's class.

"Part of being here is learning how to manage your ti---"

"And I asked for late lights, but my dad. He did a call from New York. The person on the dorm said that I could not have them.

Because I was on the phone in study hall. But this is when my father did the call."

"Well, you probably want to call your dad back tonight," I nodded, "This is not going away, Eric."

"He is coming here. The weekend. Please. Can you not..." He trailed off, perhaps at a loss as to how to frame such an ask.

"There's a procedure for this, and this is Mrs. Carpenter's class, so she'll probably have something to say."

I stood up, not wanting to drag things out more, "and just something to think about: getting a lousy grade on a test would have been preferable to...whatever comes next, whatever it is. And trust, it's a funny thing; once you break it, it's hard to rebui---"

"Please. Wait!" He stopped me with a raised palm, and fished out his phone, "I can call a person? Maybe my sister?"

"Be my guest, but I've got another class, so I'm not talk--" He cut me off by switching to Chinese as the phone reached his ear. He clearly had her on speed dial, but as nobody under fifty actually answers their phone when it rings, he was probably leaving a voice message. His sister is in the dorm where I have Thursday night study hall duty. I pointed toward the door, and he headed out amidst a rapid fire vent in Mandarin into his phone.

Sept 26

TRYING SOMETHING NEW THIS year: letting students pick some of our readings. While I think I have a pretty good sense of what works are accessible and engaging for teenagers, this seems a way to get more of a buy-in from them on certain writings. Admittedly too, I can still see that dog-eared copy of *Tender is the Night* that a teacher of mine at school had, and thought at the time, *Since he seems to have had that copy since before I was born, I wonder if anyone in my lifetime or before has told him it's a lousy book to foist on high schoolers.* Even at the clueless age of sixteen, it was clear to most of us that one of the book's characters, Dick, was in fact, a dick, and that Nicole and Rosemary were wise to put him in their rear views. On the other hand, to those of us at a school with MSRPs – Major School Rules and Policies - over our heads, getting drunk a lot in the south of France sounded like fun. Thus some of the pathos F. Scott offered was lost on us, in spite of the teacher's earnest efforts.

"Fitzgerald was trying to create something cathartic, for him, but it was ultimately too sentimental for it to work for him." I can still hear our teacher's voice. Easy to see that now, but it was not so easy amidst BC Calculus, making the sailing team and acne. Not wanting to be *that teacher* more than necessary, I threw out a long list of short stories for them to choose from, and a bit of a consensus settled on John Cheever's "The Swimmer" – maybe because some of the kids probably have pools at home, maybe because I mentioned that Cheever had been kicked out of Thayer Academy. A majority of them had it on their lists, so today we did some readings and analysis.

"This guy seemed kind of entitled," a pony-tailed redhead squinted, looking around to make sure it was okay to say this. "Just showing up in people's yards and jumping into their pools. Does he even *know* all these people?"

"Sure he does," a sure of himself coxswain in a rowing team hoodie piped up, "He calls them all by name. He knows who has a pool."

"What year was this written?" I asked, and a mousy yet poised girl with knowing eyes offered up, "1962."

"So, how was life different back then?" I posed. Responses ranged from no TV, it being illegal to be gay to caricatures from "Mad Men" and Yale being all-men – someone's grandmother was in the first class with females a few years later. Phones were all black and blacks were excluded from some lunch counters. Not bad for fourteen year-olds. Someone then piped up with, "No internet," prompting another to jump to no social media, spawning the question of how people would know each other so well without it.

"You didn't have eight hundred 'friends,'" I explained, "or followers," I had to add, recalling that this is the post-Facebook generation. "Your friends were people who lived near you. You played with them, your parents, *your grand*parents I suppose, borrowed rakes and garden hoses from each other, and had those cocktail parties that Cheever writes about. No social media. They'd walk up to someone's door and knock. Maybe they played golf together or would just ask if they could borrow a tool or rake."

"So, you'd just walk up to a house? Just like that?" Clearly doing anything without first getting the skinny about someone online or being invited to join a chat was alien to these kids.

"So what does Neddy look like?" I asked, Neddy being Cheever's protagonist making the rounds in the neighborhood's pools.

"He's probably in pretty good shape. I mean, he swims a lot," a lean cross-country runner offered.

"He's probably white," the Knowing Eyes shared without looking up.

"How do you know?" someone piped up.

"Well, how many black people lived in towns like that back then?"

"You weren't around," someone objected. "You don't know."

"It's just" the coxswain was feeling for words, "…swimming isn't a really black thing."

This drew *whats?!* and gasps, so he went on to explain that his sister lifeguards at a city pool in Boston in the summer, and that it's actually a *thing.*

"Actually," a tall girl with jet black hair and Elvis Costello glasses rolled her eyes. "the only black people there would have been the ones serving drinks, and if anyone couldn't find his watch by the pool after a swim, you can bet they'd have had the help turn out their pockets."

A few looked at her like they'd just smelled something unpleasant, and suddenly I was pulled back to Jerome's day at the Coop, and didn't want to be there. I assured her that she might be right to a degree, internally believing that she was right to an advanced degree, perhaps a first at Oxford, *summa cum laude.* Then I steered things back to character development, themes and quotes of note from the text.

"Isn't his own obduracy *his* problem?" Ms. Costello cocked her head as if this should be plain to all of us. I was somewhat sure that prior to that moment, she may well have never used *obduracy* in a sentence before. I've been teaching English for years and have used it perhaps twice, and then it was in grad school papers, never in conversation.

"His *what?*" The coxswain was incredulous, cocking his head as if to drain water from an ear.

"Obduracy," she repeated with a hint of tired aplomb.

"What the fu--" he caught himself, "heck is that?"

"It means he's stubborn," she shrugged.

"Then why didn't you just *say* that?"

"I *did,*" she rolled her eyes.

"And because she read it in the story," Knowing Eyes jumped in. "Right here," and she proceeded to read the passage with it. The two girls locked glares, and I was honestly too curious to see how this would play out to toss some ed school bullshit into things and take them down a notch.

"Yes," Ms. Costello nodded, "I read it in the story. What's wrong with that? Aren't we supposed to grow our vocabularies, especially in an English class?" At that I conceded a nod, as she wasn't wrong. What rankled her classmates was her coming off like George Will, as though this was a word she uses as frequently as toothpaste.

"Okay," I reined things in. "So, it's been suggested that Neddy is white. That everyone in the story is also. Is that how you pictured all the characters?" Heads bobbed reluctantly. "Why?"

"It just sounds like...a really white town," someone threw out.

"What does a white town sound like?" the coxswain offered. I didn't disagree with his question, but wanted someone to flush this matter out.

"Like mine," the red head thinned her lips. "Pools, people who play golf. Half the people drive Audis."

"And their kids get hand-me-down Volvos," Costello added.

"*We* have a pool," Gabby, one of the two black students in the class chimed in, not looking at anyone in particular, "My dad does laps in it mornings in the summer before work." At this kids eyed each other, as if wishing they could take something back that had been said.

"You're lucky," the other black girl grimaced, "My parents, when they bought our house? Had the pool filled in and they put a tennis court there. I hate tennis."

"Was he not a good swimmer?" the coxswain asked, drawing daggers and disbelief from most of the class. "I mean...I saw it somewhere on TV. It's that family, and the guy was in "Law & Order," they're black. They made a joke about...not being..." He knew he was on thin ice and could begin to hear it cracking beneath his feet.

"Black-ish. I saw that one," Gabby rescued him. "Yeah, there's this...myth, but it's also a thing. Black people not being good swimmers. Lots of city pools, back in the day? Whites only. Lots of people couldn't learn to swim. Not in the city." The coxswain exhaled, but Costello wasn't having it.

"That's *so*," she was about to burst. "You can't just *say* that about millions of people, that they can't do something."

"I'm *not* saying *that*," Gabby pushed back, "I'm saying that it *is* kind of a thing, and I'm black so... *Why* are we talking about this?"

"Well, we were discussing "The Swimmer," I offered, "and it's kind of related to it."

"But it's also a stereotype," Costello wrinkled her brow, "just like they did with that kid at the Coop. It's racist. It's endemic to our society."

I didn't want to go down that road, so I held up a finger to her and made a detour. "Endemic *to* something means it's native to a place and may be found only there. Endemic *in* something means it can be commonly found there." This seemed instructive, and a way to reclaim the discussion. I know I'll have more of the Jerome matter but didn't want to sort it out then and there. I went to the list of vocab words I wanted them to take away from the story, and ended up showing them a clip from the film made from the story starring Burt Lancaster.

"Looks pretty white," someone said about the town in the movie.

"And WASPy. Harvard didn't want Jews in the 1900s," someone added.

"What..." The red head was puzzled, "Where does *that* come from? How does Harvard matter?"

"You know," the coxswain cocked his head, "Our classmate? The black one who got...who went to Harvard Square shopping and—"

"Alright," I closed my book with more than a hint of annoyance, "enough about...another student. We're not gonna talk about that here. That's not what this class is about." Indeed, the university *had* been famously anti-Semitic in the past, but that wasn't what this class was about. I cracked the anthology, found "Sonny's Blues," a short story by James Baldwin, and assigned it. If they want to flush out some racial angles, Baldwin might help, but discussion-wise, this would be a Jerome-free class. "We'll thrash out "The Swimmer" more tomorrow. If you want to start on the next story, it's "Sonny's Blues" and there'll be a reading comprehension check on it Monday."

"But it's," one student piped up as he checked page numbers in the table of contents, "it's, like, thirty pages long." Moans of *what?* and *really?* filled the room. *For next class?!?*

"First of all, after our next class, the next one is Monday, four days away." I closed the book, and caught my tie in it, which prompted a few chuckles, and a, "Why do you wear---" that I cut off to finish directions. "And secondly, if you're not done by the end of study hall, pass on playing Fortnight and keep reading. This'll be posted on Google Classroom." There are kids who'd rather chew broken glass than give up Fortnight, so letting them know that I know this was fun.

Sept 29

IF YOU DON'T COACH a sport or have weekend dorm duty, Friday afternoons at school are as pleasant as they are elsewhere in the working world. While students are tearing up playing fields, a quiet descends on classrooms that allows for some planning or grading to get done, or lets you head for the local running trails or the newest brew pub. Rewarding myself with that last option seemed a good idea if I could make some headway on the "What I Learned on My Sabbatical" presentation for the full faculty. Being a bit out of practice, I failed to close my door and draw the lockdown shade once the last class left, so a few minutes into creating a PowerPoint, Glenn Olson knocked and stepped through my door.

"Mr. Minot – got a minute?"

Glenn is a pretty average student and really nice kid whose flair for the slightly rebellious suggests he should do better. His high tops and tie-dyed t-shirts make you expect that he's perpetually whistling a Grateful Dead song, but like all struggling aesthetes, there is an endeavor he throws himself into and has a talent for: cross country. Unfortunately, he tripped on a tree root during the previous week's tri-meet against Overtoun and Chiswick, and was just now off the crutches. I waved him in.

"I kind of don't understand my grade on the paper you handed back..." he offered, and began fishing the graded work out of his backpack. When students say they don't understand their grades on papers, what they mean is *I haven't read your comments which explain the letter grade, but hope you will change it since I'm asking*, or, *I haven't read your comments which explain the letter grade because nobody taught me cursive, so they might as well be in Sanskrit*. In Glenn's case, it may be that I graded his essay – one thousand words on Raymond Carver's "A Small Good Thing" – late in the evening and admittedly, my scrawl by then would not win any penmanship awards. I gestured for him to sit and we pored over his prose with my green marks on the margins – red ink is a trigger / esteem killer / PTSD catalyst. That's the ed school *zeitgeist* anyway. Here and there I pointed out grammatical lapses and spelling errors, then drew attention to the cover sheet with my directions and his intro paragraph.

"The directions asked you to reflect on the element of communication in the story – or the lack of it, not to simply retell it - which is frankly, what you did."

"I wanted to show that I read it, that I understood it." He shrugged like a driver explaining that he hadn't seen the speed limit sign. "Doesn't that count for something?"

"Sure – it shows me you read it and got the details." Then I explained to him what should have been clear from instructions in class and the handout. "But you *needed* to *show me* that you understood the missed information and presumptions on both sides in the story. And I expected *you* to be able to do that." I let that hang there as the lengthening shadows of the failing afternoon crept across my room, hoping he would catch on. Glenn is sixteen years old and has never set foot inside a public school in his life. An oldest son of a Wellesley professor and childhood psychologist, every day of his education has been in either a Montessori or local private school. Such institutions impart to students, and more tragically to their parents, that a stunning intellect is being nurtured and that true gifts reside between those ears. As students move through one or more independent schools, the self-assuredness grows, and the parents become convinced: *Our child is doing okay at a private school - must be pretty smart.* To tell parents otherwise is to jeopardize a revenue stream to the school, so in many cases, the emperor is never told that he's only wearing underwear. The thin ice which is the foundation under Glenn's feet is not his fault; he's been passed along by smiling, approving teachers for the past ten years. Now he simply had the bad luck to have a teacher who could no longer ignore his lack of subject – verb agreement. This news transformed his peach-fuzz deadpan of a face into a squinting twist of confusion.

"This is like...I didn't think it mattered. Some of this stuff. Agreement, like. I write this way for other teachers. It's never been, like, something that, like, hurt my grade."

Like: *preposition. Used when the speaker wishes to be inarticulate.*

"I get that Glenn. And it's not your fault. Different teachers care about different things. There was a teacher at my old school, Mr. Fleck, who never took attendance. But there are certain...rules...*standards,* that you, that *every* student, needs to master."

"But if you know what I'm saying, what does a stupid comma or spelling matter? My dad was telling me about some Apple ads years ago that said, 'Think different,' but that they should have correctly said different-*ly.* So, it doesn't matter, does it?"

Thanks Mr. Jobs.

"Look: when you get to the point of advertising, or being a famous writer, you can do that stuff. You're expressing yourself and have enough license to take certain liberties with language and style. E. E. Cummings wrote entirely in---"

"So," he glared at the 'C' I'd written on the corner that I'd folded up on the last page and exhaled his frustration. "And why did you put the grade here," he stabbed at the mark with a forefinger, "not, like, with the comments? It's like you're hiding it."

"I put it there so that you'll read the comments first, which explain the mark, and not dash to the letter grade and focus on that."

"But grades matter. And why did you circle 'China' when I wrote that his stories have even been published there?"

"Lemme see." He flipped the paper around to me. "Oh, you didn't capitalize 'China.'"

His eyes rolled skyward. "Like...Chinese, right? I'm taking Mandarin with Mrs. Wang. They don't even *have* capitals. In, like, the language. When you write it. Really."

"Yeah, I know, but China also doesn't have Google. Doubt you want to start overlaying all their rules here, right?"

We went around like this for a few more minutes, and it was clear that certain expectations were revelations to him. It was what it must be like when a state trooper gives someone his first speeding ticket after years of not even getting a warning from other cops.

"If you can get these rules of good writing down, Glenn, it'll make your future work much easier when you get to---" As I made this point, he peered over my shoulder to the door, such that I turned, and saw Jianyu Zhang leaning through the threshold.

"Sorry to interrupt," he tipped his head, "Mr. Minot, correct? Do you know when you might have time to talk?"

"I can go," Glenn reached for his paper.

"No, please," Zhang raised a hand to object, "Do not stop for me. Please, finish."

"Nah," Glen rose, "we're good."

"Glenn, we're not *quite* good." I implored him. "Look: could you possibly wait outside, for a minute? I have an idea. Just think about my comments and we'll get back into it shortly, okay?" Bumping his grade up a bit to honor that he was *trying* to understand his progress seemed reasonable. "There's a chair outside the door. Five minutes?" Glenn nodded, meandered around the tables and slipped outside. The kids love that chair. Big and leathery, I figured I'd have to wake him up in it when we resume.

The school's website is a bit vague on the laurels that have landed people on the Board of Trustees. Traditionally, such individuals, who are usually alumni, and present or past parents, should collectively come up with between fifteen and twenty-five percent of the institution's annual giving. It's not clear how Jianyu Zhang ended up in Sinochem's top echelon, but a degree from RPI probably didn't hurt. However he's come by it, he betrays it in true twenty-first century executive form. Gone are the suits and tattersall shirts that could be seen at my school on Trustees' Weekends; open collared button downs and impeccably pressed khakis make do these days. His lean form and slicked back hair suggest any cover of *Forbes* or *Business Week* you'd care to pick up. He strode my way with an extended hand, introducing himself with that amazing blend of humility and self-assuredness that people of his station master at some undisclosed location.

"I didn't mean to cut your meeting with that student short." He raised his eyebrows in an apologetic way. People like Jianyu Zhang are used to things going their way. While someone who is quite generous in supporting the education of young people perhaps meant this statement, he was also probably happy to break the meeting up to get to his own business.

"How is your year going?" He leaned back and crossed his legs, seeking a critique of the first month that would be both sunny and candid. The chatter was light, then he sat up a bit and got to the matter at hand.

"I gather that, during a quiz, my son Eric forgot to leave some notes he was studying in his backpack recently."

I let his words settle in, wanting to walk through this quite carefully. I was also overcome with a sudden sense of having not closed an important loop. For all the gravity of his son's cheating, it was in a class I was subbing in, so once I was done covering it, the memory of it retreated to somewhere way back in the gray cells. Kind of like breaking a glass in a hotel room: you dwell on it then, but the next day, it hardly registers until you're checking out. I hadn't reported the whole water bottle incident to Mary yet, figuring it would keep to this weekend. And now I was cursing myself for this, so I patched. "I'm not sure that's how things…unfolded." I squinted to affirm that we were in different places.

"Well, how would you describe the matter?" he asked, holding a steady gaze. I recounted the handwritten sheet inside the water bottle, and he was careful to not interrupt me, but neither did he nod in the slightest.

"Eric tells me that it was a particularly heavy week for him, and that, because he's supposed to drink a lot of water due to a medication he's on, that he put his notes on the bottle to help him review while hydrating." He waited for my reaction to this angle, which I didn't offer, then went on. "He's a very honest young man. He has never been in any trouble. This is quite a new kind of conduct for our son, and I can't help but think that there's been a, perhaps, a misunderstanding, shall we say?"

"I…can only refer to what happened. I don't know him beyond this class." I gestured to my desk. "I have the bottle I took from him during the quiz. I can show it to you."

"That is not necessary." He raised a palm and glanced away, tipping his head in a knowing way, as if to acknowledge something but also to veto the notion of actually seeing the evidence. "I was hoping that we could look at…the larger view here." I'm guessing he meant 'the big picture.' I must confess: I get a kick out of how non-native speakers of English mangle idioms now and again. Extremely driven students from East Asia are keen to show off new vocabulary and expressions, but perhaps a third of the time these exercises produce something awkward and comical. Two years ago, a young man from Hong Kong was annoyed at some peers who would not let him be part of their video gaming group one afternoon. He stormed out of the room and headed down the hall. When I asked why he was so upset, he explained it all to me.

"The...other...players. They will not let me play with them. So I now do not care. If I cannot play with them, I will go to my room and play with myself."

"Okay," I was suppressing a grin with every ounce of my being. "I can talk to them. I mean, everyone's got to live together here."

"No," he shook his head, black bangs swinging in front of his eyes, "I do not want that. I want to go play with myself."

"Mmmmm," I nodded, "Okay, but perhaps what you want to do is play *by* yourself, okay? That's probably what you mean. Try to always say it that way, okay?" He shrugged and was off. I would not, however, be correcting Mr. Zhang's English.

"S-s-s-u-u-u-u-r-r-e," I leaned back into my chair. "Let's consider the larger view." I waved him onward, not knowing precisely what tack he was taking.

"Eric may have used poor judgment...where he put his notes to help him to review before the quiz. Maybe he did. He *is, after* all, a *late birthday,* which is how you describe a very young student, yes? This could be our fault, his mother's and mine. Maybe we pushed him to be here too early, but his sister has done well here, so we think, yes, this is a good school for Eric too. To the matter of his notes, it is my thought that everything can work out, provided there's an understanding of...what could be best for him. And, for everyone involved." I nodded, but was drawing a blank as a response, so he went on. "I don't think you've had our daughter Naomi in class, have you?"

"I haven't, but then I was on sabbatical last year."

"That's right. I hope it was productive."

"It was. I'm grateful for the opportu---"

"Good. That's good. I like to support teachers. We also have a daughter here - Naomi. You are in her dorm for duty. Is this correct?"

"For study hall, one night a week, yes."

"I thought so. What is this like? Working in a female residence?"

"It's part of the job," I shrugged, "Pretty standard boarding school stuff."

"But, is there any problem being a male on duty in a girls' dormitory?"

"N-n-n-n-o-o-o-o." This direction of the conversation puzzled me, "Gotta do duty somewhere."

"Yes. But was there an episode recently? During an alarm in the dormitory? When you did a room check without knocking first, and a female resident felt rather...*awkward* at you being there and her state of dress?"

It was as if a heavy cloud had just crept before the sun. It explained in part how this man had done so well in business: he does his homework. Two weeks ago I'd knocked on a door repeatedly when a fire alarm went off in the dorm and heard no response, so I finally entered a room to find a girl in shorts, a tank top and a face cream mask. It came together like a guess in the game of "Clue" - *Naomi Zhang in the dorm with the fire alarm*. I put it in the dorm log that night, and gave it no more thought until now, and then the last piece came to mind.

"Not sure *that's* what we're here to talk about, or even that *that's* anything at all. If you're talking about a girl who didn't answer her door when—"

"I'm sure you can see how events can get blown out of correct proportion. When that happens, things, ideas about people can form, rightly or in an incorrect way, that they, the people, really do not deserve." He allowed his words to settle on me for a bit. "We all must take care to see that our actions, and decisions, are not misunderstood by others. Or have...unwelcome results." He allowed his words to settle for a bit, before continuing. "The results of one situation can impact the results of another. For good, and...maybe, not so good."

Minot's Ledge

I felt that I had a moment of silence on my side, but that was about all. He checked his phone for the time, and then it was as if a switch had been thrown. He looked up with a hopeful face and raised a cautionary finger. "If you can keep a secret, there'll be some big news about something good for the school tomorrow. Something that will enhance our understanding of our universe." There had been a rumbling that we might be getting a small observatory - basically a big telescope in a small silo with a roof that opens behind the maintenance building. Perhaps he is the donor, but framing it as if this place will produce the next Neil deGrasse Tyson was a bit much. He rose to shake my hand, which was as disagreeable as it was unavoidable. "I'm sure Eric will learn a lot this year." Then he paused and scanned the room. "He, and everyone at a place like this, must make good decisions carefully, yes?" I didn't know what to say, which was probably what he was hoping.

Oct 2

"ARE YOU EFFING *KIDDING* me?" This was as close as I'd ever heard Ralph swear when I told him about my meeting with Zhang. It was one of those gray afternoons when the low ceiling of clouds and rain from the night before made hanging in my classroom after lessons preferable to anything else. He'd stopped in with some anecdote about a former student of ours who's now at Columbia. Repeating Zhang's *proposal* back to me, he shook his head. "You *know* what that is, right?"

I nodded and shrugged. "I also know about St. Paul's, St. George's and Brooks." Among schools with scandals involving teachers crossing boundaries, these were the most notorious ones. Such events have led to a *fait accompli* for male teachers at schools: you're accused, you lose.

"You gotta go to Barclay with this. The kid *cheated.*" He unzipped his down vest and half sat on a table. "You know how kids are. Word will get out, others will pull it, and daddy's checkbook will let that kid skate through here like Gretzky."

"Everything you say is true," I loosened my tie and tilted back in my chair, "but you saw that announcement: the observatory Zhang's helping out with? Think Barclay's gonna kiss that goodbye to have my back? Bet he's got a pile of resumes in his office of kids two years out of college who he could plug into my spot for half my pay."

"Yeah, but," he held up a cautionary finger, "you get what you pay for."

"Since when does *that* matter at a school?" I sat up and jabbed a finger his way. "Remember that opening in your department a few years ago for a chem teacher? You brought that woman here who'd been to Antarctica, right? She'd had something published in *Nature* magazine or something and had taught a summer at Cal Tech right?" He closed his eyes and nodded as if reliving a spell of pain. "And she was *black!* And who'd they go with? Some kid fresh out of Wesleyan who could coach field hockey. And *she* was gone in two years when her boyfriend got into law school in Chicago."

"Mmmm," he looked at the floor, as if some solace was to be found there. "I know, I know. Think *I* didn't want a black colleague? But," he stood up and exhaled in exasperation. "This is like a poison that'll just grow here."

"You're not wrong," I cocked my head and with a sound from my phone, I reached to see a text that I could ignore for the time being. "But neither am I." He gave a hopeful wave and headed for the door. "And I like having health insurance!" I shouted after him. He shook his head in resignation.

"Your call pal. We're about keeping things honest right? Kids write up lab reports based on what they see…we tell them not to argue with officials in games, right? We don't want them to cheat, but…hell, dude: you call this kid on cheating, do your job - and *you won't have a job.*"

"What? Wait…c'm-o-o-o-o- n." I pulled a face, but he stared back with deadpan. "My *job?*"

He leaned back on a table, and looked toward the ceiling, as if doing so would help him choose his words. Then he spoke. "Remember that physics teacher we hired a year before you left? She was from Simmons and coached swimming?"

I nodded, then remembered something. "Yeah. Haven't seen her around since I've been back. She moved on to another school?"

"You *could* say that." He tilted his head in a way to suggest that I didn't quite have it right. "She had some student in her class who…wasn't about to re-write the Theory of Relativity. Not a bad kid, just not an 'A' student. But apparently her grandfather went here, and mom was toying with the idea of a big gift to the school. But then her daughter pulled a 'C' in physics. Not a tragedy, but winter term she went out for swimming, and ended up on JV. Mom had sent her to a swimming camp at Penn, and was fit to be tied. And guess who the swimming coach was?"

"The teacher from Simmons?"

"Y-y-y-y-up." Ralph nodded. "Barclay - after presumably having his ear chewed off by the mother - called her in, asked her to "do what she could,"" - here Ralph made air quotes with his fingers, "to help the girl feel validated here, and mentioned how unhappy her mother was with her decisions, as a coach and teacher, and thus Griswold."

"What did Remy say?" I asked. As our Athletic Director, Frank Remillard would seemingly have something to say about how teams are set. Ralph shook his head.

"There was a gift in play here. *Money.* That's above Remy's pay grade. But the teacher wouldn't budge. The 'C' in physics and the JV status stood." With this, Ralph hoped that silence would do its work. "You haven't seen that teacher around this fall, have you?"

I shook my head, but pulled a face. "You *are* joking."

"Hmmm. All I know is, she got really good write-ups when she was observed teaching, but come spring, she was walking around in a daze, like her dog had died. Didn't come to the end of year dinner, and…gone."

"You think calling it as she saw it got her canned?"

"I think that doing that with the daughter of someone who might write a six or seven figure check to the school wasn't smart.

No way she could know all that - first year here, real nose-to-the-grindstone type, but...we're a business. Don't want to piss off the customers."

"Wow...cream." I shook my head.

"Cream?"

"That's what Bags calls kids who aren't doing well, but whose parents pull them out of school before a break for trips to Aruba and the like. They think they're the cream of the crop, and Bags says they're like cream indeed - *rich and thick*." Ralph howled at this.

"So, you're telling me that Jiang's kids are supposed to skate through here? No bad grades? Allowed to cheat?"

Lips thinned, he rolled his eyes and straightened up. "I can't tell you what to do pal, but this guy is a trustee, which means he's already written some big checks to the school. You cross him at your own peril. *And I like working with you!*" I let his words settle on me. I slowly began to feel like one of those characters in a cop show who was presented with a Faustian bargain. "I can't tell you want to do man, but, you're already out on a ledge, having called the guy's kid for cheating - *which is the right thing to do*, by the way. Just be careful you don't get yourself pushed off."

"Are you...Really? *Really?* We have *rules*, right?" His certainty about this was the most infuriating part of it; *here's how it is.*

"Hey. Do what you gotta do, but...you ever read Charles Barkley's book?"

I squinted at him, and couldn't resist. "Yeah, right between *Great Expectations* and *Sophie's Choice*. Sorry - 'fraid not."

"Didn't think so, but here's the title, and I'll leave you with it - *I May be Wrong, But I Doubt It.*" It sucks, I know, but your job's more important than some kid who thinks "when in doubt, look about," so...just think about it." With that he hit the light switch by his door. I told him I'd catch up with him in the dining hall, but never did.

Oct 4

PREPARING THE PRESENTATION ON my sabbatical was proving harder than I thought. The trick is to convey that what I learned could only have been learned by roaming south of the Mason-Dixon line as I did. Luckily for me, Southern literature has been bumped to the hinterlands of many a college curricula. Thus, by throwing around names like Eudora Welty and Carson McCullers, I already sounded well-versed in the genre when I proposed the undertaking two years ago. A case could be made that *Midnight in the Garden of Good and Evil* and most things John Grisham has written provide a sense of certain places and people, but there's a reason Faulkner won a Nobel Prize, and Grisham hasn't.

Pulling together some Google slides at my desk, I had a premonition that there would be a knock on my door. My aunt has a photo of herself and Natalie Cole when they were together at Northfield, and when I looked up to see someone approaching my desk, all I could think about was how much she looked like the now-deceased singer. Geraldine Davis carried herself like someone not shy about sending back meals in restaurants. In a jade pant suit with a posture that a chiropractor would commend, she added a qualifier to her name as she extended a hand, "Jerome's sister."

Between hearing that and her bearing, I unconsciously stood, as if a trustee had just walked in. Her uplifted chin, engaging smile yet unblinking eyes conveyed purpose. "Hope I'm not interrupting. I'm seeing Scott Paone at four, but am early, so wanted to meet you." Ambushed is not the right word, but it made me rethink staying in my room so late. I gestured for her to sit, and looking over my shoulder, she broke into an ambivalent grin.

"Ah, Sylvie…" She spotted a photo of Sylvia Plath atop a bookcase behind my desk. It was there when I moved into this classroom, and I've never bothered to move it.

"Do you read poetry?" I asked.

"No, but at Smith, we got a lot of her there. Even if you *weren't* an English major." As Jerome is a freshman, it occurred to me that she might still be a student herself, but as we spoke, she mentioned that she'd been out of college a few years. Sylvia Plath went to Smith, and her end in London years later has probably afforded her more notoriety than her poetry, but I was pretty sure that discussing this was not why Miss Davis had appeared. She eyed a college mug full of pens behind me, and forced a smile as she cocked her head to one side.

"My great grandfather supposedly got in there," she pointed to the Harvard mug, "but he was Jewish, and they had that quota back then, so when my mother got into that place and Smith, it took about four seconds for her to make her decision."

"So, like mother like daughter?"

"Not quite. Mother is an overachiever. Had Jane Wright as a mentor while in med school - made quite an impression upon her."

I nodded and apologized for my ignorance.

"She - Dr. Wright - sort of made chemotherapy a more widely used form of treatment. Developed a catheter system for delivering it. First woman to head the New York Cancer Society."

"Wow."

"And she was Black. Still is."

Humor. That helped. Nodding seemed the best response here. To sound surprised wouldn't do, but these days to hear anything other than that she was stopped by a traffic cop for a broken taillight was a nice change.

"No slouch," was all I could manage.

"No," she offered a more genuine smile, "but neither is our mom. She managed to somehow get us to where we are while cutting her own path in medicine." She sat up a little straighter, and leaned forward. "I was hoping that you could share with me your take on what happened at the Coop with my brother."

"Sure" I nodded, recounting everything I could, emphasizing that by the time two students found me in another part of the building, Jerome was already in the security office.

"And what was that like?" she squinted and thinned her lips a bit, suggesting that this was the heart of the matter. Into my head came those images of Dr. King holding a board in front of his chest that says Birmingham Jail, and of him being bent over a booking counter as a policeman collects his personal effects, probably for walking down the sidewalk with Bayard Rustin without a parade permit.

"I kind of felt that not having been there, that I couldn't offer all that I might have otherwise, if I had, say, been in the store with the boys earlier. It honestly didn't seem necessary when I let them off the bus. Kids always roam without us, in at least pairs."

"Was the Coop's...*officer*," she seemed to have to force herself to use that title, "fair? I'm not someone who plays this card a lot, but young black men and police: not a good record."

"True. 'Course." I sat forward, elbows on the desk and my chin on two fists, thinking.

"Honestly, I haven't been in that kind of a situation before, so how they deal with, say, white kids who get cau...*accused* of such things, I don't have anything to judge it against."

"I got a slightly different version from Jerry, and...he doesn't want it out there, but he's my brother, so I'm thinking of his best interests."

" 'Course." I nodded. "And, is this a version you can share with me?"

She folded her hands in her lap and spoke thoughtfully. "Jerry says that the boys he was with dared him to snatch something from a counter at the store, and when he wouldn't, one of them grabbed it and shoved it into his pocket. Jerry swore, which drew attention to him, and as he pulled the item out of his pocket, a salesperson approached. The others kind of faded away at that point."

"Oh," was all I could manage. "Well, that's something that the Coop should know abou—"

"No." She shook her head with eyes closed, and thinning lips. "Jerry doesn't want that. He doesn't care about going back to the Coop. I mean, why would he? But he doesn't want to drag other kids into it either. You know, the whole 'snitches' thing."

This new information seemed more important than some urban quip about stitches, so I jumped in. "But if—"

"Besides," she cut me off. "The whole racial angle isn't lost on him. He doesn't think they - the Coop, the school - will believe him. I'll be sharing this with Mr. Paone, but it's for internal purposes only, if you will. Last thing he wants is to be known as a snitch a month into school."

"Even if it's in his own interest?" I pulled a face in confusion, and we fixed silent glares on each other. But she knows her brother, and as I'm not in his shoes, who cares what I think? I thanked her for letting me know this account of things.

She uncrossed her legs and stood. "My hope is that understanding this angle of everything might inform how things shake out for him. Before Griswold, Jerome was at some school outside Springfield. It had a swimming pool about the size of our living room and a middle school which was run by a real clown. Treated the kids like third graders, and my mom wanted more for him. Something happened in the dorm - it didn't involve Jerome, but they just let it slide. A campus rent-a-cop stopped a black teacher on campus to see why she was there, and his favorite teacher was spoken to about wearing a Black Lives Matter shirt. My mother couldn't believe it. Lots of eighth graders there don't go to their upper school across the street, but instead go on to other places freshman year. That's why Jerry is here. For now."

Her *for now* hung there: *we left some shitshow in western Mass., and so far...*

"So I gather you're meeting with Scott Paone at some point, and as I'm kind of a worker bee here, I'm not sure what more I can offer." I tossed a palm up and winced, feeling as though I wasn't being as helpful as she was hoping I could be.

"I read school and alumni magazines - you wouldn't believe how many pile up in our house - and when I'm online but aren't feeling academic, I read their websites. Kind of a geeky hobby I know, but we've been to lots of schools. I read that you did a sabbatical down south. Spent a year there, I saw. My guilty pleasure has been John Grisham books, and when race comes up, it's sometimes in scenarios like what happened to my brother. So I'm just wondering: have you read *The New Jim Crow?*"

"I started, but didn't finish it." I tipped my head with a hint of shame. It was a book a decade ago about mass incarceration and you can guess of mostly who. A hundred pages of it made two things clear: our criminal justice system has racist aspects to it - not news - and some books should come with a two-week supply of antidepressants. I explained that this was why I didn't finish it, feeling that as a teacher who ought to devour all *important* books, I was coming up short here as well.

"Yeah, well you can get *depressed* about it, but Jerome, a young black man, has to *live* it." I nodded and thought about the birth lottery. "So nothing about how the Coop handled things struck you as wrong?"

Harvard is kind of like a country, and when you're from a country, you don't always love it, or at least you don't love it like the people running it do, or say they do. Some of the stuff I read in the alumni magazine makes me roll my eyes: not letting the captains of sports teams join clubs, firing a housemaster who is the lawyer for a despicable criminal defendant, as opposed to an appealing one, and so on. Thus I was happy to throw the Coop under the bus for how it handled Jerome, but I couldn't tell her more than I had.

"This seemed like a good place for Jerry," she extended her hand. "Maybe it still is." I nodded but couldn't help but feel that I hadn't checked off that many boxes for her. "We sure weren't going to let him stay where he was, and Taft was out of the question after what happened there a few years ago. Who knows?"

As soon as she left I did a search for "racist" and "Taft School." With iron gates at the entrance to its faux - Gothic campus, Taft in Connecticut has tried desperately to look more like a British public school than most British public schools. Its claim to fame is that it was founded by William Howard Taft's brother. In 2018, a student from Ghana found "Go back to Africa" scrawled on his door. Some artwork by black students was defaced around the same time. So glad we're in the twenty-first century.

Oct 9

BEING AWAY FOR A year, you forget how kids don't miss much - except when they want to. As they were lumbering into my first period class, Schyler van Wyck stuck his head into my room. A capable colleague, his perpetual *rushed here from my boat* coif and blinding smile always draws the attention of any girls who happen to be in the room. Today he dropped in to ask for my copier code.

"What's the matter with yours?" I asked. There's a limit to what we can print each month, and after you hit it, you're billed for additional copies over that limit. Billed, i.e., they tap your pay. Really. It's pennies, and designed to keep copies down and be green. The irony of this policy is that nobody would suggest that our students now are as strong as they were even a decade ago, and that includes organizationally, so today we need to print out extra hard copies of things like notes more than ever. Kids seem to lose papers handed out like crazy, and you just can't expect them to listen carefully, write it all down or check class pages online, even though in many respects they're tech savvier than their teachers. It's not all their fault. They can't be expected to do what previous teachers haven't asked them to do.

"Nothing's wrong with my code, 'cept I can't remember it."

"So if you go and run off *War and Peace*, I'm done for the month." I told him.

"Relax – no Russian lit. Just a vocab sheet."

Even I had to admit that an indigo polo shirt made his eyes even more blue, which was not lost on a few female students who couldn't help but ogle him. His devil-may-care way does have a certain charm. Life for Schy seems like a country club. He's never frazzled the night before grades are due or when a college rec deadline looms. He'll stroll into a class a bit late, no sweat. This unflappable quality, and the effortlessness with which he pulls it off is not lost on others.

I scribbled my code for the copier on a Post-it note and gave it to him, noticing a few kids switching their glances from me to him and then back to me again. He held up two fingers, and pointed at the circle of sophomores around my tables. "Learn stuff," he charged them, and slipped out.

"Mr. Minot," one student asked as I was taking attendance online. "How come you're..." he stroked the front of his shirt. I squinted at him, trying to will a bit more articulation telepathically.

"How come I'm *Lutheran?*" You opened this door kid – walk through it.

"No," a few chuckles, and he pointed to my chest. "Why...do you always wear a tie?" I knew he was going there, but wanted him to verbalize it. My guess was that Schy's *tres cas* style and breezy presence nudged this student's curiosity along these lines, in that the contrast between his and my sartorial choices was clear.

Somewhere in the well of my psyche, I've been waiting for this. I filed that whole "no ties, no tiers, no tears," notion way back in my head. Schools love themes and mantras. *Character counts. Truth always wins. Serve others.* Whenever possible, put it in Latin. These work best if such an adage is part of a school's seal, which ideally was designed in the 1800s. In the absence of a time machine, this can be hard to affect just now. As we were now talking about appearance, it's worth noting that dress codes for students tend to be crafted by bored deans. It'll be a cold day in hell when I speak to a teenage girl about her spaghetti straps. That someone actually suggested a dress code for teachers tells me that at least one administrator truly has too much free time on his hands - and clearly drank a whole punch bowl of ed school Kool-Aid.

"My tie?" I tugged at the end of it. "You like it?" I gave him a hopeful grin with raised eyebrows to suggest my anticipation of a compliment.

"No. I mean, sure but…"

"What is that?" a usually quiet girl piped up. "On your tie?"

I looked down and saw the black and white bears on a yellow field of silk. "Pandas. A student from China gave me this."

The first student chimed back in, "Why? I mean, Mr. van Wyck is just, you know, not wearing one."

"Really?" I cocked my head in a skeptical way, "Are you sure?"

"Yes! He was here just a minute ago."

"Okay, yeah. So, your question is?"

"It's just that most of the teachers here - kinda like him – don't wear ties."

"Mr. Woodson does," someone jumped in. Woody is a by-the-book dean and Latin teacher who does the *Times* crossword in ink and corrects anyone, including trustees, who ends a sentence with a preposition.

"Yeah, but he's…" someone shrugged.

"He's *what?*" I asked.

If they were going to keep stalling the start of the lesson, I was going to make them work for it. Another boy caught this student's eye and waved him off this tack of discussion, which likely would have included speculation as to Woody's sexuality.

"So," I finally sat in my chair at the tables, "is there a reason I *shouldn't* wear a tie?"

"Nobody *else* does."

"Nobody might attend communist party meetings or drink pigs' blood at midnight on New Year's - does that mean I *shouldn't* do these things, just because they don't?".

"You actually *do* that?" A sleepy wallflower perked up. Glances were exchanged to determine the veracity of my statement via other people's reactions.

"In all honesty: no. But my point is – why does someone have to do what everyone else does, whether it's not drinking pig's blood or not wearing a tie?"

"Okay," A swaggering soccer star who, from the looks of him in chapel and Sunday dinner, owned all of one tie, sat up a little straighter, "but why go to the trouble of tying it? And choking on it? Aren't you making work for yourself? Unnecessarily?"

"Hmmm," I rested my chin on a fist and considered his point. "Well, honestly: tying a tie is not work. I suppose I might wear them in part out of respect for the profession. I think teaching is a good use of my skills and life. I put more thought into it than, say, if I'm going to a yard sale some Saturday."

"So," a previously silent student allowed a grin to creep across his face, "are you saying that teachers who *don't* wear ties *don't* respect your profession?"

I eyed him with a combination of annoyance and satisfaction. "Is *that* what I said? That my tie-less peers are just killing time and don't respect their responsibilities? *Is* it? *You wanna go next door and tell Mr. van Wyck I said that?*" Like a deer frozen in headlights, he was speechless. " 'Course not. I work with some super people here. And by the way, wearing a tie in one's work doesn't make that work more important than that of someone who doesn't, so let's get that out of the way." Silence. Onward. "Here's a true story, then we'll get to the reading for today." Subtly, some settled into their chairs a bit more, as if anticipating a revelation or confession of sorts. I leaned back to tell a story.

"My first job student teaching was in a small town in New Hampshire. I was new at the job, wanted to make a good impression, and also, my father, a banker, wore a tie to work every day of his working life. So I did too. I thought, 'This is what you wear to work.' Make sense?" Just about everyone nodded. "So, my vice-principal there was a really nice guy. Been in schools for years, seen it all, and was a huge Patriots' fan. Lived and breathed the team. And every Monday, if they won on Sunday or were playing that Monday night, he'd wear a Patriots' sweatshirt to school."

"Wait," one asked. "A vice-principal? In a sweatshirt?"

"Yeah. He'd been there forever. Once told me what it was like teaching the day that Kennedy was shot, OK? Really up on the career ladder. Nothing to prove. Probably a few years from retirement. So one Monday, he and I are talking in the school lobby between classes, and this UPS truck pulls up out front. Guy comes in with his cute little brown shorts, announcing that he has the new printer for the counseling office. Harry – that was the vice-principal's name – and I watched him approach us, and as he does, he hands *me* the clipboard. 'Why are you giving this to me?' I ask him. 'Got the new Ricoh 97L out there - need someone in charge to sign for it,' he says. 'Why me?' I asked, and he gestured to my shirt and tie, saying he needed the signature of someone in authority. Harry, my boss in the sweatshirt, laughed, took the clipboard from me and signed." A few heads nodded, and some grins appeared.

"So," a fifteen-year-old proponent of social justice who already looked like an angry Rachel Weiz spoke up, "you guys were *profiled.*"

I thought for a second, tapping my chin for effect, then answered her. "Yes. Absolutely. And you know what? That's what we do. We being humans. We're a very visual species. But my point is, that tie and that sweatshirt told the UPS guy something – or at least gave him a sort of impression, as to who was in charge. And the respect that it seemed to confer upon me? Misplaced? Yes. But is there a lesson in there? *Also* yes."

"That is so…" Rachel's doppelganger was clenching her fists in frustration, "so *wrong.*"

"Hmmm. Maybe," I cocked my head, "but it's happened more than once. To me anyway, so the reality is---"

"Reality *sucks!*" she interrupted.

"No," I held up a corrective finger, "straws suck. Reality is, you're at a private school with three options for lunch today, lots of hot water in showers after your sports, and unlike Malala, nobody's going to shoot you for trying to get an education. Take a breath."

They seemed to take this as a period at the end of this excursion, so the quiet that followed allowed for a segue into the Bernard Malmud reading they had for homework. Life here is pretty good, for them, and me. If a student gets upset that I was profiled as having more responsibility than I actually did years ago, she should buy a lottery ticket, for clearly she was tapped by the lucky stick if that's her idea of a problem in society. There are perhaps seven billion people in the world who wish they had only such things to fret about.

Oct 15

Email from Fred Talleyrand

Getting to Know You Meeting

Ben –

As part of the new year, I like to meet with all new faculty. As I'm new to you as a result of the sabbatical, I'd like to finally chat one-on-one. I'll send you a Google invitation for a time based on your class schedule. Looking forward to speaking with you.

Fred T.

CALLING THOSE GOOGLE INVITES "invitations" is like referring to a parking ticket as a charitable gift to the city. It ended up being last Friday after lunch, and was pretty laid back. We swapped tales of his years in France, my time in Haiti after the quake, for starters anyway. He tilted his Herman Miller Aeron chair back to emphasize how unofficial our exchange was. He reminded me of some actor I'd seen on the classic movie channel - Burgess Meredith maybe, or Truman Capote, who I knew from somewhere else.

"I heard so much about you, while you were down south," he smiled, offering up that lukewarm grin that suggested he was thinking about something that he would not verbalize directly. The shelves behind him had books on learning styles, effective classrooms and the adolescent mind, but nothing there or on his desk suggested he'd actually been a teacher himself, although posters of James Baldwin and Key West suggested a range of interests. Eventually he sat up straight and pointed to my chest.

"You're a... pretty traditional guy, I take it."

"Hmmm," I looked at the Princeton diploma over his right shoulder. Can't get much more old school than that place's eating clubs. "Not sure what that means. I write 'thank you' notes for gifts, but a good friend of mine owns a pot shop and is transgender, so, depends, I guess." I offered up some empty palms in confusion.

"Really?" he was intrigued," How is that? Is it a moneymaker?"

"I dunno. He just bought a Lexus, so could be."

"Ha! I'm like that myself, in some ways. Big on thank you notes. Always have been. Pedantic even - least that's what my brother said. Used to make a list of cards and gifts for my birthday and Christmas and would get my notes out for everything the next day, dating them all so people would know I'd gotten right on it."

"Good habit," I nodded.

"Never hurt. My sister thought I was OCD, but sometimes being that way can pay off. I mean, details matter. They send messages." I continued to nod, knowing that some detail he thought mattered a great deal was about to come up. "Last year we came up with the three Ts as a pathway forward for the school. Sort of a theme that will hopefully last beyond just one year." He extended a hand and started ticking them off with his fingers: "No tiers, no ties, no tears, the thinking being that putting the first two aside would minimize the third from students. Just trying to tamp down any prompts that could lead to anxiety among the kiddos."

"Right. I've heard."

"Good. So...you don't *have* to wear a tie every day," he pointed again. "It's nice by the way, though. What is it?"

The red and yellow paisley had seen better days, as some fraying at the tip hinted. This ambivalent tack of his was rather annoying: *I like that - don't wear it.*

"I dunno," I shrugged, "It was a gift, probably." I actually got it in Trier, Germany years ago, but didn't want to suggest that I could be bothered to recall such details, or even give much thought to ties. I have more than I need, but like tools in a garage, you just sort of acquire them. Unlike bottles of wine, though, they don't get used up, but just hang on racks like pictures in a hallway you walk past daily and never think about.

"Nice, really. I'm just thinking that it can seem a bit formal to some of our students."

"It probably does. Kids only wear ties when they have to, which is, what, four times a year here? The Founder's Assembly, stuff like that. But, I'm not asking them - the boys - to wear them."

" 'Course. Right. But, some students in the dining hall the other day - probably new this year – they don't know you, and maybe it *wasn't* you, but they were saying how some teacher seems so... "dressy" was their word. Sounds rather silly, right? But as they went on about it for a bit...It's amazing what kiddos say when they don't realize they can be heard."

"Hmmm.," it was clear that I had to tread carefully here, for he's bothering to have a meeting about ties for God's sake. "I get that not all, maybe *most*, of the other male teachers don't wear ties, especially the science guys who go mucking around on ecology class outings, but," and I leaned in to seem earnest and the opposite of what I was feeling, which was a sense of disbelief that this conversation was taking place, "aren't we, as educators, all about getting kids ready for the world beyond the school gates? In college for instance: maybe tweedy profs, maybe a Ph.D. in a t-shirt."

"Absolutely. And Family Weekend, for conferences? Absolutely. But I know where you've been, Ben. The South. Some places there can be real keepers of tradition. We don't have to do that. We're not *requiring* you to do that. Just…" He was waving his hands away from himself, as if trying to coax the right words out. I could have helped him, but, why? "You don't *have* to dress like it's always Family Weekend."

"I don't. Least I don't *think* about it. I just wear the same clothes I've had since, mmmm, heck, my first teaching job. I just don't look around at others and decide how to dress."

"Sure. I get it. You're thinking about other things. And that's great. That's why you're here, right? Times change though, and we've got kiddos here who, well, some come from feeder schools, but some come from Montessori schools, and some from inner cities, and some of them just attach a lot of authority to ties. And, and this isn't on you, but in a way, to some, depending on their experiences, it doesn't encourage positive learning."

I let this sink in for a few seconds, during which I conjured up a mental image of my tie rack. "I get it. This," I held out a bit of my tie as if displaying a soiled rag, "is what they might have called a "power tie" one time. Paisley is sort of a part of the executive armor you'd see on TV and in the financial districts. So I can definitely leave things like this on the rack if it'll keep me from triggering any kids."

"Oh, I don't know about triggering kids. It just might keep things a bit lighter. That'd be great. How we appear is often figurative, but kids can be very literal. So, it's good for us to remember that. And, be as literal as we can with them. To help with clarity."

"Hmmm. Okay. Literal. I get it." Just then I had a brainstorm that I wouldn't verbalize. Instead, I went elsewhere with things. "Any plans for scrapping the dress code for the four or so annual-

--" At that his phone went off, which was good, because, once the matter at hand is done, small talk can be excruciating. *Yeah, I really thought the Celtics would pull it out...No, haven't tried that new tapas place in town yet. Pricey?*

"Okay," I stood up as he eyed his phone, "the paisley ties are on sabbatical- I'll let you take that call." He gave me a thumbs up while answering the phone, and I headed out for a spell of Friday afternoon essay grading.

Oct 19

Ralph was rather bored last weekend, so decided we should go into Boston for some laughs. Comedy clubs have never been a favorite of mine, but since every movie out there seems to be made for 12-year-old boys, and listening to jazz in a hot club would mean we'd drink too much, that left comedy. Ten Jokes Walk Into A Bar is a cookie-cutter laugh shop with small, round tables and dark walls in East Cambridge, a funkier than average part of the city.

"You meet someone you want to...get to know," Ralph held up a hopeful finger to me as we walked there from his car, "I'll get scarce."

"Don't count on it," I waved off the notion.

"C'mon Can't be a bachelor for the rest of...I mean..."

"Why not? *You* are."

"That's different."

"How?"

"I'm a six-foot-five black man at a lily-white prep school in a lily-white town. I teach AP bio and coach two varsity sports. I have neither the prospects *nor the time* to meet someone. You, however...I know you miss her, but, and you can tell me to go to hell, but, widowers get to be happy. No law against it."

"Yeah, fine, but I am not trolling for companionship in a comedy club. And in your case, why not move? Off-campus? Or to another school?"

"Yeah, I think about it," he nodded, picking up the pace past the health food shops and progressive bookstores, "but every January when it comes time to maybe throw my rez around, I just get lazy, or swamped with college recs and coaching." Ralph is as committed to the kids as anyone at Griswold. He once scratched an interview at a better school in Connecticut, and when I asked him why, while he seemed ambivalent about a change, he confessed, "I can probably have a bigger impact on kids here than on kids there, where lots of them are on autopilot," referring to students at the school he passed on. "But we've got kids who could go either way. It's nice to get 'em on the best road, 'specially if they're at a fork, and could go either way." When explaining this, his big hands parted like a road at a fork, convincing me of the correctness of his choice, and maybe convincing himself.

"Anyway, maybe things will get social here. Y' never know," he shook his head.

"Sometimes, y'do," I shrugged. The $12 cover charge afforded us the privilege of buying $8 beers and surveying the other suckers. Several pairs of women, a few in berets, all with lots of ink. Some mixed and diverse gaggles of friends who were perhaps there to support a pal who was trying stand up, and at least one casually surly waitress. Ralph nodded his approval.

"Interesting crowd," he smiled. "The odds are good."

"Hmmm…but the goods are odd."

He rocked with laughter at that, drawing a few stares. "Where do you come up with stuff like that?"

"I was down south for a while. Some real backwaters. What they lack in SAT scores they make up for with pithy quips." Comics that some patrons knew or affected to recognize took to the small stage for short sets. Some of the stuff was pretty raunchy, perhaps because they're using material they can't employ on "The Tonight Show." Most stuck to tossing out barbs regarding the president, Michael Jackson, and off-color anecdotes at the expense of local towns with either a hint of squalor or over the top ostentatiousness.

"She said "Kiss me where it smells" - so I drove her to Chelsea," got lots of laughs, Chelsea being a gritty town on the north edge of Boston. Eventually, Billy Clubb was up there, a lean, late-20s white guy with curly red hair and a pallor suggesting that he only came out at night. Billy's schtick was similar to the others, albeit with a bit more polish to his delivery and timing, courtesy of some chops earned in New York clubs and a spot or two on Jimmy Fallon. In spite of his freckled legacy, one of his offerings had quite the WASPish thread.

"So this guy at a bus stop notices this other guy reading the Yale alumni news and mentions that he went to Harvard. The other guy says, "Well, my father also went to Yale, as did my grandfather." The first guy says, "Well, my great, great grandfather gave a dorm to Harvard. The other says, "My ancestor gave Yale its first boathouse," and this goes back and forth; my ancestors fought with Ulysses Grant, well mine fought with Washington. Finally, one of them thinks he has the clincher: "My family came over on the Mayflower." The other fellow thinks for a minute, then says, "We had our own boat."

Everyone loved it, and that it was clean and at nobody's expense seemed rare. He then went into some stories about trying to pass as a WASP in such a world, Triscuits as hors d'oeuvres, squash as a sport, not a food, and talking about things that happened at a school he attended. From the mention of certain traditions, it seemed as though he was talking about a place we knew. Ralph and I looked at each other, thinking this without having to say it. In a bit of serendipity, at the end of his set, both our glasses were empty, and as folks just off the stage usually decompress at the bar, we decided to kill two birds with one stone. We introduced and explained ourselves.

"Some of your school references sounded *very* familiar," Ralph squinted, "What school was that?"

"Place outside of Boston. I never graduated though. Just did two years there."

"How come?" I asked. As I did so, I realized this was quite impolitic, like asking why someone is no longer wearing a wedding ring. The beer, and that he'd seemed to have done alright in spite of no diploma, washed my momentary discomfort away.

"Let's just say that, when they printed the honor roll? They didn't have to ask whether 'Clubb' was with one 'b' or two.'"

"So, where was this?"

He set his drink down on the bar and even in the dim light of the room, you could see a nostalgic smile turn the corners of his mouth up. "Little place between here and Worcester. Griswold School." He nodded to himself as if some personal joke had just come to him.

Ralph and I traded grins, which caught his eye. "Why? You guys *know* the place?"

Ralph has a great way about him; a sense of humor so arid sometimes that you have to wait to see him crack a smile to realize he's kidding. "Apart from the dorm duty schedule and the copay on their health insurance plan, not much else, really."

Billy Clubb gave a knowing nod. "Yeah. It was probably only a matter of time. You guys really work there?"

Ralph and I explained ourselves, and he had lots of *Do they still?* questions, wondering how much it had changed in a decade and a half. He had Bags as a teacher and got a yellow card in a soccer game for suggesting that an opposing player had an unnatural relationship with his mother. That he remembered that the game was against Dublin School flicked a switch on for me.

"Have you been back to school? Since you left?" I asked.

"Nah," he swizzled his drink and signaled for another. "They don't want to see me again."

"You'd be surprised," Ralph cocked his head, "Kids are works in progress. Jus' 'cuz you weren't class president fifteen years ago doesn't mean you're banned from campus."

"That you've made good would be...interesting," I suggested. "You're sort of famous, and funny. That could make for a good chapel talk."

"*Me?* In the *chapel?*" His twisted face made it clear he found this a very incongruous notion.

"Sure. You know, a guy who once sat where you are made good. Bit of an inspiration for them. Tell a few jokes."

"Clean ones," Ralph held up a cautionary hand, "no 'Chelsea' cracks."

"Hmmm," Billy mulled the idea. "C'mon," he sat up and pulled a face. "I'm here," he waved an arm towards the stage, "but, *made good?* Not sure I'm---"

"You did Jimmy Fallon right?" I recalled from when he was introduced earlier, "Had a part in that Seth Rogen movie, right?" He nodded. "Admittedly, you're not Seinfeld - *yet* - but that stuff would impress kids. And it's more than any of us have done." I gestured to Ralph and myself.

I could tell the idea was playing nicely with his ego, and we exchanged cards.

The last comic was rather forgettable. Lots of, 'You might be from Vermont' jokes involving Subarus, vegans and lesbians.

Oct 23

WEEKEND DUTY IS ONE of those tasks at a school that always looms worse than it is. From Friday after sports until Sunday dinner, it means either organizing one or two diversions on or off campus for students, or simply meandering the dorms and making sure all are where they're supposed be at lights out. While previously I've taken students ice skating and white-water rafting, with some grading to do for work I'd hand back Monday, I felt no such inspiration last weekend. Instead, I was the on-campus go–to guy.

Saturday morning I was wandering through Wentworth, a boys' dorm, when "ooohs!" and "aaahs!" began wafting out of a second floor room. Years ago I might have found this odd, but with so many tech diversions now, for a bunch of teenage boys to be inside on a gorgeous Saturday morning in October was not unusual. Pity the person who, once cell phones and video games became addictive, bought stock in companies that make frisbees or baseball gloves. Inside a large corner room were a half dozen juniors and seniors in a semi-circle around another student seated in a desk chair, his roommate lurking over him, barber clippers in hand.

"Hey Mr. Minot," the boy in the chair called out, rubbing his hand over a shaved head, "Like the look?" The boy, Todd Garmin, clearly did, although why he'd suddenly go for the Sinead O'Connor look baffled me. Todd, until that morning anyway, had a shock of blond hair that he never bothered to comb, yet it suited him, and seemed to add to his appeal to a number of girls on campus. A co-captain of the varsity soccer team, his toothy smile and rosy cheeks gave the sense that nothing bad had ever or would ever happen to him. If he actually thought this himself, he had reason to.

Todd's dad is Lloyd Garmin. It's not clear whether he shepherded the creation of the GPS system that bears his name, but the notion has been floated, perhaps by those at the school hoping to suggest *Look who chose us to educate his children!* Todd is his oldest child, a junior, and kind of a big deal among his peers. His dad is a big deal on the Board of Trustees.

"Your 'look'...is on the floor," I noted. "Are you...anticipating a worldwide shampoo shortage?" At this a few of the onlookers laughed.

"Hold still," his barber insisted, "I gotta get this patch back here."

"Scary, huh? Todd looked at me again for approval.

"Will you hold still? Or you'll lose yer fuckin' ear," his manservant declared, then, looking up, "Sorry Mr. Minot."

I waved it off – it was their party.

"What gives?" I leaned on the door frame, and as I did, noticed that two others in the room had already gone Uncle Fester.

"It's a team thing," one of them offered, rubbing his bare head, "Oughtta make us look fierce, right?" I recognized a few others from the soccer squad, and he went on. "Imagine you see a line of shaved heads coming down the field toward your goal. Not fun, eh?"

"It might get me wondering, indeed," was all I could muster. Practicing their corner kicks might be more useful, I'm old school.

" 'Course!" another piped up. "We were watching this movie about gangs in New York last night, and one of them was...nasty. All cue balls."

"So, you're all gonna go Cory Booker to scare opponents?" They twisted faces at me then each other, and I realized that the political reference wasn't the most useful one to offer. "Okay, I mean, Magic Johnson. Know him?" To this they nodded and grinned, as if I'd hinted they shared anything in common with the man. "And, this from a movie?"

"Yeah," Todd nodded with glee, "Was awesome. We gotta game Wednesday. Against Westgate. Today's was scratched. Bunch of kids there got caught...something...I dunno...Our looks alone gonna intimidate them - Westgate, on Wednesday. It's home. You should come!"

"Probably will. But..." Eyeing the blond droppings on the floor, and recalling how the worst kept secret in my middle school was the gym teacher's toupee, I had to ask, "You *do* know that, people, mostly men, spend a lot of money to *keep* the hair they have, or at least *look* like they have it. It's pretty odd to get rid of it all by choice."

"We're young," one of them chimed in, "it'll grow back."

"Hey," another was suddenly unnerved, "What about the Halloween dance? And senior pictures? Aren't they next week?" This seemed like a good time for me to move on. I reminded them to vacuum up everything when done. Not sure if shaved heads is a thing in high school sports or not. I know it's a thing in parts of Idaho and in Charlottesville, but that's with bigots, who probably refer to fifth grade as "senior year," so never had to think about yearbook photos.

Oct 30

CHAPEL ASSEMBLIES ARE WINDOWS of time midweek for an all-school meeting sprinkled with announcements and often a senior presentation along the lines of *what I've learned here*. Today was one of those rare occasions when a guest speaker seemed to put a spring into the steps of all heading to the mid-morning gathering. I'd put the Alumni Office in touch with Billy Clubb after Ralph and I met him, and they got him to visit today. I saw the prodigal comedian step out of a car by the administration building during my prep period, so went to greet him. Somehow, I was surprised that he looked just as he did when we saw him at the comedy club. A brown bandanna covered much of his curly hair, and his gray hoodie suggested that he was part of the school maintenance crew rather than a chapel guest. I crossed the green at the center of all of our buildings to say hello.

"Wow," he muttered as he scanned the scene slowly. "Hasn't changed a bit."

"Well, give us a new building and it will," I offered. He snorted a response and proceeded to point out various points of interest.

"That's where I lived my last year here. Over there is where we used to sneak into the woods for a smoke. Got caught once."

"I'm sure you weren't the first."

I walked him in to meet Barclay and others, including someone from the Alumni Office to escort him to the chapel.

"Ben said you were here over a decade ago," Scott began, "Is this the first time you've been back?"

Billy nodded and hinted at a bit of shame or chagrin that he hadn't graduated.

"Well, you've got a lot of company in people who didn't make it through boarding school," I assured him.

"Yeah?" He arched his eyebrows.

"Salinger, Bette Davis, Humphrey Bogart, George Plimpton, to name a few." His face betrayed that he hadn't spent much time reading certain books or watching old movies.

"James Spader?" Barclay jumped in.

"Owen Wilson? Heard of him?" I added.

"Oh, okay. Sure." Alright, so we established that he'd seen the movie "Wedding Crashers."

I left them there so I could get some prep work done, but not before others shared a few cautions with Billy to "keep it clean" in chapel. He assured them he'd be focusing on his path from here to "The Tonight Show," and to let them know, *Hey I was where you are one day.* I slipped out.

There's something about entering a chapel for an assembly that sparks a glimmer of anticipation. It's like seeing a server approach your table with plates in a restaurant, even though what usually awaits us in chapel is seldom intellectually or spiritually mouthwatering. Not surprisingly, it's hard to be original with wisdom these days, and it's usually necessary to tap a few kids on the shoulder in the pew in front of you to remind them to put their phones away. A week earlier, Billy's visit was announced and a clip of him on some comedy tour was shown on the screen in front of the organ pipes. For the past few days, strolling past gaggles of kids in the dining hall, you could see them watching YouTube clips of his stand up gigs here and there. They were pumped. I hadn't presented the learning from my sabbatical yet, so being able to bring him to campus felt good. It's always useful to demonstrate to an institution that you can do something beyond your classroom to justify your contract.

Inside the gothic chapel, students were filing into the pews, while up on the dais, Fred was studying his announcements. He started patting down the noise the way people do when they're seeking quiet. It didn't seem to be working, however, so Scott rose behind him and raised an arm straight-up over his head. Maybe it was his blazer, or that he is perhaps a foot taller than Fred, but for whatever reason, his gesture, a universal one schools employ in pursuit of silence, worked. Fred took to the pulpit and began with announcements.

"Hats off please," and various ball caps were removed. "Varsity field hockey will be dismissed at 11:30 for your game at Worcester Academy." A smattering of *woo-woos* followed. "The bus for boys' soccer will leave at 1 PM, *not noon*, so they will *not* be dismissed early." Grumblings arose from a bunch of soccer players near the front, their shaved heads turning to each other in disbelief. Life is hard. "There will be an open dress rehearsal of "The Importance of Being Earnest" Thursday evening in the auditorium. You may attend in lieu of study hall," *Woo-woo!* "but, you must sign out of the dorm and check-in at the rehearsal." Murmuring as some of the students weighed the option. "Please get your travel plans for Thanksgiving to the student affairs office by the end of this week." *Woo-woo!* "And now our special guest." *Woo-woo-woo-woo!* Fred began rattling off Billy's comedy CV: late-night appearances, Comic Relief and bit parts in a few sitcoms. His Capote-esque lisp gave his words the feeling of someone reading the TV listings to an elderly person, reciting the names of programs he would never watch himself. "Ten years ago, he sat where you are today." *Woo-woo* and approving applause.

"Until I didn't!" Billy added from a chair behind Fred. Tittering laughter.

"I'll let him explain that," and with a sweeping gesture, "Billy Clubb." Roaring applause and phones held high for photos.

"I'd like to thank Mr. Minot and Mr. Brady for getting me back here. They came to see me in a bar. That's where *they* go to drink." Extended hoots. "When *I* was here and lived in Wentworth, *I* just had to go into the *next room*!" Major hoots, especially from residents of that dorm, and faculty eye-rolling. He worked the room well, anecdotes of his days here and PG-13 observational humor. At one point, he eyed the shaved heads of the soccer players and twisted his face.

"All the tuition your parents pay for you to be here, and they couldn't spend a little more for Rogaine?" Some of his remarks were self-effacing, alluding to his lack of acumen for schoolwork. "Yeah, I was what my uncle called 'slow.' *Real* slow. Sunday nights we could watch TV and it would take me an hour and a half just to watch "60 minutes." No great lessons, but a nudge to not follow his example. "I'm doing OK, but I don't recommend you try it my way - don't do stuff so they suggest that you not come back next year. A GED and a year and a half at Bay Path College in Springfield might not open all the doors you want to walk through in the future." He took some questions and some selfies and wrapped up nicely. Honestly, I was impressed – and relieved. After hearing some f-bombs at the club with Ralph, I was worried he'd get even with Griswold for not asking him back for senior year by going all George Carlin on us. I knew he'd be sticking around for a bit so while he was holding court with some students afterward, I slipped out.

Earl Blackabby was doing a unit on humor, and asked Billy to come back to his class for the period following chapel. I asked if I could sit in, and they both said sure. Although Earl's classroom is two doors down from mine, I've never been in it before. Like mine,

Minot's Ledge

tables are pushed together in an oblong seminar way, and he has a threadbare Oriental that helps with the old school look. Above the whiteboards, as seemingly required by law of all English classrooms, are pencil sketches of literary figures: Poe, Wharton, Whitman and others. Watching another instructor can be a good way to improve as a teacher more so than a week of professional workshops. You see things and say *I'll try that tomorrow* or observe that *This is going terribly - never doing that.* I was looking forward to this. Once his dozen or so juniors and seniors settled into their chairs with Billy at one end of the tables, Earl began at the other end.

Blackabby has a boyish way about him and is actually the youngest member of the department. When the previous department chair retired, Barclay said we'd have a big search to replace her. I nudged a college classmate of mine to apply and figured she had a good shot: she'd attended boarding school, had a masters from Dartmouth, and would have finally brought some diversity to Griswold, as our faculty isn't exactly a box of crayons. I was floored and embarrassed when they passed on her, but took joy later on mentioning casually to Barclay that she'd become the first female of color to be appointed a dean at his alma mater. There are a couple of folks who have been teaching longer than Earl has been alive, and none of them wanted the job, but neither could they believe that he got it. His dark hair isn't quite down to his shoulders, and this look is complemented with cowboy boots and flannel shirts. The rumor is he's never assigned a grade lower than a C+ to anyone, so he's quite popular with the students.

"We've been reading "Lysistrata," Mr. Clubb," he began, "Can someone catch Mr. Clubb up on the narrative?"

"Can we get selfies with him?" one boy piped up.

"Yeah!" *"Please!?"*

"Fine with me," Billy turned his palms skyward, and there was a rush to his chair with phones in hand.

As Earl tapped away, probably on the attendance page, I flipped through the pages of "Lysistrata," a Greek farce about women abstaining from sex until their men quit warring. More Q and A for Billy. *Why specifically didn't you graduate from Griswold? Did you break any major rules here? Have you ever met Amy Schumer?* Earl seemed powerless to steer things from interest in Billy back to "Lysistrata," so tried to join in.

"Maybe if you're nice, Mr. Clubb will tell you if he has a website and you can---"

" '*Course* I got a website. Clubbcomedy.com, but I don't mind answering questions. I got a few of my own. Where are you kids from?" Going around the room, he heard a smattering of states and nations, allowing him to slide into standup mode seamlessly.

"Northern Maine, huh?" He thought about where one girl said she was from. "Did you know that the toothbrush was invented in northern Maine?" She shook her head. "If it had been invented anywhere else, they would've called it the *teeth* brush." This was treated with pretty hearty laughter but not by the girl from down east. I'm unclear on how thin-skinned she was, but a few hints in her appearance and carriage suggested that her address wasn't near where the Bushes quaff G & Ts summers. At one point Billy noted how he had a teacher there in the same room we were now in. "He used to eat during class. It showed, too. Guy was a porker. He had more chins than Chinatown." This sounded distantly familiar, like out of some routine I'd heard before, but not by him. It also got some laughs, but a few Asian students just eyed each other silently. He then waded into school life and asked about the dorms these days, relaying a tale of how he rigged a firecracker to go off in a kid's room when someone turned on the light switch. He'd learned the trick from some cousin of his who'd gone to Salisbury, a school in Connecticut. "By the way, do you guys know Salisbury? All boys. Good at sports." A few heads nodded. "How many kids from Salisbury does it take to change a lightbulb?" he went on. Nothing but deadpan faces. "Four. One to change the lightbulb and three to help blow up the inflatable sheep." Only a couple of kids got that one, and they had to explain to others.

"They don't have *girls* there so when they…"

"Oh *gross.*" "That's dis*gusting.*" Several girls rolled their eyes. That seemed a bit edgy, but they were mostly seniors and it was Earl's class; I was just observing.

"Hey, beats Canterbury though." Billy went on. Canterbury is a Catholic school an hour from New York that some Kennedys passed through. "Your teacher this year will be Father Fondle," he slipped into tour guide mode, "and Brother Bugger will be your housemaster." While the priest abuse scandal certainly seemed good material for him, it probably went over most kids' heads. Eventually, Earl decided to wrangle things in, and asked him what humorous literature he would suggest for future class readings.

"Well," Billy shed his bandanna and tossed his curly red mop back, rubbing his chin. "Chelsea Handler has written some pretty funny stuff. I liked *Thank You for Smoking* years ago. Can't remember who wrote it."

"Chris Buckley," I tossed out.

"Yeah? Okay. They made it into a movie too, in case you're dyslexic and books are tricky."

"Well," Earl sat up a little straighter and cleared his throat, "this has been a treat. We're grateful to you for taking the time to be here." Less than half the period had passed, but Earl seemed to have heard enough. Coats were pulled on and chatter commenced as phones were stuffed into pockets, drowning out his parting remarks until he raised his voice. "*Check Google Classroom for the homework!*" A few boys shook Billy's hand, he wished them well, and I said I'd walk him over to the administration building. There's usually a small reception for guest speakers following the presentation and in this case it was delayed a bit on account of Earl's class. Billy actually seemed quite sincere in thanking me for getting him back on campus.

"Funny how ten years can make a difference," he said, gazing across the landscape again. Barclay came out onto the steps to greet him, thanked me for bringing him here, and they went inside. I figured I'd get a kick out of seeing Billy on TV someday and thinking back on this. It wasn't even lunch and it had already been a pretty good day. Or so it seemed.

Nov 5

THERE ARE FEW BETTER places to be on a fall afternoon in New England than a soccer pitch. "Football" fans from Brazil may say our game in the States is weak, folks in the EU might roll their eyes at our name for the game, and people in Manchester, England probably scoff at the paucity of drunken violence at our matches. That said, seeing teenagers run after a ball sure beats watching them veg in the student center exercising their thumbs on Deathcraft or Coven Hunt, two of the more popular video games at the moment.

The parents of day students often show up, which is a chance to chat with them. These days there's less conversation with them, for they spend most of the games filming their kids with their phones. Gone are the days of three-sport athletes and the desire for a varsity blanket, an award presented in spring of senior year to students who play a varsity sport six terms in a row. Kids now specialize, often focusing on one sport for years, pining for and often getting "exemptions" from sports during other seasons so they can "train" for their main focus. This often means spending afternoons throwing a lacrosse ball around all winter rather than lacing up skates, which takes what is usually good athletes off other teams as well.

The varsity soccer match today was against Westgate, a school that's slightly more traditional than Griswold and more than slightly better endowed. Regardless of a school's athletic history, soccer is always a crap shoot. One year there may be a gaggle of kids who've been playing together for three years and are a well-oiled machine, but they might all be seniors, so next year the team is thin, or some phenom from Brazil shows up and embarrasses opposing goalkeepers. Hard to tell about Westgate, but as the shaved heads of our squad gleamed in the afternoon sun, it at least looked as though the Grizzlies were a team in most senses of the word. Off to my left in the bleachers were two mothers discussing the boys' new coiffures.

"Did yours tell you he'd be doing that?"

"Mine? You kidding? We're lucky we hear from him once a week - and then it's usually to buy or send him something. We don't get consulted on grooming."

"I just can't believe Josh shaved his. Wonder what his girlfriend thinks."

"Well, it hasn't hurt Bezos. Seen wife number two?"

"Yes," she shook her head, "but then Bezos has a little more in the bank than Josh."

"Oh," the other chuckled, "sorry to hear that. I was going to ask you for a loan." They both cracked up.

"Would like to have seen *that* prenup."

"Mmmmm."

The Griswold Grizzlies were clearly pumped for the game and the first ten minutes saw them doing most of the attacking. When Westgate won a number of throw-ins, our boys seemed less confident on defense; they were more vocal than other matches I've been at, such that amidst cheers from the sidelines and a brisk wind, their calls to each other as they moved up field were audible. I only coached soccer for a few years, but didn't recall this kind of chatter from back then. Before halftime there were a few more throw-ins, and our boys' Achilles' heel became clear. A throw-in occurs when one team sends a ball out of bounds and the other team gets to toss it back in, ideally to a teammate. Often an efficient way for the receiving teammate to send the ball to another teammate is to head it to him, an inexact but darn impressive tact when one can pull it off. When Griswold first had some throw-ins, our boys could never seem to get their skulls to head the ball to a teammate. It usually went off their heads in some random direction, maybe because the ball was hitting a bare head, or because that reality was in fact painful, and kids weren't putting their all into it. If you kept an eye on the player who'd headed the ball after play moved elsewhere, you'd notice him rubbing his shiny dome, as if making sure it was still there, or nursing a wound. With time this became more evident, and it was hard to dismiss the notion that a soccer ball hitting a bare scalp led to a distinct effect that none of our Jeff Bezos lookalikes had anticipated. I couldn't imagine that having a soccer ball tossed at it would have truly stung on a bare head, but the last time I headed a soccer ball, the World Trade Center towers were still standing, and I was visiting the local Supercuts every six weeks, so what do I know? It could be that practicing with bare scalps for two cloudless days in this warm autumn had resulted in a few sunburns on top, where, usually, the sun never shines. Whatever it was, whenever there was a chance to head the ball, which usually involved both teams sending skulls up to steer it to their advantage, our boys rose to the task with all the gumption of a mouse edging toward a rabid cat. Once Westgate sussed out our team's timidity, they set to kicking the ball out of bounds off our guys intentionally, knowing they would win the throw-in.

"Gee-zus," a wincing, disgusted parent of one of our lads grumbled, "Do our guys think their heads are made of potato chips?"

"Maybe not," the parent of a senior muttered with one eye on his phone, "but they've made it clear that they're afraid to head the ball, and Westgate knows it." Behind me a few others were thumbing their phones and talking about the chance of concussions from heading a soccer ball. While I was trying to pick up more of this conversation, whistles broke in, and heads turned to the field. A yellow card was evident, and a player from Westgate was ranting at a ref who had his cautionary finger a few inches from the boy's nose. The player clearly felt that something wrong had occurred, and began pointing to Todd Garmin. Team captains bantered around the matter, then assistant coaches lurched in from the sidelines. Not sure what nudged me to, but I meandered down to behind the Westgate bench to see whether I could figure out what had sent one of them into his rant.

"He *said* it, I heard it. *Swear* I did," a fit-to-be-tied player insisted to his coach. The lean and agitated player was Black.

"Calm down. Yes. That *stinks*. And that's on *them.*" Then the coach grabbed him by both shoulders. "So: I'll talk to the ref, but you - *you* take how that makes you *feel,* and *channel* it into your game. *Put it on the ball.*" The coach jerked a thumb in the direction of the Griswold bench.

The player huffed, hands on hips, "Fuckin' skinheads." The assistant coach laid hands on the young man's shoulders and spoke some inaudible words that settled him. Hard to know what is said on a competitive field, so I moved slowly to behind the Griswold bench where the two referees had just finished a conversation with the coaches. Our guys were nodding at them in a way that reminded me of how one acts when a police officer who's stopped you for speeding lets you off with a fine that could have been a lot worse. One of the refs lifted and showed a red card to all as he headed back on the field. Todd huffed and puffed with hands on hips, and one of our coaches extended a very serious forefinger in the direction of Todd's feet.

"Use those," he said with suppressed anger, then pointed to Todd's mouth, "not that." That Garmin didn't acknowledge this directive was as telling as if he had. He sat out the rest of the game, which Westgate won 9-3. At dinner later, I fished around the faculty table to see whether anyone knew what was said during the game.

"The players were pretty close when it was supposedly said," someone offered, "so who knows?"

"Why would a kid claim that something like that happened if it didn't?" was asked.

"Well," I reasoned, "it got a kid tossed from the game. So I guess the ref believed the kid."

"Todd was swearing all the way back to the gym." another recalled. "F-ing this, f-ing that. Kid needs some decaf."

"He did score the first two goals for us," I cocked my head, just wondering, "It could be that, if you're Westgate, the kind of player you'd want out of the game."

"I dunno," someone shook his head, "This is soccer, not some Olympic ice skating trial where someone's gonna *eliminate the competition.*" A younger teacher looked baffled at the reference, so the rest of us filled in the details of the Tonya Harding episode from the 1990s. Ralph mentioned that after study hall one night in the dorm, Todd was telling stories about his summer. "Everyone – his boss, the guy next to him on some flight - everything was "faggot this, faggot that, this fag, that fag." I finally told him to put a cork in it, and later spoke to him about his choice of words."

"Did he get it? What you were saying?" I asked.

"I dunno," Ralph shrugged, "Not sure he's gonna rush out to see "The Laramie Project," but he won't be talking that way on *my* duty nights." Ralph has this calm authority about him. One look and a raised finger from him will silence a room. I wondered if the N-word had crossed Todd's lips.

"Sounds like," someone at the end of the table began, "he's got some unresolved homophobia going on."

"Not at all," Ralph held up a fork to explain, "It's quite resolved. He talks like a bigot, and can be a jerk, and that's not my first choice of a word."

At that, people at the table eyed each other, silenced by the statement. Interestingly, nobody spoke up to rebut it.

Nov 7

FOR A CHANGE OF scenery now and again, I'll grab an armful of papers to grade and camp out at a coffee shop a little over a mile off campus. It's just a bit too far for teenagers to be willing to walk to. Java Jane's isn't as good as loyalists suggest, but it beats the church coffee in the dining hall, and it's nice to support a local business. Two paragraphs into a short story essay, a teenager at the next table spun my way with a question.

"Do you teach at Griswold?" Her dark bob cut, and freckles wouldn't necessarily cause her to stand out, but some oversized, bright purple eyeglass frames would have, at least on campus, so I didn't take her for a student.

"I *do*. How did you---"

"I go to the local high school, and I know you don't teach there, but kinda look like you might be a teacher."

"Ah." Wasn't sure what that was about. Khakis and a Shetland sweater I've had since college? Admittedly, I'm grading papers. Apparently I should not consider undercover police work; I'd get "made" in no time.

"I was wondering...how Todd is. Do you know him?"

"*Marcie,*" her mother piped up from across the table. "Some things are not...You shouldn't bother people." A forty-something blonde also in a bob cut was *cross*. Her tennis tan and pink crew neck - possibly cashmere - suggested that they came here in an Audi, or maybe a Range Rover, and might have stopped en route to a riding or dance lesson.

"I'm sorry. Todd?" I asked.

"I'm sorry," the mother leaned forward, "My daughter can be impulsive."

"No problem," I waved off her concern, "I live with teenagers - they're never boring."

"So, do you know him? Todd?" Marcie's eyes widened.

"We have a few boys named Todd," I tossed my hand up in a *who knows?* way. She thumbed her phone and came up with it.

"Garmin. Todd Garmin."

"Marcie," Mother broke in. *"*This isn't the ti---"

"Mu - *ther*," Marcie spun around to glare at her.

"There *is* a Todd Garmin there. A junior. Plays soccer."

"See?" Marcie lorded this over Mu - *ther*.

"Is he a friend of yours?"

"That's it," Mother crunched the remains of a croissant into its wrapper and fixed to leave. "We're gonna be late. I'm sorry about her. Marcie, you *can't* just be *asking* people about other people's...*about other people*. Finish that in the car." She gave a wince of contrition as they rose. Heading for the door, it was clear that this discussion was not over. The rain wasn't letting up. I ordered a decaf and took my papers to a table in the rear.

Nov 9

WEDNESDAY LUNCHES ARE OFTEN pretty underwhelming, for with so many athletic contests in the afternoon, perhaps there's a sense that students wouldn't gorge themselves on anything anyway. Whoever thought as much hadn't spent much time watching teenage boys eat. After three squares a day, two of which include the ice cream bar for dessert, gaggles of them regularly crowd the snack bar after study hall for pizza and wraps at ten PM. Yesterday the grilled cheese just wasn't doing it for me, but I lingered at my table to hear a teaching intern in the History Department lecture Howard Bagwell on World War II.

"I mean, you have to admit that dropping atomic bombs on Japan was racist, right?" He was one of those well-scrubbed tweens - between college and grad school - whose combed-back mane and animated face reminded some of Ashton Kutcher. He walks around with a copy of Howard Zinn's *A People's History of the United States* under his arm. Either he's virtue signaling, or the world's slowest reader. "The *only* people the U.S. used it on were non-white."

"The same could be said of the planners and pilots who orchestrated Pearl Harbor." As he spoke, Bags was doing a crossword puzzle.

In ink. He jumped in without looking up from his paper. "You're not saying that Pearl Harbor *justified* Hiroshima and Nagasaki, *are you?*" The intern looked like he'd just been handed an outrageous bill for car repairs.

"I'm saying," Bags' patience was starting to fray, "that as the nation was at war with Japan, of *course* any act in that war would be against people who are Japanese." He squinted at a clue, huffed, and wrote the answer in the squares.

"But we were at war with Germany and Italy, and it wasn't used against *them*. And they look like us."

At the end of the table, Ralph theatrically cleared his throat, "Er…who's '*us?*'"

Bags loved it, and our Zinnophile was suddenly quite uncomfortable, stammering as he explained that Roosevelt and his generals were white, and that western Europe was as well in 1945. Ralph nodded and smiled as he returned to his salad.

"Roosevelt didn't make the decision to drop the bomb," Bags offered without looking up, "Truman did."

"Okay, but he was also white."

"I *know*," Bags' tone now had a scolding in it, "Just get your facts straight. FDR died in April."

"Okay," the Zinnophile held up a finger, "but Truman still only used it on Japan." With that, Bags put down his pen the way one does when about to gently reach for a rhetorical silver bullet.

"Not on Germany right? Think that could be because it wasn't successfully tested until July of that year, and Germany had surrendered two months earlier?" This sent the intern's eyes to our table's surface in search of a response. After some silence, Bags returned to his crossword. "A written compliment - eight letters."

"Encomium," I chimed in.

"Very good, Ben." Nice when the word-a-day calendar pays off. Our intern was grasping at something invisible with clawed hands over his plate. Eventually he went on another tack.

"Well, the allies *could have invaded* Japan *instead.* Sure, it would have been bloody, but, they were *soldiers,* not civilians, that's what they had to expe---"

"And *who* might they have encountered on their *march* to Tokyo?" Bags cocked his head as he squinted across the table. His thinning gray hair, *whatever* mustache and corduroy blazer tell most people that he's been at this academic thing a while, and probably doesn't go out on limbs he doesn't think are secure. "Not Japanese soldiers - most of them were---" At this Peter Burnham waved a finger.

"May I? Being a history teacher?"

Bags tipped his pen Burnsy's way and returned to his puzzle.

"The Japanese army was pretty thinned out by the summer of '45. Most of it was already maggot food on Guam, Saipan, Iwo Jima and Okinawa. Some were guarding allied POWs in country, but mostly, you know who the troops would've faced? Civilians - who believed the emperor was a living god. Think any of them between the coasts and Tokyo might have tried to fight off the Americans and British?"

"And the Russians," Bags added without looking up.

"Right. You *bet* they would have. Think they would have succeeded? A bunch of kamikaze widows and old rice farmers against the 82nd airborne and the Red Army? With their bamboo spears? This was long before anyone figured out how to make a bomb out of a rice cooker." Peter has a cousin who lost a leg in the Boston Marathon bombing. Had to hand it to him for working this reference into things. "They had about seventy million people left by war's end. You really think that three armies intent on defeating them, and toss in some revenge, would have killed fewer people than lived in the two medium-sized cities where the bombs were dropped?"

"But Japan could have surrendered if…if we'd given a demonstration of the bomb, say over Mt. Fuji." The intern had a bone and wouldn't let go. "If we'd shown them what it could do, they probably would have given up." I admired his passion, if not his grasp of the facts.

"And what if it hadn't worked?" Peter held up an index finger. "The bomb had only been successful once, in the New Mexico desert. And you can't say 'probably.' It's counterfactual."

The intern froze and looked puzzled. "It's...what?"

"Counterfactual," Ralph jumped in before Bags could roll his eyes at this. "Counter: opposite of the facts. Your statement goes against what actually happened - the condition you suggest never existed, so you can't say what would have happened because of it. Maybe they would have surrendered, maybe not, maybe the bomb wouldn't have worked. Can't be known."

"Like people who say, "If Kennedy hadn't been shot, Vietnam wouldn't have gotten out of hand," I added, "There's no way to know."

"It's a fun parlor game, but not much else." Bags nodded.

"*Parlor* game?" the intern asked. I took that as a good time to leave. Obviously student teachers are here to learn, and some are fantastic; they love coaching, are good with the latest technology, and are willing to live in the smallest flats on campus. I had one two years ago who knew more about poetry than our department chair. Then again, two years before that, my intern from Penn had not heard of either William Faulkner or Toni Morrison; it's a crapshoot. Something about the four of us schooling the intern on his own discipline all at once felt a bit like intellectual hazing, so rather than have Bags explain what a parlor was, I headed out...albeit, a bit too late.

In the lobby of the dining hall, Fred and Earl were deep in hushed conversation. They stood just inside the entry door by a plaque engraved with the names of Griswold boys who died in the world wars. Earl was waving his arms, suggesting frustration while Fred was nodding, hands in pockets. I'm pretty good at affecting lousy peripheral vision, allowing me to appear oblivious to something I can actually see. Just then, dammit, an advisee of mine dropped her backpack near the conspirators' feet and bellowed, "Hi Mr. Minot!" With that, Fred's and Earl's eyes shot to me.

"Ben," Fred flashed an ever so subtle smile, "Are you free just now?" This was the administrative equivalent of asking someone who is sitting in a lawn chair if he is busy. I nodded that I was.

"Could we meet? The three of us?" He waved his hand in the direction of his office.

"OK...when?"

"Well, now unless...Do you have somewhere to be?"

The varsity field hockey game at which I was going to grade some essays in the stands wasn't for another hour and a half, but I glanced at my watch to avoid appearing truly idle.

"Sure."

We walked three abreast to the administration building. Fred spotted some weeds along the path, and wondered if they were poison ivy. I wasn't sure, but didn't feel compelled to offer an opinion on campus flora. Once in his office, Earl sat down first, the way someone does when they know the agenda. Behind his desk, Fred held a steeple of fingers to his lips, contemplating how to begin.

"First of all, it was good of you to bring a guest speaker to chapel, Mr.Cubb. Especially nice that he's an alum---"

"Quasi-alumnus," Earl corrected him, "He didn't graduate." Fred raised a palm, directing him to hold his fire, then cleared his throat.

"I'm told," Fred began, "that our guest made some comments after chapel, in a class, that... Earl has been taking some heat for."

I looked from one to the other a few times and raised my palms in a request for details. Earl pulled out his phone and began scrolling.

"There was the joke about Salisbury being all boys..." he raised a finger as if to begin counting.

"Salisbury? But... it *is* all boys, right?" Fred looked puzzled.

"Some comment about *inflatable sheep*." Here we go. "Then he made fun of Chinese, which is bad enough, but I had Chinese students in the room."

"He didn't *make fun* of Chinese people." I was trying desperately not to roll my eyes, "He mentioned some teacher he'd had here who had a double chin."

"And something about more chins than Chinatown." Earl added. "One student texted her mother in Beijing, and she texted me."

"O-k-a-a-a-y-y..." Fred was trying to absorb this tennis match before him.

"Then he went off on Maine. Some toothless reference, and there's a girl in the class from there." Now he had three fingers up. "Her mother emailed me. Not happy that her daughter was likened to hillbillies."

"Ben, did Mr. Clubb liken her to a hillbilly?"

"I didn't hear that," I could feel Earl eyeing me, but I refused to look at him. "He made some joke - that's what he does - about teeth, but it certainly wasn't aimed at her."

"Her *mother* thought it *was*." Earl cocked his head.

"Her mother wasn't there," I practically spat.

"But her daughter *was*, and I'm getting heat for it."

"Did you tell her the context? Explain it?"

"She got the context. Her daughter recorded the whole class on her phone. She heard it all, including the Catholic jabs."

"Catholic jabs?" Fred suddenly looked alarmed.

"He mentioned buggering and fondling," Earl added. Fred's eyes widened and turned to me.

"Not...exactly." I tilted my head. "Some context there would help"

"And this family is Catholic. Who knows who else in the class is?"

"He made a reference to the priest abuse scandal," I explained. "which is common knowledge."

"But that's not what the class was about." Earl leaned forward for emphasis.

"What *was* it about? Or what was the plan?" Fred squinted.

"We're in a comedy unit. It was supposed to be about "Lysistrata.""

"But it never was." I'd had enough. "He, Billy, held court, and the kids took selfies and obviously recorded it. So, *why am I here?*"

"You brought him here," Earl sat back and was still checking his phone. *"You* introduced him to the community." He said this with a hint of blame, as though I had poured anthrax into the chapel's vent system.

"I got him to speak at chapel. *You* brought him to your class, which *you* couldn't control." I turned to Fred. "Everyone seemed to like it. At the time. Where did these comments come from?"

"Let's...consider, shall we?" Fred raised a palm at me. "Earl feels he's been called on the carpet by some for someone else's words. He feels as though Mr. Clubb should have...had clear guidelines set out as to his language."

"Then why didn't he have a discussion with Billy before the class started?"

"He should've been spoken to when he arrived on campus," Earl was now jabbing a finger towards the floor.

"He *was* - right next door in an office." I jammed my finger to the right. "In the chapel, things went pretty well."

To this, Earl tilted his head, suggesting he didn't entirely agree with the statement, but offered nothing else.

Fred leaned forward on his desk. "Earl feels as though there needs to be a statement that could be sent to students and parents, letting them know that what was said does not reflect the school's sentiments nor the opinions of teachers, that it was rather an entertainer doing his shtick. He thinks that both of you should sign and send it out."

"But it wasn't *my* class," I threw up my hands, more annoyed than baffled. "I was just an observer. They weren't *my* students."

"But you brought him here," Earl was checking his shoes at this point. Out the window behind Fred, a woman from the Alumni Office was walking by on her phone, which gave me a brainstorm.

"Why not have Billy issue a statement and send it to the whole class, parents included?" I offered.

Fred pursed his lips and gave a slight nod. "That might work. Earl? Think that would do it?"

He was silent for a moment, turning the idea over in his head, or perhaps just coming to terms with the fact that it was me who suggested it.

"I suppose," he put his phone away, "if it was sincere."

"You could edit, or suggest what it should say," I extended a hand his way, almost like an olive branch. "You could have final say over the wording, get it perfect before it's sent."

Fred cocked his head a bit and raised his eyebrows, the way people do to suggest that you have no cause to not agree with what has been said.

"Fine." Earl sounded like a driver who had just talked a $100 speeding ticket down to $50; accepting of it, but not thrilled.

"Good. I'll have the alumni office get you his contact info." I smiled.

"Me?" Earl straightened his neck and finally looked at me. "*You're* his contact."

"Sure, and if things went south in chapel, *I'd* be writing or calling him, but as it was *your* class, it seems like you could best explain to him the reason for…whatever you want to call what you're going to compose."

Fred eyed us both silently, as if hoping that the tennis match was over. "All of this might be a reminder," he held up a finger, "to keep...celebrities and guests on short leashes — figuratively - if we bring them to speak here."

At this I nodded slightly. No good deed...

"And," my turn to hold up a finger, "do not let students on their phones in class," I added.

"Wait," Earl shook his head, "He still would have said all that, with or without the students' phones recording him."

"Sure, but you wouldn't have a record of it going viral." I shrugged. "I don't allow phones in class."

Reminding a department chair of my personal policy on instruction seemed a bit bold, but it works for me, and in his classroom, having phones away might have helped us avoid all this.

Fred was now typing away on his keyboard, probably noting the content of the meeting. Inside I was steaming that we had to hash this out at all. I wasn't sure what else I could contribute to things, but then behind Fred's desk I noticed his Princeton diploma. That a school administrator has to advertise that he went to college is another matter - and it reminded me of Hobey Baker. In the early 1900s, he was such an amazing skater and scorer for Princeton that the college hockey equivalent of the Heisman trophy is named for him. This called to mind how a few years ago, I'd taken some students to a hockey game in Boston, and the next day, one of the kids was talking about how his mother didn't like that all he talked about afterward was the brawling on the ice. She wasn't happy about the lesson in sportsmanship that the field trip conveyed and tried to put it in the chaperones' laps.

"Can I just say here, that to fault me, for what another person said, in another person's class, it's like taking kids to a Bruins game, and getting blamed because they saw a fight break out in the third period."

Fred tipped his hand up and nodded once, indicating a possibility that he didn't necessarily disagree with me.

"Hopefully this statement from Mr. Clubb will put this matter behind us." He broke into the slightest of smiles. Earl and I rose and headed out. At the door, as Earl walked ahead, Fred tapped me on the shoulder. "You made a good case for things here, but I'm not sure if you helped your relationship with your department chair."

"Hmmm," was all I could muster. Perhaps indeed, pride goeth before the fall.

"Good analogy, about hockey, I mean," he added. His thin-lipped smile was ambiguous, but I took it in a good way.

Admittedly, I've not been a fan of Fred, but perhaps he was right about all this, and perhaps I was wrong about him.

Nov 12

Note to self: do not read email before breakfast:

> Dear Mr. Minot,
>
> I trust this reaches you well. I enjoyed our visit when I was on campus earlier this season, and hope your teaching has been good. I know that my son Eric is not a student of yours but he is looking to the future and thinks that he will be a resident in a different dormitory next year. He understands that the prefects in that dorm are all seniors this year yet he would like to be confirmed as a prefect for next year there, his junior year. The responsibility would be a good thing and I believe that he is in fact able to take on the responsibility in spite of not being a senior.
>
> The dorm faculty are an important part of the process that chooses the prefects, and we are hoping that we can count on you to support Eric's candidate effort to become a prefect in the dorm. It is early in this process, I understand, but if he were in possession of a recommendation from you that he could submit when he applies for this position of responsibility, it could greatly aid in his position to become a prefect.

I hope you can understand how important this goal interests Eric and that you can do everything in your power to help him.

Thank you.

Jianyu
Jianyu Zhang
President & CEO
Sinotech Holding Company Ltd
No.23, Wu Temple, Shatan N St, Falungong Dist, Beijing 100009, China (Houhai)

The gift that keeps on giving. I figured I was done with this slimy brood once I let his son's cheating go unreported. Now I'm supposed to put him up for prefect? Years ago, prefects or student leaders at schools were mostly seniors, kids who faculty could rely on for certain tasks. They'd take room check at night and tell kids to keep the noise down so one of us didn't come down and confiscate stereo speakers or a lax stick. With time the position has become ersatz, as there's not much asked of them anymore.

My first year here, one night I found myself doing the last check of the dorm and I found a prefect in his room, who, theoretically, should be taking check himself and coming see me to say, "All here." When I asked why he hadn't taken check, he said he'd forgotten it was his night to do so. This was about a half hour after lights out, and when I asked why he was still up - only prefects on duty could be up after lights out in order to report to the faculty - he told me that prefects didn't have lights out. Having been at the school all of two weeks, I took him, a four year senior, at his word. This got great laughs at the faculty table the following morning.

"They're allowed to smoke in their rooms, too," Bags chuckled. "Keep some matches handy in case one of them needs a light."

A generation ago, there was a bit of stick about it, at least at my school. Don Carlson was the prefect on my floor. He lived next to me, and was pretty clear: "I'm not going to go looking for stuff, but if you guys are making so much noise or smoking or drinking so that the smell or racket is obvious, I'll be in, because if *they* come in," he jabbed his thumb in the direction of the faculty apartment at the end of the hall, "they'll also ask me why I didn't say anything to them or you earlier. Remember: shit rolls downhill."

This year's prefects in my girls' dorm are average. Half the time they remember to take room check, and they prod kids to do dorm chores like take out hall trash and bag recyclables. It's not a role that truly deserves mention on a college application, but that's why kids apply for it. Apparently having done my job in the dorm weeks ago when I walked into the room of Zhang's daughter - and Eric's sister - during a fire alarm is going to dog me. I texted Ralph to see if he'd be up for some squash so I could pick his brain about things.

Me: Squash?

Ralph: Is there a *whiter* game than squash? he wrote back.

Me: Rowing. And croquet.

Ralph: Sitting down in a boat and facing backwards, and croquet. You people.

Me: Yeah we're a hoot. 5:30?

By 5:30 the squash teams were done with the courts, so we smacked the ball around for a good half hour. Between matches I mentioned to him that the best players in the world are from Egypt and Pakistan - not exactly bastions of white privilege.

"Egypt," he huffed as he wiped some sweat away, " 'Zat the place that had all those slaves who built pyramids for them?"

As an English teacher, beyond "The Ten Commandments" and some mummy movies, I didn't have much to offer, so I went into the Zhang matter.

"Wow," he shook his head as we tucked racquets and eye gear away, "I don't wanna say you're his bitch, but, wow."

"I know right. But if his daughter decides to be difficult, and I don't want that…"

"No, you don't," he shook his head more emphatically. "I get it, pal. You're doing your job, but these days? Tricky stuff."

I tossed my palms skyward. "So…I cave? And blow smoke up this kid's butt so he becomes a prefect? I've already seen him cheat in the classroom. Think I want him in a dorm with my blessing?"

"Think you have a choice? Prefect or not, this guy's a trustee." I nodded, and we both looked around to make sure that nobody could have been listening. "And once he's in the dorm, as a prefect, expect him to be asking for a college rec the following year." We traded looks that suggested we'd both had enough of a workout.

"*Geee* - zus," I pulled a school hoodie on and felt like I was in quite a box. A spell of Indian Summer had made the early evening more bearable than the calendar would have suggested.

That night there was something you might not have found on the schedule a few decades earlier - an evening athletic contest. It used to be that schools only ventured as far as a Saturday trip could take them. These days, Lawrenceville comes up from New Jersey to play schools in New England and tournaments are held in New York and Boston for schools from all over. When you see a hockey player you teach straggle into the dorm at 10:30 PM fresh from an away game, don't expect too sharp an essay on post-colonial lit from him the next day. Actually I probably wouldn't expect much from him at all. But as some parents insist that "Hockey is going to pay for college," most aren't hanging up their skates just yet. Years ago, there was a notion that parents pay for college. Now, tuition is admittedly in the stratosphere, so families seek a plan B, namely junior's slapshot. At one point a teacher of mine conveyed that the cost of a year of college was the equivalent of a mid-size car for a family. This remains true, providing the mid-size car is the top of the line Land Rover.

***

The early evening match was a basketball game against Kenarden School, a fairly local rival against whom we have mercurial success: if we win, it's a big deal; if we lose, we're not surprised and shrug it off. A seven PM game in the new gym is always a good excuse for kids to skip the start of study hall, and as Barclay, Scott, Fred and a bunch of teachers were on hand, it sent the signal that being there was more important than anywhere else just then. In addition to banners in appropriate colors representing all the other league schools we play, our, and all school gyms, seem blanketed with championship banners for every sport offered.

NEPSAC CLASS B WATER POLO CHAMPIONS, 1997
NEW ENGLAND NORDIC SKI CHAMPIONS 2007

Some of the banners list the various basketball players who've scored a thousand points or more in their high school careers. As we and every school we play has an athletic complex plastered with these veritable quilts, one gets the sense - or more accurately, it is *hoped* one will get the sense - that 1) if you play us, you should feel intimidated and that 2) if you attend school here, you will be a champion. Apart from some running back who made the NFL in the 1980s and a snowboarder who washed out of the Olympics after testing positive for weed, not sure how well the sporting life has panned out for most Griswold Grizzlies. I mention this a few times a year in class when it seems that chatter about "committing to a D-1 school" is heard. Not sure where the next Tom Brady is coming from, but I'd be surprised if it's here.

An evening game meant that the parents of day students were able to see the event. It was the first basketball game I'd seen since returning, and I'd forgotten how the game has changed from years ago. Teams don't bother setting up plays to work around being boxed out when on offense - lots of fast breaks and theatrical dunking. The latter prompted eruptions from the stands when they were for us, followed by chants of "De-*FENSE!* De-*FENSE!*"

Behind me in the stands were a couple of families I didn't recognize, which isn't surprising since I'd been away, but some of their comments hinted that they were new to this experience here.

"How has such a small school won so many banners?" "I thought they had study hours at night?" "Does the coach also teach here?" We are told that we're all in the admissions business, so I decided to be neighborly with a few answers.

"Actually, the coach teaches math here. Also coaches soccer in the fall," I offered. On the row behind me were two middle-aged white women in turtlenecks and understated suburban make-up. On both sides of them were four or five well-scrubbed teenage girls dividing their attention between their phones and the game. A deviation from this pattern emerged whenever a certain sub went in for Griswold. This was always prefaced by a gasp and a breathless announcement by one to the others.

"Todd's going in!" At this, all eyes zoomed in on the table at center court. When the louder-than-it-has-to-be horn sounded for a sub, and Todd Garmin trotted in to cover someone, the gaggle behind me bellowed their approval.

"Go Todd!"

"Todd you got this!"

"You're a fighter Todd!"

It wasn't Beatlemania, but a few folks in front of me turned around to assess this personal fan club for number seven. They squinted while conversing and shrugged, suggesting that they didn't recognize the girls to be students here. Every time Todd got the ball the gaggle exploded with encouragement, as though he were a three-pointer away from joining the thousand point club. When he was called for a foul or something else, they were apoplectic.

"What? Are you *serious?*"

"He never *touched* him."

"Traveling? Why don't you call *them* for traveling?!" At this, even one of the mothers spoke up.

"*Char*lotte! Just...let the game play out, will you? It's just a game."

A strawberry blond huffed, rolled her eyes and set her thumbs to work on her phone.

"Mother, if they *knew* what...*Gawd!*"

The mothers exchanged silent glances, then both rolled their eyes.

With 1:19 left in the game and Griswold ahead by seven, Todd fouled out.

"N-n-n-O-O-O-O-O-O-O!!!" came the protest from behind me. "That guy *flopped!*" I didn't think the Kenarden player had flopped but was slightly impressed that a teenage girl was so invested in the game and had the snarky remarks down. The louder-than-it-has-to-be horn sounded, a sub trotted in, slapped palms with number seven and as Todd strolled back to the bench, his teammates alternated between high-fives and rubbing his shiny head in fun.

"Great game Todd!" came from several of the gaggle. This was quickly followed by appeals to the mothers. "We can go now." "Can we get pizza?"

The mothers were in agreement that, for all that went into the evening, they were going to stick it out until the buzzer. After some timeouts on both sides slowed the coming of the end, they thought better of it, and picked their way out of the stands with less than a minute left. Dueling three pointers took it down to the final four seconds, when a foul by Kenarden got our point guard to the line. He sunk them both, and with too little time left on the clock, Kenarden flung the ball from half court and watched it ricochet off the backboard at the buzzer. The gym erupted, and as the coaches and players lined up for the "good game" assurances, everybody pulled on their coats and made for the doors. It would be an easy night for dorm duty with study hall already half over. I wasn't about to put a lot of stick about it, as it seemed half of the school was at the game, and it would take kids a while to get back to their rooms and settle down. I camped out in the dorm lounge and graded some essays. When it came time for 10:30 check, I asked the prefect on duty to take it. Even if Zhang's daughter wasn't on the third floor of the dorm, after her father's message, I just didn't have the stomach to knock on any doors. When the prefect came back at 10:40 to tell me all were accounted for, I thanked her and noted this in the online log. Theoretically, I should be able to take her at her word. In reality, I had little interest not to.

Nov 19

A HOCKEY GAME FEELS like the right place to be on a Saturday afternoon in winter, even if it's still technically fall. Two years ago I was the assistant coach of the girls' JV squad, and for the year I was away, the school brought in someone else for my role and a varsity coach who played for the US Women's team in 2018. They won gold in South Korea, so they found a spot for her in Admissions to justify the hire. The zenith of my hockey days was a winning goal vs. Cushing over two decades ago, and as the new Assistant JV coach was game for another season, I suddenly didn't have a winter sport to cover. I wasn't surprised when Frank Remillard, the Athletic Director, explained that the reshuffling of the hockey program meant I wouldn't "have" to be on the ice this year. The gold medalist was happy, the JV squad was covered, so as the musical chairs seemed to work, fine with me. As working at a school tends to involve the three hats of teaching, dorm parenting, and coaching at least two terms, and as I had the fall off from a sport, I now needed to check off this box. Frank and I decided to chat at the hockey game.

Frank Remillard looks like an Athletic Director - ruddy complexion, salt-and-pepper buzzcut, and a rugby player's build. He beams as his eyes turn skyward in the hockey rink as it got a new roof and some other upgrades while I was away. The stands are still aluminum benches which prompt most people to stand during games due to the cold. The girls were playing Overtoun School and by the end of the first period, nobody had scored.

" 'Preciate your willingness to let the hockey program go with the coaches we had last year," Remy pumped my shoulder. "We really didn't want to lose her," he nodded to the girls' bench, "and I figured we'd find something for you to do this term. Still gonna help out with crew in the spring, right?"

"Sure. Can't let all those years on Lake Cayuga go to waste," I nodded. A very old Cornell alum spoke to us before practice one day, and said that between the frigid practices in early spring and that we had to dodge ice flows while crews on rivers like Yale and Penn had open water much earlier, rowing there built character. As some afternoon practices in March went so late that our coxswain could barely make out the dock to land, I figured I had enough character to fill the rink we were standing in.

"Great," Remy was pleased, "As for this term, obviously you know that your department chair is going on paternity leave, but now he's going early; his wife is having twins, and she's got to take it easy. He was doing the scoreboard and time clock for basketball games, so I wondered if you'd be willing to step up."

This is a task some people quiver at doing: the notion of scoring three point shots and pausing the clock at whistles seems to terrify them, like a mistake will send the ghost of Bobby Knight across the court, lunging at their throats. Just then Barclay came through the rink door with a few people, saw Remy and waved him over. Looking every bit the Head of School in a toboggan coat and school muffler, his shock of graying hair and aquiline nose seemed to hint at his gravitas even for those who didn't know he was the Head. A few heads among the Overtoun fans turned his way as well. As Remy met him, handshakes were exchanged with the guests, perhaps friends, but more likely prospective parents or trustees. This gave me a minute to chew on Remy's idea.

I ran the scoreboard for some wrestling matches a few years back, and there was really nothing to it; basically just pushing buttons for points when you are signaled to do so. As I mulled this over, it occurred to me that this task would - obviously - be for home games only; no loading a bus and steering it through snow for games in Connecticut and New Hampshire, so rather like half a season. When I recalled how boys' basketball had a game halfway to New York that afternoon and that the ski team was practically in the White Mountains for a meet, I almost wanted to interrupt Remy and Barclay to tell him I'd do it. Their chat seemed over and it looked like Remy was heading out with Barclay's guests. I didn't want this soft gig to get away, so I dashed over to tell him I'd do it.

"Great," he gave a slight pump of his fist, "I'll get you the schedule. Thanks Ben."

As I turned away, Barclay raised a finger. "Ben, got a minute?"

"Sure. You're here for the game?"

"We c-o-o-u-u-ld watch the game," he let out, "or we could walk." With this he gestured to the door, asking Remy if he could show his guests the new gym, promising to catch up with them there. Two of my advisees were on the girls' team, and I was hoping to see them skate some more, but Barclay has a way with persuasion. He's great at suggesting something that it's clearly a directive, but his language is always ambiguous enough that it isn't an explicit command - just an implicit understanding that agreeing with him would be best.

We stepped into a gray afternoon with flurries blowing around, but failing to add to the six inches already on the ground. "You warm enough in that?" He nodded at my field coat.

"I *was* in *there*," I jabbed a thumb at the rink with a chuckle. "We're not hiking to town, right?"

He shook his head and thrust his hands into the pockets of the coat, which looked like it was from J. Press - very warm, and very, very overpriced, as I recall mother saying when she got one for father a few years back. His Loden trousers and Bean boots made him a real catalog shot. We started on the campus loop, which encircled most of the buildings in sight.

"First of all," he began, "really looking forward to your sabbatical presentation. Bet it'll be fascinating, 'specially with all the monuments down there getting re-evaluated."

"Yeah, I work that into a few slides, and it should be ready to go before the holiday break. If there's room at the faculty meeting week after next I cou—"

"O-o-o-o-o," he clicked his tongue, "That…might have to be rescheduled."

"Oh?" Most admins would rather sit on a hot stove than scratch a faculty meeting, so this was a new one.

"Yeah. I was due to go to China next month for some meet and greets, and to see a few of our trustees from there, but I heard from them - the trustees. They're in Hubei Province and apparently hotel space for functions is really tight there all of a sudden, so they want to meet in California instead. Have some big video link with families back there, but…who knows, maybe San Jose beats Wuhan this time of year, but I'm headed there a week from tomorrow, so can we see your presentation right after the break?"

"Sure. I'm ready."

"Great." He gave the kind of smile you see when someone's car starts after a day of repairs. "Also, not sure I ever said what a great effort you and Peter put in to get those boys to shore safely weeks ago."

"Well," I exhaled theatrically, "yeah. That's something I hope to never have to do again."

"I bet. Well, I don't like to think of how it could have gone sideways, so..," he turned to me with a look of Hallmark sincerity,

"Thank you." I nodded, and we turned a corner onto a freshly-salted path behind the science building. "We *have* heard from the parents of the boys involved," here he raised a cautionary finger, "who are also grateful for all you and Peter did. Please know that." I sensed that this was the last thing he'd say that I would *want* to know, and that what was coming would be prefaced by a *but* or *however*. "They *do* feel, however, that…when some fireman or EMT…chastised them for their actions, that he was…a little rough on them, and that, as their teachers, you and Peter should have…gotten him to…tone down his…language. Or at least his tone."

As he said this, he skidded a bit on a patch of black ice, but steadied himself right away. At that second, my mind went back to that afternoon - a yellow and blue New England postcard, Peter and me in T-shirts, kids in the boat. That must have been late September, and here it is in November, as the black ice reminded us, and he's asking me about some language a fireman used before Columbus Day.

"Hmmm," I scratched under my chin, for want of something else to do. "Not sure I recall exactly what was said. I *do* know they weren't happy about it, the whole episode. Something pretty avoidable. And caused by the kids, who are lucky to be alive."

"Absolutely. And there have been consequences. To be sure." he nodded. I didn't expect him to elaborate, as discipline now involves all this secrecy and confidentiality, as if every breath kids take isn't on social media. We're told to not discuss decisions of Disciplinary Committees once we adjourn from them, but by the time we get back to the dorms, it's already old news. If they skated on something, it's all high fives and Red Bulls. If they get suspended or worse, the latter of which is unheard of these days, others are in awe of them - real life Holden Caulfields. Word was that the boys were given a month's worth of weekend restriction to the dorm, community service hours, which probably meant swinging leaf blowers on a few afternoons, and had to write letters of contrition to the local fire department and Peter, for stealing his boat. None of this was ever announced - can't have that. Schools would rather endure an outbreak of chlamydia than have a student publicly shamed.

"Honestly Barclay, I remember the EMTs, one anyway, was pretty unhappy with things, but as to what was said, I don't recall the specific—"

"Well, here's the age we live in Ben: you don't have to." With that he pulled out his phone and gave a *guess what* glance my way.

"No," I stopped walking. "Really? *Really?*" He nodded, hitched his shoulders and we walked on. "So, we're looking for their phone numbers, to call them, in the boat," I'm recounting events for him, "Scott finally, probably gets them, they don't answer while they're floating toward the falls, and when they finally get to shore and are safe, they *finally* use their phones to record a fireman who showed up to save them? And *they're* pissed off?"

"Y-y-y-y-y-up. Played it for mom and dad, and they sent us a link to the recording, and made a transcript of it."

"Huh," I shook my head. "No good deed..."

"Agreed. But they, the parents, are saying that you two should have...stepped in to smooth things out. Not have let the language go unaddressed."

"Barclay." Now it was my turn to raise a finger, but I paused as a couple of boys headed for the rink passed us. "Forget that this was a major cluster you-know-what that could have ended much worse, but didn't. Even in a different, better situation, I'm not about to play language cop to a fireman. These guys run into burning buildings. I don't even know what was said but...sorry. Bringing them up short on whatever it was?" I looked away so that he wouldn't see my eyes rolling.

"Well, on the recording, you can hear him use the word "dumb," and that really set one parent off. Her son had an IEP before coming here - you'll keep this to yourself, right? - and he'd been doing better here. She insists that that word really hurt him. He's *not* dumb, she says"

"Well, he did a darn good imitation of dumb that afternoon, and while I don't recall what the EMT or fireman said, there was nothing that I could really disagree with. It was a stupid thing, and they were lucky to be on dry land." He nodded ever so slightly and headed up the steps to the old gym, where I had a flash. "Wait a minute. Scott was there. What does he say?"

"He got there just as things were winding down. Didn't hear the EMTs."

"Okay. What does Peter say?"

"He's my next conversation. As it was his boat, he might be a bit tender about all this, but he's lucky he can store it here on campus. He's had to get a lock to fasten the boat to the trailer."

"So, now what? I mean, where's this going?"

"The parents would like you - Peter and you - to explain why the EMT resorted to the language he used. And...if you wish that in hindsight, you'd said something to him about it, that you mention that to them. On reflection, so to speak."

I let this sink in for a bit, and turned his words over in my head a few times.

"Rather like, "I wish I'd stood up for your son more when the EMT dressed him down for stealing a boat?""

He offered a perfunctory chuckle and looked away. "I know, it's delicate, but they are kids after all."

"Yes, and they *did* steal someone's property. And when we tried to reach them, they *wouldn't* respond with their phones, but they *can* turn them on when someone rightly takes a tone with them? This doesn't seem like something to which I need to say "My bad." I mean, a cop doesn't say that when he stops someone for speeding."

I stopped and faced Barclay, and as I did, atop the highest pole on campus outside the new gym, I noticed the flag luffing in the flurries over his shoulder. "We can get all hierarchical here - who was in charge of whom, and all that, but any situation involving local authorities - police, firemen, whoever - whatever happens is their call. They've got the badges or the hoses." I held my palms up in a sign of surrender, "I'm just lucky they're there. We all are. And —"

"Look," he put a hand on my shoulder, "we're all grateful for all they do. And I know, pardon me for bringing it up, that a lot of them were lost tragically on 9/11, and that the events of that day touched you in a very…If you'd rather I stick to asking Peter if…"

"This is *not* about…*9/11!*" As I let those words drift across the common before us, words I had actually yelled, I realized that my tone probably made this quite unconvincing. I scanned the campus as if the end to my statement was on a banner hanging from a dorm window. "When I'm wrong, I apologize. When I'm not," I shrugged, "I don't."

He looked at me without a word, pursed his lips and exhaled. For a second I thought he might throw my own words back at me: *You're doing a good imitation of someone who* thinks *it's not about 9/11,* but he didn't.

"I'll speak with Peter. I'm not finding fault with you, Ben. Or with Peter. Just trying to keep everyone happy."

Not everyone.

I told him I was headed back to the game to see my advisees - get some points in that way, in case I'd need some with this whole mess on the river back on the stove. He spotted Remy and that party coming out of the new gym, smiled and headed to catch up with them. I took the long way back to the game, texting Peter to meet me later, and before he meets with Barclay. Back at the rink our girls were ahead 6-2 in the third period. Each of my advisees had scored a goal.

Dec 2

To bminot@griswold.org
From bcsears@griswold.org
Re A Repose and a Request

Hi Colleagues -

I'm writing to a select few of you for two reasons:

1 - A grateful parent sent a variety of gratitude to us that I'd like to share with you at 5 PM Saturday at the Ford Cottage. I've checked and none of you are on duty tomorrow night. As always, there'll be non-alcoholic offerings as well.

2 - Some requests have come my way from some international parents that I wanted to share with you which could lead to some very interesting professional development and travel. I'll elaborate in person when you're here.

Regrets only!

Barclay
Barclay Crowninshield Sears
Head of School
Griswold School

THIS HAD BEEN SENT to seven or eight of us on campus, yet none of us had any idea what it was about when we spoke of it at lunch. Not sure why there weren't more details offered, but as drinks were noted, it wasn't likely to be an announcement of a mass layoff.

How I'm going to handle the Zhang-prefect-rec matter is another thing about which I have no idea. That I *have* to handle it is incredibly annoying, but one thing my father said that only took me twenty or thirty years to appreciate is that one can indeed get more flies with honey than vinegar. Not sure what the flies are in this case, but there's certainly a bitter taste in it all. Saturday was the first day I ran the scoreboard for two games, and as it went well, and as a dram of something interesting at Barclay's awaited later in the day, I figured I'd dive into the Zhang matter while in a good mood. I went to see Eric in his dorm room, so he could at least tell his father that I spoke to him. That notion from "The Godfather" about keeping your enemies closer came to mind. It turns out that Eric lives with Hiro Yamanashi, a sophomore from Osaka. Recalling a class on East Asian history and what I learned of Sino-Japanese enmity, it seemed that whoever put these guys together as roommates was having fun with that notion about keeping enemies close. The door was mostly ajar, and their room was a three-dimensional Pollack painting: laundry, video game consoles and ramen cups - some empty, some new - everywhere. An odor had me suggest opening the window in spite of the season. Hiro was working a console frantically, glued to a monitor on his desk. Had I set his bed on fire, not sure he'd have noticed. Eric was beside him in a yellow Palm Beach sweatshirt critiquing his game and sipping a sixteen-ounce energy drink.

"Eric - I...understand you'd like to be a prefect next year."

"What? Yeah. I guess." His eyes never left the screen. The words floated like those of a transit cop when asked how late the trains run; he needs to respond, but does so in an indifferent deadpan.

"Okay...can you tell me *why* you'd like to be a prefect?" A very exciting development on the screen overrode my question, so I repeated it.

"Well, it's a good thing, right?" I didn't respond, waiting for him to look at me. "It is, right?"

"It's an important responsibility," I nodded and took a seat on a desk chair, "so if someone does it well, it's good for the dorm, and for...what teachers and dorm parents will say about the student."

"And.." the game beckoned for perhaps fifteen seconds before he could complete his thought, "for college, yes?"

"It *is* something that students can put on college apps, yes."

"Because I want to run the Asian Student Alliance too. That would look good too, right?" His English seemed to have improved since our last encounter.

I nodded and scanned the floor underfoot. "Part of the task is getting kids to follow policies, like keeping rooms clean for inspections. So for instance, if you saw a student's room looking like this," I waved my hand over the health hazard about me, "you'd want to encourage him to clean it, and tell him you'd be back to check it in an hour."

Hiro's clicking kept me from getting a prompt response, but a sigh suggested a setback on the screen, yielding an *uh-huh* from Eric.

This was like one hand clapping. I looked about the room, just for some sense that there was more to him than plagiarizing and ramen. Under his bed was a tennis racquet and a few cans of balls. "You play tennis?" I pointed under the bed.

His eyes followed my finger to the floor, and at once he pounced to where his racquet was, using it to shove the yellow cans of balls further under the bed. He then stood, swinging the Wilson 200T as if returning imaginary serves with it. "Yeah. Long years. I want to play in the spring. My father sends me to a camp in summers. Last summer I go to a camp in Arizona." Apparently his English is still a work in progress.

"Good," I stood. This should keep dad at bay for a while. "Let's talk again about this. The prefect application process doesn't start until March, OK?"

"OK," was uttered without a thought, the strings on his racquet having just become quite interesting. As he studied one to see if it needed tightening, I told Hiro and him to "make good decisions tonight" - Griswold-speak for "Don't break any rules'" - and took my leave.

The Head of School's residence on the highest point on campus, Ford Cottage, is one of those Georgian brick homes with white pillars that probably makes some people think that it would be great to be a headmaster. Anyone who's spent more than a month at any school has probably been disabused of this idea. Raising money, keeping alumni and parents happy, praying that HR does thorough background checks on all hires, getting emails from maintenance saying that the HVAC system in the science building is failing - and it's a twelve-month job. I teach summers just because you can't sail every day and it's fun to meet colleagues at another school, to swap tales and ideas. Some Heads of School probably like all the travel in spite of complaining about it. No Red Roof Inns for sure, and schmoozing with trustees worth seven and eight figures probably convinces some Heads that they are on a par with them, if not financially, at least in their own professional realm. The shoveled and sanded walk leading to Ford ended at a banister wrapped in holly garland that edged the steps to the top one, where a boot scraper was rusting away. Perhaps, like most boot scrapers at houses built after 1900, it had probably never had any boots scraped on it. Several of us converged at the oak door, the person I knew best there being Ralph. Before any of us could reach for the knocker in the lion's mouth, Barclay opened it, and that rush of holiday warmth and smells that one imagines on the set of a Hallmark Christmas movie met us before we stepped over the threshold.

There are certain rules to how such homes must be adorned: oriental rugs, tall clocks, Chippendale chairs, paintings that suggest either Currier and Ives or Winslow Homer, a fourteen-foot Norway Green Spruce with white lights only and on such nights, a roaring fire. In a red cashmere sweater and tartan trousers, I half expected Barclay to break into a song by Perry Como. He had that glow about him that suggested all was right with the world, or at least the world inside the school gates, or maybe that house. On a table sporting a seasonal centerpiece was a charcuterie board, flanked by what looked to be mulled wine. Some spirits in bottles I've never seen before beckoned, all of which were encircled by old fashioned and wine glasses with the Griswold crest.

"Where did *these* come from?" marveled a math intern, admiring the stemware. "I've never seen them."

"They're tough to see," Ralph piped up as he studied the cheeses. "Few years ago, someone decided that having the school crest on something meant to hold alcohol was not a good message to send."

"Who decided *that?*" asked someone else.

"Someone who clearly had never been to a reunion weekend in June." Ralph offered in a flat tone with a hint of incredulity.

"This is true," Barclay reappeared after hanging coats up, "but that Bud truck will *not* be back this spring." He forced a grin in a once-bitten-twice shy way. Four years ago at reunion, some alum who worked at Anheuser-Busch had a truck with taps on the side brought to campus. By Sunday morning the area in front of the art building looked like fraternity row after a Michigan-Ohio game. When a trustee found a Soho cup that had doubled as a urinal on his Jaguar' hood, the temperance rumblings started. "After we...after it was decided to stop having the glasses made, the school bought all the ones left in the bookstore. Certain functions like *this* are when they have been used." He raised his libation and took a sip. Note to self: avoid use of the passive voice. *Mistakes were made.* Sounds like a documentary about Watergate.

"Geez," I was reading the label of one of the bottles, "this scotch is old enough to vote."

"Help yourself Ben," Barclay waved an arm over the spread. "Everyone. Please."

Shortly, we were all sipping and nibbling, basking in the warmth of the room. It was as all functions are now: from Christmas sweaters and Santa ties to jeans. I wonder how the better clothiers stay in business. I donned Royal Stewart trousers simply because it would probably be the only time I wear them all year, and it's nice to justify them. Once everyone had settled in, Barclay sat on an ottoman by the tree and began. He started with what's a common boilerplate for all meetings: ticking off laurels and accomplishments of the year so far - team records, gifts to the school, finalized plans for a new weight room in the gym. Then he pulled back the curtain.

"A number of our international parents would like their children here to experience a real American Christmas, whatever shape that may take. A lot of them have in mind rooms like this one - fires, trees, maybe some caroling and skiing...and snow; things and experiences that just aren't part of life elsewhere, like China. Obviously we can't guarantee snow, but you get the idea. We're reaching out to domestic families and alumni to see who'd be willing to host about two dozen students from China for the break. We're confident that our families will step up, but just in case, it's nice to have a fallback plan. That's where we're looking to you." He scanned the faces about him, which were frozen.

"You want us to…" Ralph was squinting at the oriental at his feet, "follow up with parents who haven't responded when break gets close?"

Barclay thinned his lips and gave him the *ask* look – an earnest, pleading glare as he cocked his head to one side. "Actually Ralph, the hope is that some faculty will step up to take some students in for the break, to really add a *family* aspect to our role with students. We would of course *compensate* you for this – having someone in your home for two weeks, feeding them. Even a stipend for a few Christmas presents for whoever you host, for every student you have."

"*Every?*" I straightened up, and probably didn't have a very accommodating face just then. "As in, *more than one?*"

"Well, Ben, think - thousands of miles from home, some students would probably like a friend or roommate to pass the days with. That would also relieve the host of entertaining one lone student, naturally."

"Wait." The new science chair was moving her hands up and down as if simulating juggling would help her to understand matters. She reminded me of Jodie Foster, and not just looks-wise – unsmiling, unmade up, a voice that it was hard to imagine having ever told a joke. "We're being asked to spend our break with…the people we assign *homework* to, whose *rooms* we inspect. We smell their breath at check-in to see if they've been vaping. And have them in the spaces where *we* may wanna vape?" She was at two schools out west before a partner in med school brought her east. "I mean, 'course I *don't* vape, but…*really?*"

Slowly, almost fearfully, the math intern raised his hand. "Will we be…are we supposed to be like, foster parents? Getting them to brush their teeth and everything?" His red curly hair, and small sometimes timid eyes suggested he was only a few years older than our seniors, although he was several years out of college.

"The idea is that we provide a welcoming home away from home," Barclay offered with a sweep of an arm. "You wouldn't be checking to make sure toothbrushes are wet at bedtime." He must have sensed that this was an irregular ask, and that it wasn't selling. Given some major gifts that have come in over the past few years, clearly he's a good pitchman, and probably figured that this would sell eventually – but Tomoko Yamanashi might have been the biggest spanner in his works tonight.

Tomoko joined the History Department five years ago after spells at schools in Rhode Island and Connecticut. Straight from Japan, she plowed through Georgetown and Penn and found herself at St. George's near Newport where she was ignored when she started reporting that some of her girls had been touched sexually by the athletic trainer. "I've been in mosh pits that were more thoughtful than that place," she likes to say. "No wonder Tucker Carlson is so...*yeesh!*" she shakes her head sometimes, recalling one of the school's alums. By the time the story of the trainer exploded, she was at The Gunnery, a small school in Connecticut miles from nowhere. By her first Thanksgiving there she was looking again, and the following September she was here, with a no-nonsense bob cut and a Border Collie she jogs with before dinner. She brought some new electives to the department, led the field hockey team to an undefeated season and is a notoriously hard marker. The kids know she's tough and still like her because they learn so much from her. If she's still here in a few years, we'll be lucky.

"Barclay, this is a charming idea. Really. But you *do* recall the school in Rhode Island I was at right?" She leaned forward in her chair and put her glass down to make her point with both hands. "Full disclosure: after three and a half months, I'd really like my break to be student-free. But: even if I was all in on this, the idea of having students staying with faculty for two weeks...Do the words "St Paul's" mean anything to you? Not saying we have the kind of creepy guys that they had, but, wouldn't we be opening ourselves up to, who knows what? Suppose some kids don't like being told to turn down their video games or make their beds, and they decide to respond by making the host out to be creepy." At this everyone's heads turned to neighbors in a *hadn't thought of that* sort of way.

I spent a month in Japan, hardly in entirety, but based on that experience, Tomoko is the least Japanese Japanese person I've ever met. No bullshit or obfuscation from her, whereas I found most people in Tokyo too polite to be terribly direct on many subjects. Here she was laying it right out: some unhappy kid could ruin a teacher's life. In an age when you're not even supposed to tutor a student with your door closed, she had a point.

"Tomoko," Barclay gently extended a hold-your-horses hand in her direction, with an expression as if he'd just been told by a dentist that he has three cavities. "I'm sure that nothing would inspire a student to take the initiative to accuse a teacher of something out of hand." Oh, *really?*

"Barclay," she tipped her head to one side, incredulous, "we're not even supposed to ride alone with kids in our cars. So, in terms of boundaries with kids, *which is it?*"

A few others had questions that suggested more curiosity than skepticism as to the proposal, but Barclay's glow was gone. He now looked like he was listening to a plumber telling him that it wasn't his sink, but the septic that needs work. I actually felt sorry for him, so tossed out a lifeline.

"You did say that, as lots of families have been asked, that, it might not come to housing students here, right? And, what about the roommates of these students? We took our roommates home for weekends when I was at school. Have families also been offered, I dunno, stipends for food and such?"

"N-n-n-o-o-o-o Ben," he turned to me. "We could, but families that offer to take some students, we don't want to insult them with offers of charity."

"Might not be a bad idea," I cocked my head. We have kids here on financial aid, so not all families are rolling in money, but I didn't feel like exploring the point. I might have an out if it comes to this, as my cousin who'd stayed in my house last year brought her cats. I'm fine with them, but lots of kids are allergic to, well, *everything* these days. And Remy the A.D. is taking the fam to Florida over the holidays and asked me to watch his German Shepherds, Zeus and Rolf. Whenever international kids see him walking them they give him a wide berth. These two animal presences might make me a less desirable host if we get that far. Ralph raised the point of how novel this notion was, which seemed to crack the door a little bit, and Barclay added to the picture.

"Honestly," he exhaled and affected a look of being confounded by something he knew or didn't know. "A number of our students, Chinese students, are from Hubei province. Seventeen, to be exact, and several of their parents work for the government there, and...I don't know how much you may have heard, but there's been an outbreak of something in a city over there. Some flu or something that's pretty serious. The parents sound rather unnerved by what they know about it, which is more than I know about it. Doesn't sound widespread, but the parents have asked us to keep their children here for the break rather than have them go home until this virus, or whatever it is, blows over."

"Obviously, we want to do what we can for our kids Barclay, and keep their parents happy," I offered a slightly hopeful smile, just to counter the mood about us, "but when it comes to Christmas and New Years'...I mean suppose on New Year's Eve someone wants to ha—"

A *boom!* from somewhere on campus stopped me cold, and everyone's eyes darted between the windows and each other. I'd heard cannons fired on the USS Constitution once, and it reminded me of that same sound. At first, thoughts run to the obvious: a boiler in a dorm or a gas grill mishap. Around the circle, everyone looked baffled while Barclay checked his watch, then spoke.

"If I'm right, that's probably Earl's gender reveal party near the rink. For his twins." We all looked at him with squints that asked *Really?*

"He told me he wanted to do it, so I told him to pick a time and place when not many kids would be around. He asked to use the old cannon we start the final cross country race of the season with and got some streamers from a party store."

"Loudest streamers *I* ever heard." Tomoko cocked her head and pulled a face.

"Y-y-y-e-e-e-s-s-s," Barclay reached for his phone. "They were, *weren't* they..."

People eyed each other amidst pregnant pauses, and a few rose and pulled out phones, probably to let family on campus know that we hadn't been targeted by North Korea. Others took this as a good time to top up their glasses. As we did, the math intern looked out a window, and twisted his face.

"Isn't the pep rally *next* week?"

"Friday night," Ralph was reading labels on bottles at the table.

"S-s-s-o-o-o-o," the intern leaned in, almost touching the windowpane with his nose, "why's the bonfire lit now?"

At that there was a rush to the windows. On the back side of the hockey rink there was a five-foot high pile of campfire wood that was to be lit next Friday at the start of the Griswold Goalfest, a three day hockey tournament we host. A few hours before the first game, the bonfire is lit and team captains as well as coaches rally the school faithful to cheer the Grizzlies onto victory all weekend. Thus it was surprising to see flames licking their way through the pile six days early. This scene across the way did not provide Barclay with any *pep*.

"What the—" and his phone went off. He looked to see who it was, and raised the phone to his ear in a manner suggesting he thought it might bite him. "Earl? Did your event possibly have anything to do with there being a fire behi—" He then proceeded to listen, and stomped into the kitchen for the call. Attention returned to the windows. It wasn't a roaring blaze, but next Friday it is supposed to be, and unintended flames at schools are frowned upon. Phones started dinging, and people began reading aloud the texts that they were getting. *You can't be serious. What was he thinking? A teacher? Earl? Too funny.* As the messages came in, the picture emerged. Earl Blackabby's gender reveal party involved fireworks, which are illegal in Massachusetts, but as anyone unfortunate to have found himself at a meal with him since September will confirm, he's very excited about having twins. He always talks about some cousin in New Hampshire who owns a fireworks store there. As the story dripped out, the relative apparently brought down some July 4th stock for the event, along the logic that a one-time blast, as opposed to a fireworks show, wouldn't attract attention, at least not from the kind of authorities who enforce things like laws and such. Earl bumped the cannon after he lit the fuses in it, causing its barrel to drop downward, and instead of skyward, the salvo shot across the parking lot and into the woodpile. This combination of brazen whim and foolish hubris seemed like something you'd expect from a fraternity house, not a high school department chair, although it has been pretty well established that some people who go big on gender reveal parties are not the Lord's best work. If I was about to become a father, I might want to have people in for food and drink, but since I'm not, from afar, I consider the whole concept beyond stupid. As more details dinged in via text, Barclay emerged from the kitchen pulling on a parka with a look suggesting that he'd soon be in someone's face. This was matched by his determined gait for the door. He turned for a minute.

"Help yourselves to…everything. Watch the fire here. Stay as long as you want. Sorry. I need to tend to this."

Everyone waited and sipped quietly until Tomoko at the window told us he was safely away from the house, at which point chatter and laughter filled the room. People shook their heads at it all, and some began joking about whether I'd become the new English chair once Barclay impaled Earl on a campus lamp post. "I think I'd rather chew glass," I responded.

"Whoa!" Tomoko actually stepped back from the window, and in the panes, a brighter light from outside could be seen. I moved next to her and saw why. What had been a docile collection of flames reaching out of a pile of wood was now a ten-foot high ball of fire.

"What happened?" I asked Tomoko.

"I dunno. It just...*poof!*"

We could see people converging on the hockey center, which was probably the last thing Barclay or Maintenance and Campus Security wanted. Between the lights from the rink and the fire, we could see Barclay meet up with a heavy set fellow - quite likely the head of Campus Safety. He then turned to a shorter person and started a very animated conversation with him. This was probably Earl.

Countless sounds, even if not investigated, are chalked up as *a car backfiring*, although either due to how cars are now made or to my limited life experience, I cannot recall ever actually seeing a car backfire. Something beyond just sounds was at work outside - small sparks were leaping out of the blaze, and soon they became small flares, then bigger ones: *fireworks*. Not all of them could escape the pile of wood and brush, but those that did were quite entertaining. When the cannon has been used for the season-ending cross country meet, we've always called the local fire department just so they'd know that we hadn't stumbled upon an old munitions dump under a soccer field and were finishing it off. The fire department hadn't been called in advance this time, and they hadn't mistaken it for a car backfiring, for ever so distantly, then louder, sirens began to fill the evening air outside. The red lights flickering off school buildings followed, and soon two trucks and several smaller vehicles had pulled to a stop by the rink.

"Huh," Tomoko chuckled to herself and made for the charcuterie board, "Didn't know there'd be entertainment." A few of us meandered out to Ford Cottage's wraparound porch and watched the figures silhouetted against the blaze confer. From within the burning pile, pops could be heard, and a few streams of sparks shot out from it. Two of these whistled skyward and exploded overhead. These couldn't be part of Earl's gender reveal announcement, for his intent was not to have the cannon aimed at the pile; this was something else. The fire department arrived, but no hoses were deployed, and students had begun to gather at a distance. Adults, probably administrators, waved them back, but as the flames were now perhaps twenty feet high, they were no doubt visible from most of the dorm rooms on campus, and more moths were inevitable. Behind the rink were woods and a series of trails, which is where we could see kids migrating once they were shooed away from one side of the spectacle.

"Since that was going to be lit next week anyway..." the math intern began.

"They're probably not going to put it out," I shrugged. "It's *supposed* to burn - just not now. I expect they'll just get more wood for it before the tournament."

"It wasn't 'sposed to burn like *that*," Ralph pointed his open beer bottle at the scene. "That had *help*." There were a few nods, and questions were floated about the whimper of fireworks that emerged from the bonfire. The notion seemed agreed upon: while Earl's lousy aim was a head scratcher, the blaze was more than what was intended for the following week. The occasional *pop!* could be heard even from where we were, sounds like smothered firecrackers.

Back inside a discussion commenced: should we stay or go? Barclay clearly had an agenda to discuss with us and had put on the dog for it. The two-alarm intermission, however, had been quite a curveball for him, and wasn't over yet. With this on top of the river incident that the EMTs had been called for in the fall, he was probably getting an earful from the firemen Once done, he probably wouldn't be in a mood to hear why his host family idea was a bad one.

"I can talk to him," the school counselor offered. A somewhat austere Joan Didion doppelganger who I'd guess is pushing sixty, she was on her phone to someone. I've never had much to do with her, but these days, a counselor for kids at any school has enough to do without getting to know colleagues. Barclay's wife was away, so she seemed to be the *de facto* hostess. "This is just a strange time, but I'll talk him down when he returns." We all offered to help clean up, but she waved it off. "I didn't have lunch," she chuckled, hinting that she'd make more things disappear. "But take what you want." Some of us eyed the expensive bottles before us, but figured they weren't exactly like half-filled Soho cups that we should walk away with.

Dining hall fare is notoriously lame on Saturday nights, the expectation being that some students have gone home for the weekend, some teams are still on the road, and others will order food to be delivered to the dorm. The local pizza pub does lots of the last one, so knowing that we might not run into too many students there, I took Ralph up on the notion to split a pie.

Apollo Pizza is your garden-variety small-town establishment. A hole-in-the-wall half a mile from campus in our one-stoplight town, its fare is smothered in cheese and oil, promising a heart attack in every slice, God bless them. It's also apparently a bit too far for students to walk to. Sipping PBR from the tap as we waited for our pizza, I recounted the year so far with Ralph. Eventually, I noticed the corners of his mouth turning up. He seemed amused but I doubted it was his beer.

"Have a joke you want to share?"

He shook his head and laughed to himself. "Sorry man. But the problems you white people get yourselves into. It kills me."

"Sorry?" I squinted at him with no idea what he was talking about.

"I'm just thinking: that picture of a sailboat in Barclay's house got me on it. You had that thing this fall when two kids took Burnsy's boat for a joyride on the river, and you had to save them, and now they're on you about some fireman's language to the kids. You caught some kid cheating on a quiz using his water bottle - and it's a trustee's kid, and dad's dangling something over your head 'cuz you did your job in his daughter's dorm. Then you invite some comedian back to campus, and the guy pushes some people's buttons in Earl's class once he gets here. That's a freaking hat-trick, dude."

I couldn't argue with him, so I gazed out the window of our booth. It had begun to snow, and the cars outside were creeping through it silently as their beams picked up the huge flakes.

"Yeah," I took a sip. "Probably should have stayed down south." I peeled off my coat. "Hard to screw up in South Carolina. When the state was the first one to secede from the Union, some northern politician noted that it was, "Too small to be a country, but too big to be an asylum.""

"Too big to cut loose too." Ralph nodded. "Too bad it's not an island we could just ignore. But think of it: a loose sailboat, and an unruly guest speaker. It's…"

He could see my eyes widen, realizing that I didn't find these various shitstorms cannon fodder for his amusement. He sat up and leaned in, raising a qualifying hand as if he thought I needed restraining. "Sorry, but if black people had…*only* those kinds of problems, God, life would be..." He whistled and glided a flat hand through the air to suggest smooth sailing.

"Okay," I tossed my head from side to side, hinting that I didn't totally disagree with him, "but hardly the fall term I wanted to have after a year away. I was hoping to feel, you know, recharged when I got back...but it's been...just one thing after another."

"I know man," He raised his glass to me, the head of beer falling inside it. "But my first year teaching: hell, I *wish* I'd had your problems. Black at Nottingham - not sure what I was thinking. I wore a Red Sox cap to a game in the Bronx one time. *That* was easier than that whole year at that place." Nottingham is a school near the New York border - apparently not a bastion of diversity.

"That Sox cap at Yankee Stadium wasn't very smart." I looked to see where our pizza was.

"No it wasn't," he nodded. "Pretty stupid, but self-inflicted. Now, look at Jerome here. New kid. Gets nudged into something at the Coop. Maybe he did get prodded, or not, but that's neither here nor there, 'cuz he's Black – never good with a cop or even a store cop. Not exactly of *his* making. None of it."

"No argument. Gee - zus, I was there." I swallowed half my beer, "I dunno. Is it my imagination or is everything this year really fucked up?" I looked at Ralph as you might a doctor who had test results in hand.

"Hey," he held up his palm and pointed to his skin with a finger from the other hand. "See this? Things *always* been f-ed up, far as I can tell. Never known otherwise."

"Hang on a minute." I had a text from Peter about Barclay wanting an apology to the parents of the boat thieves. They'd finally had the conversation that I had with Barclay outside the hockey game weeks ago. He said Barclay had pressed him, but as the victim of a crime, he didn't feel as though his path should be one of contrition. At that I fetched another round.

"I'm good, thanks." Ralph waved this off when I brought them to the table.

"Fine," I pulled his to my side of the table. "I'm not."

Jan 6

WINTER AT A BOARDING school has always been like living inside a bipolar bubble. Coming back from break, there's all this energy. The dorms are clean for a bit and the kids are looking forward to games every Wednesday and Saturday. Shaking off snow as they enter the classroom, the red cheeks and tousled hair suggest some old covers of *The Saturday Evening Post* during the holidays. By mid-February however, it seems like half the students in any dorm would like to stick forks in their roommates' eyes. The cloistering that comes with not being able to toss a frisbee or lacrosse ball around on the lawns, combined with anxiety over college acceptance news and incomplete FAFSA forms really winds up a lot of kids, and makes living with them sometimes as much fun as flossing teeth.

Turns out that teachers weren't asked to house students over the break, in spite of Barclay's pre-holiday ask. A combination of parents and alums stepping up helped, as did a dose of reality: the kids would happily retreat to hotel rooms in New York or Boston that their parents pay for and just play video games for two weeks between breaks to fetch more energy drinks. This all scratched the big ask from Barclay. Honestly, with a spare room offering two twin beds, the notion didn't bother me on one level as much as I initially thought it would. My concern was that if I was watching a Celtics game and spit out some nasty language at some point from my couch, six weeks later, a former guest who didn't like his grade on a quiz or my "no" to a request somewhere on campus would mention hearing a teacher swear. Why borrow trouble? The Chinese kids were stuck stateside over the break owing to that bug going around back home. Some will also stay nearby in March as well, and then get sent to another school for the summer to work on English and garner feathers in their caps for college apps. Not much of a childhood, but from what I hear about the air quality in Beijing, maybe it's a wash. Monday I sent my proposal for the sabbatical presentation to Fred, Scott and Barclay. An online offering of perhaps forty slides, it should run twenty minutes or so on the takeaways from my months down south. A PowerPoint that provides a sense of what the elective will cover should do it. As I tapped out the introduction to it in an email, it occurred to me that perhaps two-thirds of the people in the PPT images are black, and that the three people who would give me the nod to present it are all white, as am I. This being a New England boarding school, this is not a revelation, and I suppose a reflection of the pipeline more than anything else. Deans and Heads of Schools have been in the game for a while, so it's kind of like the Supreme Court: you get there by being a federal judge who was once at a white-shoe law firm after clerking for a justice following law school at Yale or Harvard. Not that many people of color could start checking off those boxes decades ago. They're coming, but it's pretty much a white ivy boys club. Same with the schools. While Milton and Groton have had black Headmasters, the pipelines are still pretty much white.

In a case of 'you couldn't make this up,' as soon as I sent my email to the troika, I saw an email from Mary Carpenter.

Ben -

FYI Jerome is looking to go to another school next year, or at least his family is. As he's my advisee, his sister emailed me about it, and mentioned to be expecting a request for transcripts and recommendations on his behalf. I know what happened at the Coop wasn't your fault, but we both know the administrators can act...contrary to what they may know. They might want to blame someone for what happened there if he leaves Griswold. Just thought you might want a heads up.

Mary

Well, that's why we have an Admissions Office that sends out catalogs.

Jan 8

RUNNING THE SCOREBOARD FOR the basketball games is not a bad gig. I really like hitting the horn when there is a sub. Today the boys beat Overtoun. At one point while setting a pick in the game, Todd Garmin was flattened by a power forward from the other team. A foul was called, but he was slow to get up, and came out for a bit, not going in again until the second half. He still has that shaved head, which I thought he would have grown out by now, as the other guys on the soccer team have. There was a yell from his gaggle of admirers, those local girls who seemed fascinated with Grizzly basketball, especially whenever Todd was on the court, and he reached up to massage his shiny head every time they were vocal to acknowledge it. When I look at my old yearbook photos, I wonder why my parents never told me to get a haircut.

"They probably did," Ralph said when I mentioned this to him one time, "but you probably didn't listen to them. Listening is not a great talent in teenagers." Maybe so, but if I thought that I could have had an all-female fan club as Todd does by shaving my head, I would have gone all Uncle Fester early on in my school years. Breaking down the scoring table, a couple of Todd's groupies came by. Doe - eyed, apple-cheeked girls from town, one was glued to her phone's screen while the other twirled some blonde locks between her fingers. This one cocked her head to the other side to speak.

"Excuse me, but do you think Todd should be allowed to…to play so hard?"

"What?" I was unplugging the wire from the shot clock. "It's not my call. I just run the board."

"Right," she looked away a bit, as if a good response was to be found in the stands. "But…did he get hurt today?"

"Well, he still got some minutes in the second half after that foul.. and six points too."

"O-k-a-a-a-y-y-y-y…" She wasn't getting some answer she wanted, so I suggested she ask him herself.

"He'll probably be in the student center in a bit. After a shower. I hope."

At this her eyes widened, affecting a slight alarm. "What do you mean, "You *hope*?" Here I wanted to be a bit delicate, but also to make a point that's been gnawing at me for years. It used to be that everybody showered in locker rooms after games. Those days are gone. Nobody does that anymore, at least not in the gang showers in school gyms. You couldn't go to meals in sweats or anything athletic after a game. You had to change to eat in the dining halls. Those rules and policies have gone the way of black and white TV. I conveyed all this, but raised the palm to assure her that I wasn't being critical of how her generation was swimming in this unhygienic status quo. "Hopefully the boys are showering after the game in the dorm - that's all I meant." At that there was a text ping, which I sensed was mine. As if on cue, the girls turned on their heels and were gone. *Happy to help you.* Manners seemed to have gone the way of showering in gyms after basketball games.

Text:

> Mr. Minot - Jerome's sister here. Short notice I know, but I'm taking Jerome to dinner tonight and wondered if we could meet for coffee before then?

Even if Jerome was heading to another school, it didn't seem that anything since the Coop episode would involve me. Precisely *because* it was not clear what she wanted to talk about, I suggested a diner by the town library at 4:30. Jerome's sister waved to me in an almost friendly way from the door as she entered. She strode toward the booth in a long tweed car coat with a satchel on a strap over her shoulder which I'm guessing was made of leather or alligator. She said she recognized me from the school website. After small talk and her tea with lemon arrived, she placed her elbows on the table and made a steeple of her hands over the steaming mug.

"You may hear that we're looking for another school for Jerome. I didn't want you to hear about this like some rumor or game of telephone, or because we thought that what happened at the Coop was somehow on you."

"Your parents – do they have some schools in mind? Thank you for the heads up, by the way." I raised my mug to her.

"My mother does. But I'm here since she's on loan to the CDC and is off to Washington State. This virus that showed up there is spooking lots of people in Atlanta."

I nodded and offered what useless crumbs I could about the disease which apparently had arrived in the northwest via some tourist who'd returned from China.

"There's been some," she waved a spoon around as if doing so would help her to find the right word. "some stuff in the dorm. Nothing particularly awful, at least not by boarding school standards, I know - I was at school - but little stuff: things missing from the room, remarks…more than microaggressions. And…maybe he's just homesick. Again, I don't want you to think that this is because of how you handled the Harvard Coop thing." She leaned in to make her point. "I've *been* there. Cops, even rent-a-cops, and black people - not a good record. And his advisor, Mrs. Carpenter, she says good things about you." Not sure why that is but nice to hear. "I was wondering," she squinted a bit, suggesting a hint of uncertainty, "This business at the Coop: anyway that might find its way to any schools he's applying to?" I had to think on that one, and the crash of a few dishes in the diner's kitchen didn't help my concentration.

"That's really not something I know. But, as far as I *do* know, they simply send schools the grades and recs, and as he is still here, there's no suspension or withdrawal or anything disciplinary on his record, so nothing officially untoward."

"Wow. *Untoward.*" She broke into a grin with a nod. "You *are* an English teacher. Sounds like the kind I had at school. But," she tipped her head in a bit, "you and I both know that some things have a way of getting communicated…unofficially, especially if there are sour grapes about someone looking to go to another school."

"I can't see it working its way into things. If something did, and that came out as a factor in a decision that worked against Jerome, well, that would open up a can of worms here, right?"

"I suppose." She formed two fists under her chin. "But some people have a way of avoiding consequences. Not just adults and kids, but institutions too. Those boys who he said…I don't know, cajoled him, dared him, stuck the thing in his pocket…whatever. It's been like that forever at schools. There's a whole peer pressure thing from older kids. Aren't their parents involved at the school?"

At that I shrugged. One of the boys' names is the same as someone who co-chairs the Parents' Fund but it's not an uncommon name, so I played dumb, which comes quite easily to me.

"Where's he looking to go next year?"

"My mother has the list, but I'm doing the groundwork, so to speak. Some day schools near D.C., Lawrenceville in New Jersey I think. Northfield Mount Hermon 'cuz I went there, and one more school in Connecticut. I can't recall which one." Here she sat up straighter and cleared her throat. "One thing though. Maybe it's nothing but, there aren't any skinheads here, like a club or anything, at the school? Sounds crazy I know but …."

"What?" Now I sat up a little straighter. "No. *God* no. What gave you…" and before completing that sentence, I knew what she was referring to: the soccer baldies from the fall. Either some photos showed up on the school's Instagram page, or Jerome had mentioned them. I explained the team shaving their heads in the fall, but she said that there were supposedly still a couple of kids with cue ball heads now in mid-January.

"Well, there's one I know of, but he might think it's intimidating on the basketball court - and it saves them time in the shower." She forced a chuckle at that.

"Yeah, probably." She sipped her tea. "I just had to ask. I've got an aunt in Charlottesville. Her daughter was at that rally there where that girl died. You just think about these things, even more now than before. Seems like it should be otherwise. What *year* are we in?"

"I know. Strange Days. And not in a good way, but—" Just then she got a text. Checking her phone, she apologized for having to respond to it, working her thumbs faster than I ever could. I drained my coffee as she finished.

"I should go get Jerome." She got organized to leave. "Give you a lift?"

"Thanks. I drove here." And as I stood, I got a text.

"Now it's my turn." I said.

"No problem. Thanks for meeting me." She gave her warmest smile yet and was gone.

***

The text was from Fred Talleyrand about a meeting to discuss my sabbatical presentation over lunch tomorrow. At least it's finally scheduled, but I'm still not sure what's to discuss. There seem to be people who, if they couldn't schedule and attend meetings all day, would have very little to do during their waking hours.

Back on campus I pulled into a spot between the dining hall and the gym since dinner was starting soon. Getting out of my car, I gave a start at hearing my name bellowed.

"Ben!" One of the athletic trainers was yelling as she bounded down the steps from the gym. A grad student in physical therapy, someone said she reminded him of Lena Dunham. Unadorned and perpetually in sweats, she's good natured with a voice that carries. "Where you been? Not grading papers I bet."

"No, matter of fact I wasn't."

"Didn't think so. You left your grade book on the scoring table."

"Oh *shit!*" came out loud enough for some students nearby to hear. Thankfully, this resulted in just passing chuckles; they love instances that reveal us to be human. I was more worried about someone having seen kids' grades in my book. They share everything anyway, but when a teacher does it by, say, handing a lousy test back to the wrong student, now someone else knows who got a 57 on it, and it's cause for a couple of meetings.

"Don't worry," she held up a calming palm. "I saw it just after you left and grabbed it. It's on my desk in the training room, and the door's unlocked." She pointed over her shoulder with a thumb, and I gushed gratitude as she headed on to dinner.

Grabbing my old school rank book from the trainer's desk, I closed the door and headed out a different way. Outside the weight room I came upon a figure kneeling on the floor with his back to me, head down and arms raised as if asking some deity above *why?* Not seeing a prayer rug underneath, I felt obliged to inquire. Coming around front I saw Glenn Olson with an open backpack at his knees.

"Glenn." I put a hand on his shoulder out of reflex. "Are you okay?" A student of mine whose writing is pretty average, his work at least suggests that his father, a Wellesley professor, doesn't polish his papers for him; would that this could be said of more students here.

"Hi Mr. Minot." From under some *whatever* bangs, he looked up at me like someone who had just soiled himself. A red hoodie is his go-to top most days, so he's pretty recognizable.

"What are you doing on the floor?"

Exhaling, he gave an extended wince, squeezing his eyes shut as if this was necessary in order for him to answer me.

"The top came off my Powerade. In my backpack." He reached in and pulled out a dripping gray box. "And I had the battery cover off of my calculator." He eyed the device with a combination of despair and lament. It was a graphing calculator, a Texas Instrument device twice the size of what I used twenty years ago. Per my niece, they cost about $150 these days. Glenn began flipping some pages of a math text and a notebook, both of which were now colored in various designs of red Powerade. He remained on the floor, transfixed as he leafed through what looked like Rorschach tests in thin blood on each page.

"Can you still use the books? Is there someone whose notes you could—"

"Fenway!" He threw the books against the outside of the weight room wall, looking that way, not toward me.

" 'Scuse me?"

He buried his face in his hands. "My father is from New York. Loves the Yankees." He heaved a deep breath. "He says *that* instead of something else when he's really... pissed."

A novel idea. This would have spared me a number of episodes in my youth that I'd be happy to never relive.

"So look," I stood up and fetched his text and notebook. "Do what you can with these. They still look fairly—"

"It's not just them. Fine. I can probably get the notes again, but the *calculator*," He breathed in and out deeply. "I've got a pre-calc test tomorrow morning. *Tomorrow*. And, without a calculator, I'm..." He was stuffing everything into his soggy bundle, then pulled out the empty Powerade bottle and stared at it.

Not sure what struck me just then, but there it was. Something rose to the surface. There's an unwritten policy about teachers not being alone in a car with a student. Obviously there are times that this gets breached, such as when a ride to the ER is needed during duty after a student jumps down six stairs in the dorm and hears an ankle crack. By and large, it's something to avoid. Here, however, it seemed like the kid was in a bind, and I honestly didn't sense that what I had in mind would lead to a problem. On a more basic level, if we're here for the students...

"Do they have those at Staples?"

"What?"

"Graphing calculators. That's where you get them. One place anyway right?"

"Oh. Yeah. I got mine online but, yeah, I know some kids who got them there." He was checking the other compartments of his pack, not looking up.

"There's a Staples at the mall. Probably still open. If we go now, you can still make dinner."

He looked up at me baffled. Then his eyes widened with incredulity. "What? You'd.... *drive* me there?"

"If we can go right now, yes. *Right* now." I jabbed a thumb toward the door and he got to his feet. Glenn held his dripping backpack out to one side as we headed for my car.

"Put it in the trunk," I told him.

"Holy sh—" He caught himself. "Sorry. This is just, like, super nice of you Mr. Minot."

"Well, looks like you could *use* something nice right about now. Not a problem. But let's keep this between us, okay? School policies and all."

As we reached the school gate, he pounded a fist on his knee. "Crap. My wallet."

"Your wallet?"

"It's in my room. Can I go get it?"

I thought for a minute. "What dorm are you in?"

"Wentworth. Second floor."

From where we were, Wentworth was perhaps the furthest dorm on campus. This wasn't a big deal, and I get that he didn't have his wallet. Most days I don't have mine on me. When everything such as meals is provided for you and you walk to work, you don't need it. But if he went into the dorm, I was pretty sure he would come out with three friends once word spread that there was a ride off campus. I was in a charitable mood, but not that charitable.

"Don't worry about it."

"But, I nee—"

"I'll cover it. You or your folks can pay me back. Let's just get there."

Between the lamps atop the gate posts and my dashboard, I could see what almost looked like shock in his eyes. "It'll be faster this way, okay?"

"S-s-s-u-u-u-r-r-r-e...wow. Thanks."

This was something his advisor might do for him, or might not.

The TI 84 Plus 6E Graphing Calculator has high resolution, a full-color backlit display and is able to import and use images. Not sure if it's a bargain at 119.99, but there were only two of them left at The Crossroads Mall Staples store, and after 5:50, there was only one left. Glenn smiled to himself ever so slightly as it was rung up, and I gave him the receipt.

"I'll have my mum Venmo you the money tomorrow. Or we could get my walle—"

"Talk to your mom and that'll be fine." I gave him a theatrical glare. "I know where you live."

"Batteries?" The checkout woman looked over her glasses at Glenn.

"Oh, shi— Yeah. Can I—"

"Go get some." I shooed him in the direction of the battery carousel.

The cashier rolled her eyes with a grin. "Did he think it was solar powered?"

At a red light on the way back to school, Glenn was negotiating the packaging of his purchase which was firmly entombed in clear plastic when he asked a question from the passenger seat without looking up.

"Why would you…just, like, do this for me, Mr. Minot? I mean, it's nice and all, but I didn't need it for, like, your class, and like…" He turned to me as we began to creep behind a student driver as the light turned. Cars going in and out of the Applebee's and Taco Bell ahead of us had our student driver riding the brakes, and the darkness was now sprinkled with flurries..

"Hmmm." I didn't have a profound answer for him.

"I mean, I'm like, super grateful. It's just that not everyone would do this." Then, from some place where the brain keeps long buried memories, came a vision of Bert Clough, an English teacher of mine at school. The image, which prompted a smile that probably baffled Glenn, was one of Mr. Clough in a corduroy blazer and tartan trousers, leaning back in a chair as we tried to make sense of some work by Twain or P.G. Wodehouse in a senior humor elective.

"Senior year at school, there was this girl. One day she was out of sorts. She was supposed to buy a cake mix so the girls in her dorm could bake it for their dorm parent's birthday, but she forgot. We were in the library and the teacher on duty was Bert Clough. I had him for English. As a joke, I asked him if I could borrow his car to drive to town to get a cake mix to impress the girl. There was no way a teacher would let me borrow his car, but I thought he might know when the next shuttle to town was. He said he needed cigarettes anyway, so "asked" if he could come along. I can see his car now - a red two-door Toyota. He asked if I could drive a stick, which I couldn't, so he said that it would probably be better if he drove. I got my cake mix, and the girl was thrilled."

"*How* thrilled?" He leaned over a bit with a *details please* hopeful grin.

"Ha!" I couldn't resist a chuckle. "It was great to see her face when I handed her the cake mix, okay?"

"A-a-a-a-n-n-d?"

"And do you want to *walk* the last two miles back to campus?" He sat back and held up a palm of surrender. "Point is, Mr. Clough just did it. Drop of a hat. Probably didn't give it another thought. But here I am. Thinking about it all these years later."

"And he bought cigarettes while he was with you?"

"Probably. I didn't notice. It wasn't a big thing back then. If a teacher smoked, they were adults, so who cared? Not every burp or curse word got relayed to parents, like it does now. We didn't care about some things in those days. Things back then just didn't cause mushroom clouds or trigger kids the way everything does now."

Glenn gave me some acknowledging nods as he wedged the batteries into his TI 84 6 C Graphing Calculator with high resolution and the ability to import and use images. The flurries were tailing off as we pulled back onto campus. Fishing his backpack out of the trunk, he paused and looked at me thoughtfully.

"This Mr. Clough - is he, like, the reason you became an English teacher too?"

I looked up at nothing except the last few snowflakes blowing in the glow of the campus lights. "Not specifically. But I suppose, in some way, probably. I mean, if I hadn't liked my teachers or English, I'd probably be doing something else."

"Huh." He stuffed his new device into his hoodie's pouch. "You should email him. Tell him you still remember that story."

"I should, but," I clicked my key fob to lock the car. "he died years ago. They found him with a lap full of student essays he was grading. The pen was still in his hand."

Neither of us said anything or looked at each other. Breaking the spell, a gaggle of ebullient kids came bounding out of the dining hall. Glenn thanked me again and was off to 'Build your own burrito' night.

Jan 14

THE LUNCH MEETING ABOUT my sabbatical presentation had been moved to 11:30. This carved into a prep period of mine, but as I was free, hard to argue. As I settled into the captain's chair in Fred's office, I still had no idea why we were meeting. I'd sent the presentation up the pipeline, so they could either approve it or tell me to change something. Scott and Earl were late, so Fred took a minute to finish up an email. I pulled a handful of essays to grade out of my backpack, so naturally two paragraphs into the first one, Fred was done and had a question.

"So," he drummed his fingers on the desk and leaned back with a neutral smile, "still going for best dressed I see." He was gazing at my tie. "Is that a skull on it?"

I looked down, affecting that I needed a reminder as to what I was wearing. "Yes. It's a Leakey tie. He was an anthropologist who did a lot of work in different parts of Africa. Profits from the tie go to a museum in Kenya that's trying to preserve some old sites the museums dug up years ago."

"Oh," he squinted as if the answer vaguely interested him. "So, there was a purpose to buying the tie: you're interested in archaeology?"

"Not really. I just want people to think that I was a member of Skull and Bones."

"Oh," he sat up a bit, as if confused. "But, you didn't go to Yale, did you?"

"No."

"Oh." He squinted in confusion.

"Sorry - just kidding. It was a charity thing. I'd never suggest I went somewhere I didn't. I wear this on Halloween. The younger students get a kick out of it. It's nice to put in a plug for saving a little slice of the African continent too."

"Oh," he offered. Small talk and banter didn't seem to be in Fred's toolkit, but this was his meeting, so I was happy to wait. The awkward silence was broken by him launching into an account of a trip he'd taken to some of the former French speaking colonies on the continent years ago. The details he recalled regarding the makings of a family dinner in Algeria suggested a photographic memory, as I heard way more information about foods like rechta and dobara than will ever be useful to me. Midway through the recipe there was a knock at the door and Scott walked in.

As he's starting to go gray, Scott has come to look like Kevin Spacey. While I'm probably not the only person to think this, out of fear of triggering anyone within earshot with the mention of that name, I doubt that any other colleagues have actually verbalized this to him. Hard to know what's going to set some people off these days. Two years ago a new male member of the science department spent half of the faculty meeting glaring at his female department chair who was wearing a "Kiss Me I'm Irish" button. It was St. Patrick's Day. When she caught him looking at her, she gave him a wink, which colleagues often do to each other just to say 'hi' when they're too far apart to speak. Later it was learned that after she asked him to join a few colleagues at a pub that night, he had complained to HR afterward that it could all collectively be interpreted as a very passive case of sexual harassment. At the next faculty meeting, there was an announcement that faculty should refrain from any verbal, written or other expression that "could be seen as possibly advocating any activity not in keeping with respectful values as stated in the school handbook." That meeting went on about half an hour over the allotted time, owing to the discussion that followed this announcement. The next day I ran into Bags sitting in a corner of the library. On the breast pocket of his shirt he had a yellow Post-it note on which he'd drawn a shamrock and written "Slap Me I'm a Trigger." Upon seeing me, Bags mimicked a quick and harried removal of the Post-it. I wagged a finger at him, and we both rolled our eyes.

"Sorry I'm late," Scott held up a palm of surrender. "Conference call with a parent ran long. Earl won't be coming." In addition to me taking over the scoreboard for him, he's stepping back from more and more duties as his wife's due date approaches. In his impeccably creased khakis and well-pressed blue button-down, Scott gave off a sense that nothing terribly bad was going to happen to him this day, or at least that a conference call that ran long would be the worst of it.

"This shouldn't take long," Fred slipped on his wire rim glasses and opened his laptop, presumably pulling up my script and the PowerPoint presentation of my sabbatical. His asides as he scrolled through it reminded me again of Capote's voice. I'd seen interviews with the author years ago and hearing Fred read my words in that tone made them sound like someone else's. "Looks good." Scott raised his eyebrows as he tapped through the slides on his phone. Fred seemed to approve as well, asking *What's that part of the Delta was like? The schools you visited - on average, about how many AP courses?* and so on. After five minutes of this, Scott had a question.

"Just curious. Did you ever hear any conversations about reparations for slavery down there? Or an apology for the history of it?"

"Not in so many words," I cocked my head. "Now and again, someone would mention righting wrongs. A couple of people thought one way to do it would be with free tuition at State schools for some people. I really just tried to let people talk rather than steer them. I wanted to get a sense of where peoples' hearts and minds are, check out some contemporary Southern literature, and see how it mirrors the present South. Or doesn't."

"A-a-a-n-n-n-d?" Fred looked over the top of his glasses for a response.

"It's all there." I gestured to his computer. "*Southern* literature isn't a big common thread in a lot of schools. Some writings by Thomas Pierce and Taylor Brown came up a few times, but no Grisham. No teachers seemed to like Welty, and Falkner wasn't a staple of English courses, to my surprise. You can't really use a broad brush either. The Delta and Panama City are not Atlanta, and vice versa."

They traded brief glances, and Fred tossed up a hand, suggesting that Scott should take things from there. They both sat up a bit straighter.

"Someone mentioned reparations, which are, I suppose, apologies of a sort." Scott removed his glasses. "Brings to mind something Barclay wanted me to mention. He was wondering if you'd given any thought to patching things up with the parents of the boys who got an earful from the fireman after the boat incident." It took me about five seconds to grasp this lane change. I had three scenes replaying themselves in my head: Peter's boat heading downstream with two teenagers in it, the fireman and his comments, and Barclay raising the point outside of a hockey game before break.

"O-o-o-o-o-h-h-h." I nodded, theatrically affecting a tone that the penny had just dropped. It suddenly occurred to me that discussing my presentation was not why we were there. "You know what a segue is, Scott?" I kept my eyes on a crystal paperweight atop Fred's desk.

"Sure." He was thumbing his phone now.

" 'Cuz that wasn't one."

"W-w-w-e-e-e-l-l-l-l..."

"In fact, as an English teacher I would mark that as a non sequitur. Yeah. Let's see: *did you hear anything about reparations down south? And will you apologize to some parents because a fireman said something to them that any reasonable adult could agree with?* Yep. Non sequitur. Look it up. Got *The Elements of Style* in my classroom."

Both of them exhaled, and Scott rubbed his brow as if my point had caused a sudden rash on his forehead.

"Well," a rueful grin appeared on Fred's face, and he eyed Scott. "He's not wrong." I got the sense that this part of the meeting was Scott's idea, and he wedged it in once he learned Fred and I would be speaking.

Scott conceded this with a nod. "Okay. But," His chest rose and fell, which seemed for effect. "nobody's saying you said anything wrong or inappropriate. You didn't. The kids were just rather, er, *rattled* by the fireman's comments." Here he turned in his chair to face me. "Which apparently were pretty harsh." He raised an eyebrow to convey the seriousness of his point.

"Wait," I raised a finger but didn't point it. "You were there too, right? Why is this on me?"

"I was there, yes." Scott nodded. "But I didn't witness the exchange. The rant, if you will. I was speaking with the nurse and one of our safety officers."

"Well, I didn't have that pleasure. I suppose I envy you that, but it still wasn't a situation where I was going to tell that guy to reel it in. He runs into burning buildings. I teach kids the difference between metaphors and analogies. He can say whatever he wants."

"Sure." Scott leaned my way a bit more and glared. "But we're here *in place of their parents,* remember? What do you think their folks would have said if they'd been there?"

"Honestly? Not a damn thing, except I bet they'd have been embarrassed by their kids' actions. Maybe they'd have laid into them as well. What *could* anyone say? They'd done something really dumb. It was theft, let's remember, and someone told them as much. And more importantly, they could have died. But no, he didn't use an *inside voice* there. The EMT. I don't see the harm."

"He called them 'dumb,'" Scott cocked his head. "That word's a lot more loaded these days."

"He said that what they *did* was dumb - and he wasn't wrong."

"Look Ben, I'm not second-guessing what you did, but—"

"Well, you're doing a pretty good imitation of someone who *is* second-guessing me." I could see Fred taking in some breath at this. He leaned forward a bit on his blotter.

"I think we're at what might be called an impasse." Scott and I looked at him, and I shrugged. Scott exhaled and pursed his lips. It occurred to me that this was the most polarizing exchange I've ever had with him, and I was not enjoying it. "As I wasn't there, I can't offer much." Fred held open his hands in a way that suggested we were done. We all rose, and Scott checked his phone. Again. If he was looking for the time, it was a minute after the last time he'd checked it, so I'm convinced that this is a tic of administrators. Perhaps it was born of their concern that somewhere was a fire they'd need to put out, but it's honestly annoying to observe so often. You're not really present if you're doing that, and unless you're a brain surgeon on call or the President's Chief of Staff, the frequency of it is ridiculous; you're not that crucial to the world remaining on its axis.

"You're not wrong, Ben," Scott was pulling on his North Face parka. "It's just that, it's nice when we can all pull together."

"No argument with that." I was fishing through my pockets for all the keys and fobs one needs to get into everywhere on campus. "Look, when I'm wrong, I apologize. When I'm not, I don't. And I don't think that throwing a volunteer fireman under the bus is what we ought to be looking to do." Fred thinned his lips at this and squinted, as if chewing on my words. "If Barclay wants to throw me under the bus, well, technically, since he can tell me to coach girls' JV lacrosse next term or fire me, I guess he can do that too, but...sorry guys. That idea just feels wrong."

This forced a slight grin out of Scott. "I don't think we're *there* - Barclay firing you, I mean." He zipped up the parka. "I've got another meeting. Thanks folks." He turned and disappeared out the door. I wasn't much in the mood for small talk, which is about all that Fred and I can manage together. I mentioned having to grab a computer charger from my house before class as an excuse to not have lunch with him. This was accurate, if not entirely true.

Jan 20

DURING THE WINTER MONTHS, the school's cross-country course is given over to snowmobilers. Although all the trails are on school property, to be a good local citizen, letting it be known that people not from the school are welcome on campus is something a lot of schools do. We also let some youth hockey teams use our rink during the winter break, the idea being that such acts make us seem less of a privileged cloister where kids make jokes about *townies*. Having kids take a sailboat for a joyride doesn't quite further this effort. I'm guessing not a lot of folks at the local fire department were in touch with our Admissions Office in the fall asking for school catalogs and interviews for their kids. Thanks to the snowmobilers, the cross country trails are basically groomed enough so that I took to them for a run this afternoon. It was one of those gray mid-winter afternoons when the barren trees and steel sky make for a nice gothic effect. These days can also make one want to move to Bermuda now and again.

The cross country course follows the river for a bit then weaves into the woods behind the lower fields. Thankfully, Thursday afternoon is not peak snowmobiling time, so I had the trails to myself. Around the three mile mark, I was in the zone. It's not like a switch is flipped and you're in it, but you just find yourself thinking about a lesson you're planning, what you need to get at Stop 'n Shop, a library book that's overdue, just anything but your knees or the hills you're running. It's a good feeling. One downside to it is that you don't always pay attention to what's underfoot. Coming over a small bridge that sheltered a culvert, my right foot came down on something slick and down I went. Several words my grandmother never heard me say came out, as my ass landed on a thoroughly packed patch of snow. I was pretty sure that nobody else was dumb enough to be doing what had landed me on my tail, so wasn't worried about scalding any tender ears with my swearing. I got to my knees and realized that beyond having a literal pain in the ass tomorrow, I wasn't paralyzed, which was of course nice. I studied the area that sent me flying, and there it was. Half buried in snow was a yellow canister with black writing on it.

The way it was wedged into the snow, it looked like it had been there a while. After such spills, I usually convince myself that I'll remember that it - a hole, a root, whatever I trip on - is there, and yet the next time on that path I inevitably stumble on it again. The afternoon sun had softened the snow around the can, so I decided to dig out the offending object. Pulling it from the snow, I turned it in my hand. Smaller than a can that might hold tennis balls, it was a laminated cardboard. Some canary yellow paint was still intact, but some dents and scuffing suggested that others had trod on it. I could make out a colorful word that was still evident: Krakatoa. Streaming stars in a range of colors conveyed that this thin tube once held some fireworks. Such things are illegal in Massachusetts, but there are always people who smirk at that reality, considering it merely the government's opinion of something people should not possess. What had me staring at it was the container's condition; it didn't look like it had been exposed to the elements since last July. After a few weeks by the roadside, beer cans look worse. From somewhere in my head, the air bubble came to the surface; I'd seen a can like this before and not last July 4th. I brushed some more snow off what was sure to be a sore butt shortly, and got on with my run. I left the canister there, not feeling like the litter police at that moment.

Feb 6

NOW AND AGAIN THERE'S a press release, a bit of breaking news or an announcement that suggests the title of a Ray Bradbury book: *Something Wicked This Way Comes*. Such was the case with an email blast this morning from Barclay.

> *To: All Griswold Faculty and Staff*
> *From: Barclay sears, Head of School*
>
> *No doubt we are all aware of the myriad problems the coronavirus is currently presenting across the US and the world. The tragic consequences and the impact of this scourge are evolving daily, and as a community where the safety of all is a priority, it is felt that certain steps must be taken to guard against an outbreak on campus. Therefore, following the February 21 to 24 long weekend, all members of the Griswold Community will be required to wear face masks while on campus until further notice. This policy will apply to all students, faculty, staff and any visitors to the campus.*
>
> *All members of the community will be issued surgical masks prior to the end of classes Friday and are expected to wear*

masks at all times while at school, including during classes, passing time in the hallways, and in all common areas.

The final paragraph of the email was a blend of some sugar coating of the situation courtesy of some ed school pablum with a sprinkling of "the only thing we have to fear…"

Feb 8

BECAUSE HE'S NOT IN any of my classes or my dorm, I've honestly had nothing to do with Jerome since fall term. Last Friday was the end of Science Week, when students work in groups of four on projects grounded in certain themes - light, sound, chemical reactions, going green and such. Most of the collaboration occurs during study hall when groups of two boys and two girls create something that will teach others and that they'll be proud of. Thursday evening, Jerome was part of two pairs working in the dorm lounge while I was on duty. As they took turns reciting key points of their project in advance of the next day's presentation, I caught his eye. Once they were done and the girls took the trifold of their project upstairs, I waved him over to the table where I was grading papers.

As all teenagers do, he seemed half a foot taller than when we first met in the fall, and he appeared to be outgrowing his jeans and red Nike hoodie. He affected a quiet deadpan when I gestured to him to the Butcher Block chair near my desk. He flopped into it and eyed the papers on my desk, perhaps only because doing so allowed him to avoid eye contact.

"What's new?" I sat back.

Minot's Ledge

He shrugged, in a manner suggesting that it was the most banal of overtures.

"Nothing?" I pressed. He gave a most economical nod of his head. "Everything is old?"

"Everything's...the same," he managed, and started fiddling with a strap on his backpack.

"I hear you might be leaving us?"

This prompted a pursing of the lips. "Don't think so." Now, this was a surprise. Given what his sister had told me, I didn't know how to suggest that I perhaps knew more about his future than he did. Or perhaps I didn't.

"Oh. I got a sense from your sister that—" I stopped myself when immediately his gaze met mine. For a few seconds, he seemed to be deciding how he felt about my knowledge on the matter.

"My mother's..." He pulled his phone out of a back pocket and began scrolling it with his thumb. I leaned forward to keep him from falling into the well of his little screen. "She's busy with this corona thing, and I guess it's getting worse."

"Is she pretty involved in this virus battle?"

" 'Is now." He leaned back and looked skyward, as if counting the ceiling tiles.

"So," I sat back too, wondering how and where to go from here. I was reminded of an adage I once heard on one of those British murder mysteries on PBS Sunday nights: the easy thing about telling the truth is that you never have to think about how it goes to get it right. Thus there seemed little point in suggesting that it was just a random guess that he might be going to another school next year.

"I ran into your sister when she was last here, and she made it sound like you might be going elsewhere. Another school."

"I was." He gazed across the lounge and spoke without emotion. "Then I wasn't." Then he finally looked at me. "Like I said, my mom. She's busy."

"And are you okay with that? Staying here?"

"Doesn't matter. I'm here. I'm okay with…whatever."

"Well, it's better if you *want* to be here."

He looked at me, almost *through* me. I can't recall a teenager taking my measure with a stare as he did then and there. He held me in those steady brown eyes. A few girls burst into the lounge from study hall in the library, giggling and talking over each other as they headed upstairs. This distracted him a bit.

"It's just school," he shrugged. "Lots of schools out there. School is school."

"Yes, school is school, but schools can be as different as apples and oranges."

He offered a barely detectable snort at this blurb, which probably could have come out of any issue of *Independent School* magazine.

"*You* like it here?" he asked in a matter-of-fact way. This is always a question that must be handled carefully. Indeed, it's nice to have health insurance and long breaks in December and March as well as a free online subscription to *The New York Times* and being able to walk to work. Tasteless fish every Friday for dinner does wear a bit thin, but there's a French press machine in the teachers' lounge. Then again, some hockey players who were recruited here can skate so well that their eighth grade reading levels are overlooked, and the Admissions office employs some deadwood simply because his or her spouse teaches here, and a request was made to help find a role here outside the classroom for the idle partner. Do I like it here?

"I like teaching, and this place just gave me a year away to study what I teach."

"So, you like it here? Like *everything?*"

"Everything?" I raised an eyebrow. "Do you know *anyone* who likes *everything* about something?"

He looked away for a bit, settling on a sunset mural over the plasma screen on the far wall.

"What's with your ties?" Out of the blue, this offering clearly broke the glass on the non sequitur gauge.

"My *ties?*"

He turned it back to me. "You're like, the only teacher who wears a tie. What's that about?"

Funny how the mind works.

"Mr. Bagwell wears a tie sometimes."

He chewed on this, then sat up.

"Yeah but not always. You: always."

This was true, but perhaps he hadn't noticed that Bags' neck was not that accommodating of silk knots. His wispy gray locks blowing every which way, raspberry nose and corduroy blazer that could be older than me all suggested that he was not obsessed with his appearance. He might get a tie around his thickened neck now and again, and does for official school functions, but that Jerome has noticed such things was interesting. I told him the tales of the shabby vice-principal being mistaken for a janitor in defending my sartorial choices, wondering why our chat had taken this turn.

"Was he Black?"

"Who? The vice-principal?"

"Yeah."

"No."

He nodded ever so slightly. "Guy on the dining hall crew at my last school. He was the only Black guy working there." I just nodded in rueful acknowledgement. "Math teacher there. *He* wore a tie."

"They're a special breed, math teachers," I offered. "Some of them insist that true math teachers use chalk on blackboards. No white boards."

Looking at nothing, he nodded. "Tough class. Didn't like it." Things seemed to have stalled, and I stole a glance at the essays I still had to read. "Learned a lot from him, though."

He turned back to me with a deadpan for perhaps two seconds, then got up and made for the door.

Feb 20

BETWEEN SCOREBOARD DUTIES, THE winter short story project in two of my classes and overall sloth, it's been a while since I've added to this log. I've got a stack of papers I'd rather not read, so this is a good time to catch up.

Like a new video game or a restaurant someone suddenly discovers, lacrosse is one of those sports that seems to attract players who never gave it a thought before seeing a game a year earlier. From its Native American roots, it seemed to flourish mostly in the Mid-Atlantic States and private schools for generations. Just before the millennium, it began to spread to public schools in affluent US suburbs. In doing so, it lured countless baseball players from the diamond. They were glad to be brandishing a stick instead of standing in right center counting dandelions while no balls got out of the infield. Some years ago it became a thing for spring teams at New England schools to head south for the March break. There they practice and scrimmage against each other - squads fleeing the perils of March in Massachusetts. That this migration involves lacrosse has always been an eye-roller for me. Those guys suit up for battle with helmets and carbon fiber sticks, looking downright like gladiators. You'd think they could endure some late March weather in New England; guess not. Today's all-school meeting being the last one in February, the final itinerary of the lacrosse team trip to Orlando was shared. Feet were stomped and players were reminded to be at Logan Airport three hours before the flight. Three to four players perennially fail on this count, sometimes prompting a verbal dressing down from the coach outside a duty free shop or ticket counter.

The entire school headed to the chapel after two periods on Thursday. Out of the dorms, classroom buildings and the Prestley Student Center, teenagers and adults emerged, all trudging as one might do to a teeth cleaning; not in dread, but neither with gleeful anticipation; it *is* after all, late February. The flurries that swirled around campus at breakfast had not let up, and as we crunched along the shoveled paths, as always, there's hope that something interesting might be announced. Rumors of a headmaster's holiday tend to float around school, and once in a great while, something big: a movie star is coming as the commencement speaker, or that the dining hall bought a pizza oven.

The chapel is a stone structure that recalls H.H. Richardson, but wasn't designed by him. There's a clock atop its carillon, and the simple architecture inside reflects the Congregational roots of the school's founder. Sunday services in the building were phased out in the 1970s, along with neckties for boys and Greek or Latin as a language requirement. Ironically, it was the school chaplain at the time who pushed to have Sunday chapel made optional, his logic being that faith should not be forced upon people, and that he didn't want to preach to people who were *required* to be there. Inside, students file down the left and right aisles, lurching into pews and inevitably, at least one boy in each pew has to be reminded to remove a hat or hoodie. Faculty sit on a dais in front of the organ, and once everyone is settled, the student body president steps to a pulpit to quiet things down. I've never had the girl who presides up there in class as a student, which is too bad, as she's rather poised and businesslike. A no-nonsense Katie Couric type, she runs through announcements.

"Girls varsity hockey is playing Overton this afternoon at three, so come out and support them. The soup kitchen visit by the Community Service Group has been rescheduled to next week," and so on. Eventually things are handed over to Scott, who reminds us that the recycling bins are not trash bins, and that if food containers continue to be found in the library, it will be closed one night a week. He usually concludes with an anecdote involving a historical figure that will teach us all something or a quote by someone from the *1000 Things I Wish I'd Said* volume that sits on his desk. Today in keeping with Black History Month, his closing words were from James Baldwin. With that, he handed things off to Barclay.

Gone are the days when the Head of School might teach a class and look in on sports contests on a Saturday afternoon. Between fundraising and meeting with the physical plant crew which likes to point out which deferred maintenance projects can no longer be deferred, the person in the big office can be downright scarce. Even with the annual trips to Hong Kong and Tokyo and the sprawling Georgian Head's house, I wouldn't want that job. Anyone who actually did covet that mantle probably thought differently after the assembly today.

I couldn't suppress a grin as Barclay took to the pulpit. His neckwear had me mentally thumbing my nose at Fred. His Loden blazer fit in perfectly, and he smoothed a Bruins necktie down as if to call attention to it, saying, *See? A tie, but of a Boston sports team. I'm a cool guy!* Beyond his salt-and-pepper shock of hair and ruddy complexion, a slight clenching of the jaw suddenly made him seem older. He kept flattening clothing against his chest and stomach, as if breakfast hadn't settled well. He looked up with a sanguine expression, then launched into a brief recap of his recent East Coast swing and how all the alums he saw are fascinated with what we're doing here at their *alma mater*. He then congratulated Girls JV hockey for being undefeated with three games left in the season. Foot stomping and *woo woos* ensued. He pressed on.

"Even if you're not in Mr. Burnham's "Current Events and Issues" class, I'm sure you've heard about how the corona virus has encircled the globe, exacting tragic consequences in every corner." He then launched into a stream of grim statistics surrounding the virus which seemed to have sprung from some wet market in China and is now killing people on every continent. "Just this morning, Dr. Nancy Messonnier of the National Center for Immunization and Respiratory Diseases announced that as a nation, we should be collectively braced for, and I quote, "a disruption to everyday life that may be severe.""

Barclay had now taken on the tone that a doctor might while telling a patient that in some previously good results of blood work, something has in fact been detected. He paused, taking in the scene, and had even the most fidgety kids rapt.

"As you, our students," after which he turned over his right shoulder to look at us on the dais, "and our faculty will likely be traveling over the break in a few weeks, there's a genuine likelihood, owing to the law of large numbers and the many states and nations from which everyone hails, that the virus would arrive on campus when you return in late March." At this, some students could be seen turning to neighbors in alarm, perhaps wondering if we were to be kept on campus to avoid Barclay's scenario.

"It would seem that we must all adjust to this evolving situation, but we are at Griswold, a school that has weathered two World Wars, the 1918 influenza epidemic, and a presidential assassination." This recalled Barclay's JFK fixation. Although he was born the year of the moon landing, a bookshelf in his office would have you think that he'd spent his early years sailing off the Cape with Jack and Bobby. It did not, however, seem the time to point out that

Griswold was founded seven years before McKinley was shot in Buffalo, so he was actually one presidential assassination off.

"For your well-being and to limit the spread of this virus, we've chosen to obviate this dangerous scenario of people bringing it back to campus after break." (Obviate: *verb*, meaning to avoid. Used when the speaker wishes to remind everyone that he has a master's in English from Columbia.) "To that end, it has been decided that following the break, Griswold will switch to remote learning which you will do from home."

Students' heads turned left and right, and then phones came out. Among the faculty, there were puzzled winces. Many of us have conducted classes with guests streamed into them online but haven't taught an entire lesson to a computer screen. In the row facing mine across the dais, some of the more senior teachers were trading *he cannot be serious* looks over their glasses.

As I thought about it, the consternation I could see on their faces might have had another source - that we were being informed of this at the same time as the students. More so than many aspects of life, school is hierarchical, and it is so intentionally. Some teachers revel in that reality, cutting the lunch line, for instance, and when students raise eyebrows, simply offering something like, "When *you're* a teacher and not a student, *you* can do this too." Honestly, as information about this virus and what to do about it changes every few days, I couldn't be bothered about not being clued in on this before the kids, as it wouldn't change anything.

The buzz in the pews didn't subside, so eventually Barclay had to quiet them, and then he went on. A schedule and protocols for employing Zoom technology would be finalized and shared in another week. "Maybe with us, too?" Bags muttered. After saying that parents would be informed of this plan by email blast before lunch, he slipped into sage mode - quoting Walter Reed and sounding Churchillian. "We will all sit together in this space again. Science and human nature will prevail."

"Hmmm," Bags wondered aloud, "Didn't those two forces combine to create Zyklon B gas and the atom bomb?" I affected a chuckle for him. There was never any danger of me winning the biology prize my senior year at school, so frankly I'm happy to defer to the CDC on all things surrounding this virus. Currently though, even in their hands, things currently seem as clear as mud.

Concluding his remarks, Barclay turned around to us and asked if any faculty had announcements. From somewhere behind me, the yearbook moderator announced that the publication's staff will meet in her faculty apartment, not her classroom, after dinner. As no other hands went up on the dais, Barclay dismissed the seniors first, and the rippling pews followed them to the aisles and out through the vestibule into the flurries. As they did so, Barclay turned around to let us know that he'd have a word with us once the chapel was empty.

"So," he dropped his shoulders and shoved his hands into the pockets of his blazer. "I assure you that this decision was not made lightly. The trustees, the county health commissioner, some peer schools, we had lots of input. There was no shortage of discussion on the matter."

"There was with *us*," Bags piped up. Barclay cast a wary glance his way.

"Well, what would discussing it after we received all that input have accomplished, Howard? Think of some faculty children. If their parents knew, and they knew, other kids would know, and we would have been getting calls and emails left and right before we'd firmed things up."

Someone said this suggested that a request of faculty not to share the news with their children wouldn't be honored. Another person piggybacked on this, asking if the concern was that not all faculty could be trusted to keep something confidential. Now Barclay was on the defensive, arms folded over his chest, his eyes looking about, trying to guess where the next spitball was coming from.

Always someone with a good sense of how to take things down a notch, Ralph spoke up from behind me.

"Perhaps what some people are concerned about Barclay is that we're about to head back to class, facing rooms full of students who'll have questions for us, and we haven't been told any more than they have."

Barclay nodded and repeated his point that an email would explain all shortly. After a slightly awkward silence, Ralph cocked his head. "I suppose we could walk to class slowly, and pull up some CDC stats from online to drive the point home with the students."

"Great idea!" Barclay pointed to Ralph like a president might gesture toward a favorite reporter at a press conference.

Bags harrumphed, "One of those damn cooler heads that always prevails."

Barclay held up an index finger as a sign of assurance. "We'll be tweaking things over the next two weeks, proceeding with the expectation that things will be better come the fall. So: Admissions will keep doing their jobs as well, we'll select prefects for next year, but, I'm afraid that the Spring Fling is a casualty of this. If there's a bright side, those of you who offered to chaperone that dance, you're off the hook."

Now the hard questions emerged. *What about course selections for next year, which usually happens in the spring? Are the kids going to take their AP tests? Do they have to clear out their rooms for the year?* From Barclay's half-baked answers, it was clear that not all the details had been thought through or even thought of. Eventually, Scott piped up that many of these issues would be made clear shortly.

"We just wanted to get the word out so families could begin to make plans for their children learning at home." He then looked up at Barclay, and with an upturned palm, made a suggestion.

"Perhaps the next faculty meeting could be devoted entirely to crossing all the Ts on this?"

Barclay eyed him with no expression for a few seconds, then pointed his way and spoke.

"Yes. Let's do that." He clasped his hands and nodded to us, hoping for agreement. As most of us had a room full of unsupervised teenagers to get to, folks were happy to head out. Outside in the late February morning, the sun was trying to break through the milky sky. At the bottom of the chapel steps, a light bulb clicked on in my head: the next faculty meeting is when I'm due to present on my sabbatical, and spring term is when the new class is to be rolled out.

"Wait a minute," I thought out loud, stopping on a shoveled spot of pavement. "This means—" And with that, Tomoko plowed into me after slipping on the chapel steps.

"Oh. Ben. Sorry. I didn't see—"

"No, my bad." I waved it off. "I was spacing out."

"Wow." She tossed the long end of a red, crocheted scarf over her shoulder. "These meetings are *usually* a snore. Then this. All spring online? That'll be fun."

"Not sure it's the term I'd use." We started walking to our classes and she gave an exaggerated shiver, then looked at me.

"Aren't you freezing?" She was eyeing my open field coat. As I was processing that my presentation might not happen, and that the new class would not be taught in person, I hadn't noticed the wind chill.

"Not really. Just thinking. I guess we'll all figure this out. It's just," I shook my head, half studying the glazed path underfoot as we walked. "A lot to think on."

"Have you used Zoom?" she asked, stepping carefully on the black ice beneath us.

"I went to a demo on it a few months ago. They said they might use it when kids are in the Infirmary, or are suspended and we still want them to get some learning done. Never saw this coming, though."

"I just wish Barclay had just asked us, or even told us before announcing it. It seems like that would have been the—"

"The *respectful* and right thing to do?" I muttered.

"Well, I was going to say 'courteous,' but your word's fine."

"Yeah, but I do get that this thing is pretty nasty, and people are dying from it. The solution here though, does screw up a lot of things. I mean what about commencement?"

"Yes!" She stopped and froze. "He didn't mention that."

Losing events like Spring Fling, the prom, and commencement would really take something out of the seniors' last term here. Not exactly a recipe for building a strong base of young alumni. Looks like I'll be teaching my new elective without all the faculty knowing about its details or my year away. Not a big deal, but first masks, then spring term in-person scratched. Never dull. Dull might be a nice change.

***

By 3 pm, I'd read Barclay's email three times. His FAQs were helpful, but he seemed a bit pedantic on some points. When part of an online class, if a student needs to be absent from a screen for any period of time, she/he/they should use the screen device to raise a hand and ask to be excused. When they're learning from home? Mr. Minot? Can I leave my kitchen table to go to the bathroom off the kitchen? Really?

It didn't take long before the reactive emails started flooding in. An advisee of mine, a junior and likely baseball captain, asked about the season, and how college scouts would see him if there are no games. (They won't) Another student asked if I'd write her a college recommendation, noting that she'd planned to ask me in May once she pulled her average up in my junior-senior elective. (Ask me in April.) A girl in the dorm where I have duty sent out a faculty-wide email blast about the yearbook, which usually results from lots of layout meetings in the spring. (Don't count on much of a yearbook - and look for an especially thin section on spring sports.) All valid questions. There's a reason Barclay makes well into six figures. I stopped checking my inbox after dinner.

Feb 26

Email

Dear Mr. Minot,

Obviously, Griswold is taking the coronavirus very seriously which is wise. It is hoped that this scourge might be under control by the fall so that the school year can begin in session. Assuming that this occurs, I'm sure you recall that Eric is seeking to be a prefect next year. I am told that this process involves an interview with several adults which usually takes place after the March break. Eric will be completing the year from our home in Vancouver, so as this interview will not happen in person, it would be good if you provided the recommendation for him before he departs next month.

If you CC me when you send it to him, that way I can alert him to check his inbox, which he is not always very diligent at.

I wish you good luck with the new style of teaching ahead of you. My daughter says that her dorm is very orderly when you are on duty there.

Jianyu
Jianyu Zhang
President & CEO
Sinotech Holding Company Ltd
No.23, Wu Temple, Shatan N St, Falungong Dist, Beijing 100009, China (Houhai)

ote to self: some emails are best read late in the day, ideally after a bourbon with a bourbon chaser.

Mar 10

WEEKEND DUTY. IN WARMER months, a Saturday event might be a trip to Six Flags, but this month it's thrifting - taking kids to various thrift stores to buy clothes they will consider great finds, and later refer to as *ghetto* because of where they got them. Today I took a minibus full of students on such a hunt, and at our third shop, a quasi-Goodwill place called One More Time, the students discovered a trove of funky clothes from the 70s. In ten years, they'll wonder why they bought them, but at that moment, they were must-haves. A couple of girls in the group had Griswold sweats on, and while they were slinging hangers of sweaters along a rack, a petite girl in her early teens with tight red curls ran up to them arms outstretched as if seeking to touch them.

"OMG. Are you from Griswold?" The girls exchanged silent glares of *ennui,* and one of them nodded. "Wait. Of course you are." The redhead rolled her eyes at her question. "Can you tell me? How's Todd?"

The Griswold girls traded deadpan looks. "Todd?" With a slightly bored gaze, one of them raised her palms in a sign of helplessness.

"Todd *Garmin*," Red insisted, in a tone suggesting that a last name shouldn't be necessary. "You know him, right?"

The two girls eyed each other warily, then one of them managed a "Y-y-y-e-e-e-e-s-s-s."

"So how *is* he? He hasn't posted for a while."

"Posted...what?"

"You know."

The Griswold girls squinted at each other, and one said, "Not sure we do."

Hearing this from the other side of the clothing rack, I approached.

"Excuse me," I smiled and leaned her way. "I'm a teacher at Griswold. Can I—"

Out of nowhere, a lean woman in a bob cut and capri pants emerged - probably the redhead's mother. I got the distinct sense that she was slightly unnerved that an adult stranger was talking to her daughter. I explained that I'd heard the girl inquiring about a student at the school.

"Oh. Yes. Well, we'll hope for the best." She looked down at her daughter and with a hand on her shoulder, directed her away from us. "Come on honey. There are some items I want you to tag." She threw me a perfunctory smile, and walked away briskly, as if she needed to put change in an expired parking meter.

"What was that about?" I asked the girls. Both shrugged, and went back to slinging hangers along a metal rack.

"They have some neat ties over there, Mr. Minot." One of them pointed across the room with her lollipop, not looking up from the clothes she was swiping.

"Thanks. How 'bout you pull that mask up. You too." I pointed to her wing girl. Not sure if she actually thought they were nice ties - some poly stuff from the 70s so wide you could land a plane on them - or just wanted me away. Probably the latter.

"Other people in here don't have masks," one of them protested. "And we're not on campus."

"Yeah, but I don't think this virus cares about that."

Eye rolls, followed by compliance.

At our last store I picked up a copy of *Moby Dick* for fifty cents. I'm not a huge Melville fan, but we're reading *Billy Budd* later in class, so thought I'd give his opus another chance. Reading it at school years ago in Chuck Hamilton's class, I learned what a phenomenon was - a rare and remarkable event. This referred to how when Billy was hanged on a ship, his body did not sway on the rope. Funny the things you remember.

Mar 11

ON SUNDAYS AT SCHOOL, everybody seems to be somewhere else. A quiet hangs over the campus, like an invisible fog that nobody dares disperse by speaking loudly or moving from their rooms. As a result, it's a good time to track someone down. Shepherding Eric Zhang to become a dorm prefect for next year had the feel of asking Alex Rodriguez if I could take a selfie with him. You hate to reward wrongdoing.

I chewed this over in my head during a run on the cross-country course. The late winter thaw had reduced the few miles through the woods to a muddy trail. No surprises on the course this time, so just a good long think.

If there was a way to assuage the slimy father, I couldn't see it. Time was when some parents would let certain transgressions and the consequences be lessons to their kids. My junior year at school, the commencement speaker was a famous journalist. His son was a year ahead of me and had been caught drinking a few days earlier. As a result, he didn't graduate. Not just didn't walk - he didn't get a diploma, as it was his second offense. They had him stay in the school infirmary and piped the commencement ceremony into his room so he could hear his father give the address - which his father did. Dad didn't pitch a fit, a la *Forget what my kid did or you can forget my speech*. I wouldn't want to have been the kid, but wish more parents were like that father.

I didn't bother to shower after the run before going to Eric's room. Teenage boys are impervious to unhygienic situations. There are a few rooms in dorms that look like a landfill after a tornado, so Eric could deal with my sweat.

Walking down the hall on his floor, I heard yells suggesting that someone was having a match held to his toes. Picking up the pace, I found that the screams were coming from Eric's room. I knocked in a panic, and entered without waiting for a response. At his desk, Eric was leaning forward in a chair, headphones covering his ears, thumbing frantically at the controls as he stared down a video game, his eyes six inches from the forty-two inch screen.

"Eric. Eric. *Eric!*" The third try with my outside voice got his attention. His buzz cut of the fall had mushroomed into a black mop-top suggesting The Ramones. Peering between his unkempt bangs, he saw me, and continued tapping away. Truth be told, I was in no danger of winning any prizes for behavior when I was at school. Weekends were known to have me studying the effect of alcohol on the human body. That said, I never told a teacher who came knocking on my door to wait while I continued to do something pointless, even if it was fun.

"Eric," I insisted. "This is about *your* prefect application." My volume was such that I'm pretty sure everyone on the floor now knew that I was there. With this, Eric paused "Dungeon Fighter," a game which is all the rage with students from Korea and China, and slipped the headphones down around his neck. He was squinting at me over his right shoulder, suggesting that my visit was most inconvenient. "We should talk about your interest in being a dorm prefect next year."

"Okay. Now?"

"Yes. Now." I pulled out his roommate's desk chair and proceeded to tick off the character traits that the committee would be looking for in him. "Lots of kids want to be prefects. At least they want to put it on their college applications. So somehow, you've got to make yourself stand out."

He nodded, and said he'd already submitted the application.

"What? *When?*" This was news. I leaned forward.

"Sometime, days before now."

If his application goes over like a lead zeppelin, he'll never get to the interview stage, which dad might blame me for.

"Okay. So. I need to get a letter to the residential life office and ask them to pair it with your application." He gave me a slight nod. Perhaps he's never written a rec for someone that he held in contempt, so couldn't appreciate my task.

"If you get to the interview panel, they'll ask you all kinds of hypotheticals." He cocked his head in confusion. " 'What if' questions. *What if the kids on your floor are noisy after lights out? What if someone has a microwave in his room? What if you suspect someone's been drinking?* When teachers are not on the scene and you are, you can come find us, but you might have to make a decision about another student. It might involve the student's health."

Again he nodded, with all the interest of being told by a dentist that his next cleaning is in six months.

"And then there are room inspections. We have them on Thursdays, which you know, but if you can do a walk-through ahead of time, you can tell kids to clean things up so that when *we* do them towards the weekend, we don't come down on them for being slobs." More nodding. I had the distinct sense that I was a lot more concerned with this outcome than he was.

"Really," I stood up. "This matters." It was slightly demoralizing that I was coaching him on this so that I could continue to have a job, but there it was. "So, this room is okay," I made a sweeping gesture for the floor, "but prefects should get kids to put stuff from food deliveries in the trash." I pointed to a Domino's box on a dresser. "And Mr Burnham, who's probably going to be the dorm parent in the senior dorm? He's a stickler." Eric looked askance. Bad word choice on my part. "Details are important to him. Doing things right. So be sure that people aren't just kicking stuff under their beds. He'll check there too, so you have to—" with that I lifted one side of a twin bed slightly to show how Peter might do so, and there they were.

Strewn among a hoodie, three sneakers and an SAT prep guide were four cardboard canary yellow canisters. Two of them with labels bearing the name Krakatoa. I stood there for a few seconds, making sure that I was seeing what I was seeing. Then, it came to me: the spill that I took on the cross-country course a month earlier. Before that, the premature bonfire by the hockey rink set off at Earl's gender reveal party. The fire department found some spent canisters in the debris after it burned out.

"Eric." I lowered the twin bed back to the floor and turned to him. "These are *fireworks*." He held my gaze for a few seconds, then looked down as the mayhem of "Dungeon Fighter" rolled on in some loop that his hitting *Pause* had prompted.

"*Eric*, these are—"

"These are Chinese culture!" He insisted, looking up, affecting a defiant tone. "Our new year was last month. But here, only food one night, and some red paper in the dining hall."

"But, fireworks are against sch— forget school rules. They're illegal in Massachusetts." This left him searching for a response. He began fiddling with the strings of his GAP hoodie. "And, they are a fire hazard, just like—"

"These not used. See? They are there." He pointed to the bed. If his father really was one of China's savviest businessmen, and Eric was thinking that unexploded ordinances under his bed weren't a big deal, this didn't speak well for how strongly the intellectual DNA ran in his family.

"You're going to have to come with me." I reached under the bed and gathered all the canisters under my arm, asking him if there were any more about. He shook his head, but I did a pretty thorough search anyway - closets, dressers, everything. Nothing else. I waved him my way and headed for the door. Not hearing him behind me, I turned. Eric was now standing, hands on his desk chair, as if waiting for me to depart.

"Come on." I looked at him. Then my gaze became a glare. *"Today."*

He remained frozen, as if paralyzed by the request. It wasn't as if being told to obey an adult was a new experience for him. His eyes went to his phone on the desk, as if it was some kind of lifeline on a TV game show.

"Eric, coming with me *now* is really the best thing to do. The alternative will not be fun, especially for you." Nothing. If there's one thing that years at school has taught me, it's that arguing with a teenager is pointless. "Any more in here?" I held up a canister. He shook his head. "You sure? Lying wouldn't be a good move here." He insisted that there were no more. I was seething over his refusal to come with me, to the point that I had to leave. I'd be back with someone to do another search - who knows what I might have missed? After a few seconds I stepped into the hallway. At the stairs I turned, but he still wasn't following me. This was a new one: in your face defiance. It's not as though I was going to physically carry him to the weekend dean's office though. When one comes upon a student violating a school policy, it's commonly accepted what happens next: he hands over the bottle, she coughs up the cheat sheet during the test, and there's an unspoken *you got me*. This wasn't the case here. It was kind of like thirteen o'clock - never been there.

It being Sunday afternoon, I wasn't sure whether Scott would be in his office when I knocked, but he was.

"Scott," I was floored. "Didn't expect you to be here on a Sunday afternoon."

"My daughter's having some friends over. Can't hear myself think there. What's up?"

I flashed the yellow canisters from under my arm, which prompted a theatrical dropping of his jaw. He turned to his computer screen, asking patience while he finished a thought. Looking back at me, his eyes widened as they cut to the tubes under my arm.

"What the…"

"Better put any cigarettes out. Happy New Year." I then explained how and where I came by the items at hand.

"Eric Zhang? Really?" Scott offered a wince as if he didn't want it to be true. "Shit."

Newsflash: teachers do not like catching kids in transgressions, no more than they like handing back tests with scores of 37 out of 100 on them. Lots of people, certainly lots of kids, think otherwise. I finished explaining everything that transpired in Eric's room.

"He *wouldn't* come with you?"

I shook my head. Scott then stood. Wearing a plaid flannel shirt, he crossed his arms over his chest and moved from behind the desk. He tapped his chin with an index finger as if activating his brain by doing so.

"Leave those here with me." He pointed to a kindling box by a fireplace in his office that probably hasn't been used since black and white TV was a new thing. "I'll get on it."

I walked to the box and placed the canisters there in a gentle way. "So: now what?"

"Well," Scott paced to nowhere in particular. "He *actually refused* to follow you here?"

"Yeah. Honestly, I didn't think you were here, but I figured the walk to your office would cure any constipation he had and let him know at what level this whole thing was."

"Okay," he said, strolling back behind his desk and settling into his Herman Miller Aeron chair. "I'm on it." He began tapping away on his desktop computer.

"I had to talk with him about applying to be a prefect for next year. This conversation was in *his* interest." At this point, Scott nodded, gazing at his desktop's screen. "By the way, there's more." I proceeded to mention how an earlier run in the woods had uncovered another such canister that had been fired off. I added how the local fire department had found some canisters at the embers of the bonfire by the hockey rink that had gotten out of hand, and that Eric's room should still be searched again, if only for effect. Scott was clearly kicking this around in his head. "Since you *are* down here, don't you think he ought to be made to come down here? Now? If you come with me, you could be the good cop. He disobeyed a clear directive from a teacher after all."

Scott nodded slightly, never taking his eye off his screen. "We're definitely going to sort this out. What happened today, including what you found." At this he held up two defensive palms. "Sounds like this dog won't hunt. I just…I want to get the full picture, including the student perspective."

I looked at him intently, conveying that I wanted to be sure I'd heard what I thought I'd heard.

"Well," I took a chair before his desk without being offered to do so. "Think I *gave* you the full picture. Those aren't cans of tennis balls over there." I jabbed a thumb in the direction of the canisters in the kindling box.

At this, he launched into some bite-sized version of a vignette, which included the adage that where one stands on something depends on where one sits.

"Sure. Like *Rashomon*."

At this he squinted, then held up a palm and pulled a face in confusion.

"It was a Kirusawa film about the same events seen through different eyes."

Scott tried to effect that he was impressed. "Didn't know you were a scholar of Japanese film?"

"I'm not. But I'm also not someone who thinks that we should consider teacher accounts and student perspectives equally. We're a hierarchy, right? I didn't pull that stuff out of my ear."

"Yes, of course Ben. It's just that..." he waved his hands about as if trying to reel in the word he was looking for. "We have to get this right. Look at the child as an individual. And remember the big picture. We're here to teach them. They're works in progress. He's not going anywhere. " This was perhaps as close as he would get to admitting that the largesse of Eric's father toward Griswold, present and future, could color how this matter would be handled.

The big picture: metaphor - used when the speaker wishes to dismiss certain realities in order to suggest priorities that might override any present concerns.

"Let me process all this. I'll start an email thread - to which you should indeed add your two cents. By nine AM tomorrow?" He looked at me over his reading glasses in a silent plea for agreement.

We held each other's gaze for a few seconds. He stood up to break the spell.

"We good?" He lowered his head to give me an inquiring *we still friends?* plea with his eyes.

"Scott, I just told you a kid had—"

"I know what you told me, but he's not going anywhere, and..."

"And his father has given us some equipment in a building, so we..."

"Ben," he scowled, and planted his fists onto his desk. "This is complicated. I'm on it."

Another brief staring contest, which I broke up, and said nothing. It's one thing to call a student a liar when she insists that she has no idea how a bottle of rum turned up in her desk drawer. It's another to insult a superior. Even if he deserves it, I want my powder dry on all this before I press on. And I like my on campus housing.

Mar 13

THERE'S A SCHOOL MENU app, and on it, I read that dinner tonight was tilapia with brown rice and mixed veggies. That made tonight's decision easy: I walked down to GHOP, the Griswold House of Pizza. When they mention it, students borrow the F sound from *enough*, so it's pronounced *fop*. I was intent on at least one Foster's Lager with my meal, and felt pretty secure that on a Tuesday night, I wouldn't encounter any students there.

A nice constant about indie pizza places is the warm, red vibe they all have. Parked in a booth with a stack of mail from the previous week that I hadn't read, I tried again to put the weekend episode with Eric and Scott out of my head. In addition to a copy of the latest *Atlantic* magazine and offers for two credit cards I don't need, there was my letter - the contract offer for next year. Usually contracts come out right before spring break, so people have a couple of weeks to consider them. They put them in our mailboxes, noting that we are invited to return for next year for the following salary. We read it, and a few weeks later, sign it and turn it in. Or don't. Or, you don't get one. That's the way it is at independent schools. No teachers' union. Year to year, and they'd better like you. I actually think that this can make one a better teacher, knowing that you have to re-earn your job every year. But if some administrator doesn't like you, be afraid. Not being "a good fit" is the umbrella reason given for when people are not renewed, but there's always more to it. Perhaps a teacher assigned some low grades to some athletes that kept them from being eligible to play, so a big team had a terrible season. Maybe the teacher ran a dorm that was anarchy, or perhaps he looked like the guy who broke up the Head of School's first marriage - it can be that capricious. If a school just wants someone out, not being *a good fit* for the school culture is the boilerplate reason often given, and that's that.

My letter noted a modest raise, with the description of the duties that I've been doing this year, expecting that I would do them again. As I read it, I couldn't help but start grinding my teeth over Scott's imitation of a jellyfish on Sunday, and this made me more impatient for food. Walking up to the counter to wait for it, I gazed at the bulletin board covered with local notices. Garage sales, computer repair, math tutoring and the like. Pasted on to a notice for a car wash that happened two weeks ago was a Post-it note with three simple words on it: Pray for Todd. Not sure why, but I couldn't take my eyes off it. The sliding of a large oven spatula into a Blodgett oven and the words *"Pizza up!"* broke my trance. I ordered another lager and took everything back to my booth. Before I finished my first slice, I had dribbled some grease on my contract letter. Bit of a metaphor, that.

Mar 14

AT 7:30 IN THE MORNING, I parked in the far corner of the dining hall and poked at my scrambled eggs until the coffee reminded me of how to use a fork. This morning it was pretty much just faculty and staff at breakfast, as a delayed start of classes was put in place to allow for the faculty meeting of how we'd be teaching remotely next term. Thus it was kind of surprising when Jerome came bouncing into the dining hall then made his way to the cereal table. Once he spotted me, however, he was on a mission. Beating it my way, he pulled out a chair and asked if we could talk. His eagerness and big brown eyes suggested that this was a rhetorical question. I tossed up a hand for him to continue.

"My sister was in New Hampshire this weekend, and she went to some school. I never heard of it, but she said it looks nice. I was wondering if you ever heard of it. I heard you know a lot of schools."

"Well, I've been to a lot as a coach, and people in my family have attended some that we don't play so that's a few more but..."

"Plimpton. That's the school? Know it?"

Now this was a rather delicate matter. Plimpton is a school in The Lakes Region of New Hampshire which indeed has a nice campus; I helped drive the cross country team there years ago for a meet. Lots of schools have nice campuses. And all of them have reputations that don't work their way into the catalogs. Plimpton's is that it gets whoever didn't get in anywhere else, or has been kicked out of somewhere else. As a colleague who had student-taught there once said, "No dress code there, but hard to imagine that many of them will be wearing ties in their careers, so why should they practice tying them?" That was pretty snobbish, but we got the point. When asked to explain that at lunch, he went into a litany of the disciplinary issues he found there. "Thing is," someone else at the table who knew the school chimed in, "the place is so desperate for kids, they don't kick any of them out, no matter what rule they break." A few others at the table nodded. "Nice outlet mall in the town though," someone added.

"They got a turf field a few years back, then they scratched their football program. Not too clever," another person added. This was the extent of my knowledge of Plimpton, none of which I'd share with Jerome. It must be the right school for some who are there.

"I've been there once," I nodded. "What does your sister say?"

"Just that it looks nice."

His sister was no slouch. I couldn't remember where she'd gone to school, but my sense was that she and her mother had higher hopes for Jerome than Plimpton. Also, this would be his third school in three years. They want to get it right.

"What brought her there?" I started in on my room-temperature eggs.

"She was shopping. Some outlet mall near the campus, I guess. So, you know it?"

"I know *of* it, and," I looked at him, then at a portrait of some past headmaster on a wall over his shoulder, hoping it would help me to at least *sound* wise. "There's a right school for every student, probably more than one. But New Hampshire is...not too diverse a state. I'm not saying that people there is racist, or, maybe like that rent-a-cop at the Harvard Coop might have been. But, you might like a place that attracts a wider variety of people, or is closer to a city. For weekend activities."

"So, it's all white?"

"I'm sure it's not *all* white." I was sure about this because such schools tend to fill their beds with kids from China. Lots of them. "When you get off campus there, it's not Boston. You like farms?"

He returned my hint of a smile. "So, you don't think I should apply there?"

"I can't tell you much more than I've said." I wanted to give him something like hope, or at least more than I had offered already. "I think you should cast a wide net. I really do." At this his eyes brightened just a bit. "By the way, why are you up? You do know it's a delayed opening, right?" I wanted to eat.

"I'm hungry." With that he stood up and made for the cereal bar, throwing a "thanks" over his shoulder.

I was really hoping there'd be Danish at the faculty meeting, for by the time I left, my eggs were stone cold.

***

With its shorter periods and the last one of the day dropped, the delayed opening schedule to make room for the faculty gathering was bound to mess kids up. Teachers too. The schedule runs periods A to F. This would mean that anyone who teaches the same classes D & G blocks would lose G and now have one section of that class a day ahead of the other section as a result. This is usually the work of an administrator who does not teach and wouldn't think of the issue, with the exception of an administrator who only teaches G block, who may have in fact proposed it.

At the back of the large conference room was a table of croissants, bagels and a few boxes of Dunkin Donuts coffee as well as some handouts explaining how remote teaching would go. Barclay was up front, offsetting his salt-and-pepper coiffure with a tattersall shirt open at the neck.

"If we can get started, we'll get out of here early," he began as I found my seat. "First I want to thank Ben Minot for his understanding. This week's faculty meeting was going to host his sabbatical presentation, which is being postponed so that we can cover this. I'm sure it'll be worth the extra wait."

I returned his smile at this. From the other end of my row of chairs, Peter leaned forward and shot me a facetious grin that mocked the accolade *good job!*

"Many of our peer schools are also going remote following their spring break, so we've got a lot of company on this new journey. We're all in the same boat."

"I'd rather make a swim for it." Bags leaned forward to share that with me, just loud enough for half the room to know he'd said it. For the next half-hour, Barclay scrolled through a PowerPoint presentation while referencing the handout which covered Zoom instructions and policies. The daily schedule for the term was a bit truncated, the thinking being that our fifty-five minute periods were too long to keep kids riveted to a screen. A demo class was played for us, the checkerboard of faces all appearing to be thrilled to be there. In spite of FAQs that covered most matters, there were a few stupid questions. *How do we take attendance?* (Same way - see who's on your screen.) *What if a student on Zoom is out of dress code?* (Barclay: encourage her to recall she's being seen on camera. Me to self: who cares?) The big ask involved international students. In some cases, teachers will be asked to Zoom at odd hours to accommodate groups of students on the other side of the world, namely in China and Korea. This news prompted lots of groans.

"Barclay," a voice came from the back of the room, and there was a hint in just that one word that the speaker was not all in on this plan. "We're doing this because of a virus that *came* from China." This turned heads, and sure enough it was our hale football coach who teaches one section of algebra. "Couldn't *they* work themselves into *our* schedule?" Silence. In all candor, I'm guessing that he wasn't the only person feeling this way, at least in terms of the schedule. Jumping back on to Zoom at 9 p.m. to do it all over again for three kids in Shanghai would definitely quash one's evening. Not sure anyone else would bring up the point of China being the source of the virus, however. Also, I'm pretty sure that with the exception of perhaps a couple of maintenance people, the coach's Don't Tread On Me and Trump stickers on his F-150 are among the few on campus.

Barclay paused, possibly wondering if such a comment warranted a meeting with the coach later. "We want to do all we can to help our students learn - wherever they are." This prompted a question from another corner about teaching the same lesson a few hours later to work with kids from the west coast. And so it went. With lots of things actually covered in the handout, it seemed that this could have been accomplished via email. Eventually Barclay eyed the tall clock in the corner, thanked us for rearranging the day, and I got up to kill off the continental breakfast.

The exit from the faculty meeting was sprinkled with skeptical mutterings. As this new *journey* has a lot of passengers, surely the first few weeks of it will be a shakedown cruise. Bags had stomached his fill of the nautical analogies that had been offered, and shot me a withering glare as we pulled on our coats.

"Fresh hell," he grumbled, reaching for a Dunks box and shaking the last few drops out of it into his mug.

"Eh?" I reached into a box of Munchkins.

"Dorothy Parker. "What fresh hell is this?" Before your time."

"Before yours too. I'm an English teacher, remember?"

He shrugged and buttoned his coat to brace for the late winter dampness outside. The overnight flurries were now just the odd flake caught in the wind, and a low gray ceiling hung over the campus. We picked our way carefully through the slush underfoot, and Bags thought out loud as we headed to the classroom buildings.

"What if a student forgets to bring his Latin book home for break?"

"Hmmm. Good question. Is there an online version?"

"Probably. Haven't used it though. Am I supposed to scan the pages from the text and upload them to Google classroom in case kids don't bring them home?"

At that I stopped in place. Now a bit ahead of me, he turned back with a puzzled look. "What?"

"Did you step out of the meeting or something?"

"Y-y-y-e-e-e-s-s-s-s," he was just slightly piqued at the question, "Why?"

I took a deep breath. "That might have been when Barclay mentioned it. We're not using Google classroom for the rest of the year."

Bags winced. He looked older than his years now. His wispy gray hair, JPMorgan mustache and rough-hewn eyes reminded me of some British judge in one of those PBS series who had just heard something in his courtroom of which he didn't approve. "What?"

"Can't. We've got students in China."

"A-a-a-n-n-n-d?"

"China won't allow Google in the country. Too much stuff on it that makes their government look bad."

"Their government *is* bad. But *this* is just for assignments for school."

"Tell that to the people whose policy toward Taiwan is 'marry me or I'll kill you.'." I held up two defensive palms. "Not my idea. Really. You picked a bad morning to drink too much coffee before the meeting."

Bags' classroom is on the first floor of our building. I always like going there. More than any other room on campus, it's frozen in time: pull-down maps of the Roman Empire, a picture of the Coliseum, movie posters of films like "Ben-Hur" and "Spartacus." It smells like old books and dust. I fished the handout from my backpack and showed him the section that discussed the new LMS - the learning management system. All schools have them - online programs we use to take attendance, post assignments, and the like. Google Classroom is one of ours. He tossed his coat and scarf onto his desk chair and sighed.

"Heroin," he muttered.

"Excuse me?"

"Heroin. That's what they're like to schools. Schools like ours, anyway."

"That's what *who's* like?"

"Not my term. Wish I could take credit for it. Charlie Neils - he's the first one I heard it from. History teacher at a girls' school in Virginia - maybe Foxcroft, or Madeira. I can't remember which one. I'd meet him at the AP grading meetings in June, and we got to talking about the influx of Chinese students at schools." He held up a palm before I could speak. "Now, I have some wonderful students from there. Two years ago one of them got the Latin prize. But, once we started taking them in big numbers a few decades ago, because they're full pay, we can't get enough of them. Other schools too. Idyllwild, that art school in California? Forty percent are from China. I met a woman from Hong Kong over the summer whose child was admitted there, but she wouldn't send her because she said she would just speak Chinese all the time. The smaller schools, the ones that don't get the cream of the crop? They can't compete for all the better domestic students. They, like us, go to Beijing and Shanghai to fill every spare bed. So now, what happens in September? What if this virus is still with us? Will they be let back into the country?"

"September? Hell, we just walked through slush. I'm not there yet."

"Well, I hope someone who works here *is*. Think: we're nineteen percent international. Some great kids, from all over, and that looks great in the catalog photos. But what if corona is still around by then, and they can't get back into the U.S.? Seventy-five percent of that nineteen percent is from China." He leaned back on his desk and folded his arms in front of him. "That's a lot of empty beds."

"Okay, but lots of schools must be in the same boat."

"They are. Especially ones with ESL programs. To them, kids who don't speak English are an ATM. But once you get used to them, how do you function without them? Like Charlie said: we're addicted to them. *Heroin.*"

A clever analogy, albeit one with some accuracy that was unsettling.

"So what's the alternative?"

At that he pointed to a class photo from the 1960s to the right of one of his maps..

"That's before my time. I'm not saying it'd be good to go back to those days, but…"

I walked over to look at it closely. Mostly white kids with flat top buzz cuts, and a few with manes slicked back, probably with Brylcreem. Blazers and skinny ties. The caption said National Honor Society Inductees, 1963.

"Like I say, I'm not looking to get back to those days, but getting kids here from Connecticut and Pennsylvania was a piece of cake back then. Now, if we're going halfway around the world for nearly a fifth of our kids, and if this virus isn't all gone at the end of the summer…"

With a very vague idea of how the next few months are going to play out, I honestly hadn't thought as far ahead as Labor Day. Sometimes, with his quotations from Pliny the Elder, it seems like Bags is of another era, like that device from Timex in my room that needs a new battery. But even a stopped clock is right twice a day.

Mar 15

PETER BURNHAM IS AS bad as me when it comes to letting classes out on time. I like not having a working clock in the room. When you have one, kids keep eyeing it, trying to *will* it into releasing them. Sometimes a good discussion runs long, so my kids have to dash to their next class. Nobody dies. Peter has a better excuse than I do.

"The thing with history is that they keep making it," he says. "When I started teaching, I didn't have to cover 9/11, 'cuz it hadn't happened yet. There's always more, except when it comes to class time." Earl Blackabby, my department chair is quite the other way. With his wife's due date approaching, the most dangerous place to be on campus was between him and his car at three PM. Not sure what his teaching methods are, but his classes are always released early. No skin off my nose, but considering what families pay to send kids here, they ought to get a full period out of the teachers. Today was no exception. As my students were working on a writing prompt, I looked out the window to see kids from Earl's junior - senior elective bounding into the quad, and spontaneously starting a snowball fight. In the middle of it all was Todd Garmin. He has an orange North Face parka and Yankees cap that make him recognizable everywhere. Seeing him, I wondered why I was supposed to pray for him, as the note at GHOP implored.

The winter sports season is over. Translation: none of our teams made the league playoffs. With no more basketball, Todd would probably be either in the student center or his room by the time my class got out. We've started reading Melville and I want to get their take on a theme I've hinted at, and mentioned, and written on the board. With ten minutes to go, I told them to finish up. When the last student handed in a written hard copy, I started streaming a clip from the 1962 film "Billy Budd" for them to watch while I dashed to the printer. I copied each essay and once back in the room, handed out the originals.

"I want you to type up your essay as is, changing nothing in terms of the syntax. *Nothing.* You may clean up spelling and punctuation, but I want your word choice and word order unchanged. Just type it. Double spaced, 12 point font. Drop it into Google classroom by 8 a.m. tomorrow."

"Why can't we change our words?" one student asked.

"Because I want to see how you actually think and write out of your head - not after you check *SparkNotes* or some online Melville site."

"But if we change something, wouldn't it be to make it better?" another wondered.

"Sure, but it could also be informed by something other than just what you had in your head when I asked you to write this without referring to the text. And I'm assuming all the essays reflect that you all read carefully. Oh, and I've got copies of your handwritten ones, so don't bother changing the originals before you type them."

"So, why don't you just read those?" the first questioner pulled a face.

"Have you ever seen hieroglyphics?" Crickets. "Really? *Nobody?* Nobody's ever seen a mummy movie?" Blank stares. Brendan

Fraser, call your office. "They're ancient Egyptian writings. Hard to decipher. Like some people's handwriting. When things are typed, I can read essays easily and get them back to you quickly."

"But, it's more work for us."

"Yes, but the easier it is to read your writing, the better mood the teacher is in when it comes to grading it. You *want* your teachers in a good mood when they're grading."

A few of them eyed each other with pursued lips and tipped their heads, suggesting they got it. Once they all cleared out, I made for the senior boys' dorm.

Todd is one of a handful of juniors who, owing to the need to give rooms in another dorm over to a faculty apartment, lives in a senior dorm. Unlike other houses, this dormitory has fewer rules, based on the notion that seniors need to manage some independence before college. Doors can be closed during study hall, there are no lights out, and room inspections are rarer. This last policy was abundantly evident when I knocked on Todd's door and he bellowed, "What?" prompting me to enter.

A college friend of mine who went to Lawrenceville had a mother who rolled her eyes at what slobs boys can become after a while in a dorm. "Send a kid to boarding school, and after a month it looks like he never had a mother," she used to say. Here though, we were way beyond untucked shirts and hair screaming for a barber. Sweats and tank tops were strewn such that they covered almost as much of the floor as the wall-to-wall carpeting. Empty Poland Spring and Powerade bottles on desks, dressers and windowsills. There were two Domino's boxes that I was not about to open. One of them sat on an unmade bed. Note to self: if Todd or his roommate invite me to their homes in ten years, or ever, decline.

"Mr. Minot. 'Tsup?" Todd turned around in his desk chair to see me. There's a garden-variety jock look about him. Ruddy complexion, with eyes and a smile that betray a charisma of which he's aware. He's the kind of BMOC that when I was a freshman at school and he said "hi" to you, you were surprised and secretly thrilled. As I didn't have him as a student this year, he no doubt wondered why I was there, but was unflustered.

"Having a good year Todd?"

"Not bad." I made small talk referencing a paper he wrote in freshman English for me, his college plans and how I'd enjoyed watching him play from the scorer's table.

"Yeah, we had an okay season." He nodded, switching his gaze from me to a phone he was thumbing.

"How about you? You okay?" I leaned on a dresser and loosened my tie.

"Huh? Me?" He looked away for a second to think why he shouldn't answer in the affirmative. "Yeah. Why?" With this he began to massage his shaved head, as if to check the height of the stubble.

"I've had a few fans, if you will, at games, ask me specifically if you were okay. Someone at a coffee shop too. She figured out that I worked here and made a point of asking me about you."

He went still, not liking where this was going. Not that I *knew* where *that* was, but onward.

"Well," he put his phone down on his desk and turned toward me more directly. "I know some local kids through some day students. So they know me. It was probably one of them."

"Yeah, I get that. They weren't Griswold students. But, they also sounded, kind of, *worried* about you. I didn't hear them asking about any other players."

"What can I say?" He flashed a prideful smile. When I didn't return it, his vanished.

"Well, do you need to be prayed for?"

At this, it almost seemed as though his face got thinner. The wheels behind his uncertain eyes were turning.

"What? Pra—No. I mean…" This had been a curveball, and he twisted his face, trying to decide how to respond. "If someone wants to, like, pray for me to, you know, get into my first choice next year or something, I'm fine with that. I mean, everyone talks about where they want to go, right?"

"Yeah. I think that's not it." I explained the Post-it note at the pizza shop. He said he'd made some good friends in town, and that maybe one of them attends a nearby Catholic School.

"I know some of them can be kinda, you know, religious. Catholics I mean."

"So," I pulled out his roommate's chair, eyed it carefully for detritus and sat. "I got to say, Todd, I've never seen other kids - kids who don't even *go* here - be so concerned with a student here, asking like they think something's wrong with him."

He held his breath. "I'm good." He insisted. "Real good. Ready for lacrosse season."

"You sure? 'Cuz this is New England. Best hospitals in the world. Really. If there's something some people know that the school doesn't, well, we can't help you." I certainly didn't want anything to be wrong with him, but I didn't want him to be the jock who wouldn't admit to something out of fear of losing a spot on a team for it. "Really? You OK?"

At this he stood up, raised the bottom of his Celtics Jersey and slapped a flat stomach. "Hundred percent. Really." I cocked my head to one side and gave him a look of skepticism. "Is that really what you wanted to ask me?"

"Yeah," I leaned forward. "You see, when you're here. We're responsible for you. If you're not okay, we need to know." With this, he slapped his stomach again to emphasize the perfection of his abs.

"Nothing else you want to…to share?" Honestly, I don't like that word. We're not talking about a sand pail between ten-year-old kids at the beach. Ed School psychobabble dies hard.

"No. I'm good." He put hands on his hips. "We good?"

"Guess so." I stood, forced a smile and wished him a fun lacrosse trip to Florida. "Be sure to cover that head down there."

At that his smile wilted ever-so-slightly. "Will do." As the trip had already been paid for, even with the season scratched due to everyone learning remotely, the team was still heading south. Couldn't let all the plane tickets and SPF 50 go to waste.

I left pretty unsatisfied. Maybe just because unlike him, I had no groupies in high school. But not just that.

Mar 16

HEADING INTO LUNCH TODAY, Scott caught my eye in the lobby of the dining hall. He waved me his way and slipped back into his office. Inside, in the corner by the dormant fireplace, a school towel with the brown stripe down the middle of it was covering the munitions I'd left there days earlier. Scott stood behind me and closed the door. In one of the wing chairs before his desk sat Barclay.

"Hi Ben." Barclay's open collared shirt suggested a day with no visitors. Scott gestured for me to take the other chair and walked behind his desk. His navy Shetland and wide wale chords suggested casual, which I sensed this meeting was not.

"Ben" Scott began, making a steeple with his forearms atop his blotter. "As to this matter of fireworks, we've talked to Eric, and we wanted to catch you up on it. First of all, great catch. We're darn grateful that you spotted those…items in his room." With this, he sat back a bit. "As you can imagine, he's really remorseful. Not just for the fireworks, but for how he disobeyed you by not coming with you when asked."

"He's learned that such behavior is not acceptable." Barclay was twirling a pen between his fingers as he spoke. "His father was none too happy to hear about that. Such conduct won't stand here. That's been made clear to him."

"Oh, okay. G-o-o-o-o-d." I looked from him to Scott and back. "Is there a reason I wasn't part of that meeting or conversation?"

"We roped his father into it, and he's been traveling. A different time zone every day. The times when we spoke with him - all over the place, really - sometimes we had a half - hour notice. We had your thread about the matter. Scott sent it to me, but didn't want to pull you out of class when we finally got his father on the phone."

"Uh-huh." Here I had to choose my words carefully. "I could have kept the kids busy with something while I was part of it."

"Anyway. We think we've got it sorted out." Scott looked hopeful. "Talking with Eric's father shed a lot of light on things. I'm sure you know he's quite a businessman. No doubt he's gotten to where he has by putting lots of pressure on a lot of people."

"And Eric has felt this, too," Barclay jumped in. "Pressure from Dad."

"Well, if he's truly been under a lot of pressure, that ought to keep him on the straight and narrow." That was the best I could do.

"Well," Scott cocked his head to gently disagree. "Yes, but as surely you *know*, different people respond to pressure in different ways. Eric is a half a world away from home, yet dad is always *there*. In his head."

"In his own way, a subtle force of nature." Barclay leaned forward for emphasis. "In business, and elsewhere. No doubt with Eric too. Certainly here, and in a good way. Some things around here are going to look very different thanks to him."

With that, I knew. I felt something similar when I got my first college rejection letter. This was all wired. A done deal.

"We've met with Eric, and his father was part of that meeting via Zoom." Scott picked things up. "It is abundantly clear to him that fireworks are *verboten* - here, and in the state as a matter of law. The seriousness of this matter was really brought home to him. We think that some cousin at a college in New Hampshire where they're legal got them for him. And he's going to do a deep dive on this matter. Eric, that is. He's going to do an independent study next fall with the fire department in town on fire safety. Going to spend one afternoon every week down there. He'll be assisting with fire drills here on campus and make a presentation on his experience at term's end."

Both of them looked at me, waiting for a reaction. Knowing this, I offered none. The silence got to them, and Barclay broke it.

"In a bit of symmetry, Mr. Zhang is going to upgrade the sprinkler system in all the dorms over the next two years."

I held his gaze for a bit, making sure I'd heard him correctly. My gut instinct was to respond with words that would shock my mother. *He's going to upgrade…* I wouldn't have cable TV if it weren't part of my housing package here, and serendipitously as it turns out, last night I watched "The Maltese Falcon" on TCM. As I quietly seethed in the meeting, a line of Sydney Greenstreet's in the film came to mind: "In the heat of action, people often forget where their best interests lie, and let their emotions carry them away." Must watch that channel more often.

"His. Father. Is…" I paused between each word for effect, letting them hang there, elongating the lunacy of it all.

"It's actually a good outcome," Scott piped up, "The learning angle of it for Eric, an upgrade for the physical plant. And, by the way, perhaps you've heard of the push across the nation for restorative justice? There was a piece about it in *Independent School* magazine." At this he reached into his pocket for a phone. "I'll send you the link." *Independent School* is the trade journal of the industry. Nobody but administrators reads it, and maybe not even them, but it looks great on office coffee tables. I turned to Barclay.

"I covered an ESL class one day this term for Mary, and taught about speech tenses." I let that hang there for a few seconds to make him wonder where I was going with it. "I detect the past tense in your sharing all this. So, I gather it's all a done deal, yes?"

"It really does seem like the best outcome for all, as Scott explained." Barclay permitted himself the hint of a self-satisfied smile.

"Well, certainly for Eric it is." I tipped my head. "I seem to recall a kid from Philadelphia two years ago who had a candle in his room. He got a week's suspension."

Scott touched a finger to his lips to help him remember. "I think I recall that case. Yes. Right. Well. Yes. There you see, there was an open flame. Truly a active and present danger to the safety of the whole dorm."

As I also recall, truly, that young man received a ton of financial aid to be here. Eric's father could perhaps pick up the school's entire financial aid budget for a year and not miss it. Must be nice.

"Also," Barclay held up a finger to make his point, "with the students headed home soon, there seems little point in trying to schedule a Disciplinary Committee now. Students have already booked travel plans for the break. Playing with schedules and departures right now would just wreak havoc in some corners."

It occurred to me that I could mention how the notice of a suspension could at least go in his file, or that a suspension could be served next year when we're all back after this coronavirus thing. It also occurred to me, however, that as the matter would appear to have been settled, there was little point in doing so. It seemed like they'd thought of all of the *buts* I could throw out and had rebuttals for them dry and ready before I walked in.

"We just wanted to make sure you understood how the matter was resolved. And how grateful we are to you for catching this. No small thing." Barclay was nodding. "And Eric *will* be writing to you about his actions. Neglecting to follow you to Scott's office when asked to. *Unacceptable.* And he *gets it.*"

"I think," I looked up at a banjo clock behind Scott's desk, trying to figure out how long I would have to eat lunch, "they used to call that being disobedient."

"Absolutely," Barclay assured me.

Nothing I wanted to say would change things and what I did want to say would only get me fired. I stood, mentioned that I had a class after lunch, and headed out, leaving them in their chairs, perhaps surprised at my reticence. Thank God for TCM.

***

I couldn't eat. I pushed open the door from the dining hall building with more force than was needed, and almost knocked Bags over.

"Careful Ben!" He held up two palms of surrender with a surprised look. "I hope to die at the hands of a jealous husband, not by a school door to the head."

"Sorry Bags," was all I could manage. I walked the wide loop of campus at a brisk pace, trying to process and burn off what had just happened. The walks were slushy, but between what I'd been told and my Bean boots, I didn't care. A stiff breeze had the American and the Griswold flags rippling straight out from the two poles at the center of the quad. I turned away, suddenly bereft of any faith I had in at least one of them. Back behind my building sooner than I thought, it was like a switch had been flipped. I went to my room, emailed my 12:50 and 2:05 classes, stuck a note on the door and went to my house in search of car keys.

Thrift shops can be closed early in the week, and if the one I had in mind wasn't open, I'd just make a long drive of it. My mother wouldn't be caught dead in a thrift store, but whenever I show up in some shirt or sweater that I got at one, I get the "Oh, is that a new shirt?" from her, usually with a tone of approval.

Pulling into One More Time, the shop that I visited with the students a few weeks earlier, I noticed the license plate on a Subaru by the door, 1MRTYM, which was encouraging. Inside, I made for the register and found the proprietor on the phone. She was negotiating some estate sale, but I caught her eye and rummaged in men's shirts while she finished. After a few minutes, she was done and made her way over to me. Over forty but not fifty, she had the same scoop neck sweater and capri pants appearance as when I was there earlier. Under her bob cut, she had a slightly quizzical look; not many people seek out assistance in a thrift store.

"I'm Ben Minot," I smiled. "I teach at Griswold and was here a few weeks ago with some students."

"Okay…" She looked truly baffled.

"When I was here, a girl asked our students about another student at the school."

"Mmmmm. Hmmmm." She nodded slightly, in that way people do when they're absorbing information, but don't yet want to offer their own.

"I was wondering if…well, you seemed to put an end to that discussion. It was on a Saturday. A few weeks ago. Does any of this ring a bell?"

She looked at me carefully for a minute, saying nothing. Switching gears, she looked over my shoulder with brighter eyes and called out, "Everything with a red dot on it is 25% off." In a far corner of the store an older woman thanked her for the information. She leaned in to whisper to me. "You can't count on people to read signs."

"No argument." I nodded. "I'm a teacher. You can't count on them to read *period*."

"So," she straightened up, "Yes. I remember. My daughter - she helps out on weekends. She noticed the girls and asked about Todd Garmin."

"Yes. Yes." Progress. "Todd Garmin. Exactly." I felt like I'd just found my keys after looking for them frantically. "I was wondering if you know why your daughter inquired about Todd."

"Oh, really?" She squinted as if confused.

"Well, honestly, she seemed concerned about him. Like there was something wrong with him."

"Well," she folded her arms and winced a bit. "She, er, of course, we, certainly hope he..." and then she pulled a face, looking for how to finish her point. "*We wish him the best.*"

"Uh-huh." I leaned on a rack of men's trousers. "And is there something in particular that makes you and her *want* to wish him all the best?"

At this, she fixed me with a gaze and clasped hands behind her waist. She thinned her lips, choosing and parsing her words carefully. "I lost an uncle to cancer. Fifty-two years old." She spoke in an emotionless monotone. "I can't imagine what it's like for a patient or his family to go through it when we're talking about a teenager."

At this I returned her stare but couldn't speak. Eventually, her no-nonsense glare nudged me to respond. "I'm sorry," I held up a *wait a minute* palm. "Cancer?"

"Yes." She looked away for a moment at nothing in particular. "I wouldn't wish it on my worst enemy." There's an expression I could do without. Certainly there are certain things I wouldn't wish on most people, but for my worst enemy, of course I'd want only the worst. But that's me.

"Well, I'm sorry about your uncle. Truly, I am. It sounds as though you're suggesting that...Todd has..."

"Not saying the word doesn't make it go away," she scolded me.

"Cancer. Is *that* what you're saying?"

With this, her eyes widened, and she folded her arms over her chest again. "Do you *really* teach at Griswold?" She frowned into a skeptical squint.

"I can assure you that I do." This sudden change in the climate sent me reaching for and showing her my school swipe card. "I have to say, I know that some medical matters are confidential, but that's something that would probably have been on our radar. A student would be on a leave of absence. Getting treatment somewhere. There'd be memos, telling all of us to be mindful of what to do to help a student work through this, and all kinds of accommodations. I mean, why would we be making him do homework if he should be getting treatment? Honestly I haven't heard *any* of this."

Her face was now a mix of simmering anger and slight confusion. "You have seen him though, right?" She pointed to her hair. "The effects of the chemo?" She brought a hand down to her forehead to cover her eyes and steady herself. "I'm sorry. I have a son who's almost his age." I let this all sink in for a bit. New territory. If a student has experienced a seizure for any reason before or while at school, we get an email about it at the start of the year. We even get a list of all the kids who are allergic to something and what could trigger a reaction. Cancer seems like something that they'd make us aware of.

"Could you tell me how you came to believe this about Todd? And, ah, by the way, what kind of cancer?"

"Non-Hodgkin's Lymphoma. It's usually diagnosed at a late stage in teens, and that's apparently the case with Todd." Her tone was now one of matter-of-fact impatience.

"And you know this because..."

After a sigh of frustration, "He told Sandy - my daughter. And he has a blog. "Todd Will Beat It." He posts updates after his trips to Dana-Farber, new research, how he's saving money on shampoo. Got to admire that, being able to laugh during all this. Sandy and he are quite close. She's perhaps *too* concerned about him, for her age, but what can you do? Teenagers, right?" I just stared at her. "How do you not *know* all this if you teach there?"

"Good question." I held her gaze and went into that list of all the medical conditions that we're made aware of at school. We then engaged in another staring contest. She blinked first.

"My daughter is extremely, hmmm, *invested* in this young man's health. And, in this young man. You're suggesting that h-e-e-e-e…"

"I'm saying that this is all news to me. And," I weighed holding something back, then thought, *why?* "I was present when the whole varsity soccer team shaved their heads last fall. It was a group thing. A way to intimidate opposing teams. Todd's kept his head shaved. Why? I don't know. Maybe for basketball. Maybe to save time in the shower." I shrugged and cocked my head, hinting that I didn't quite believe the second possible reason.

"Or maybe to get inside my daughter's pants."

Maybe Todd's motives were not simply that, but regardless, this just didn't ring true. The lone customer in the store approached with some red dotted items and One More Time's owner guided her to the register. I lingered as she rang up her purchases. After she bagged the women's blouses and thanked her, she looked up at me with wounded disappointment, and something else. "Would you like a cup of tea?"

Behind the register, she set to working a Keurig, and produced two cups of something. I couldn't be bothered to notice what it was. She elaborated on her daughter's infatuation with Todd, adding that his blog included suggestions of all the things that he likes to do "while he can."

"How many people follow this blog of his?" I asked.

She shrugged. "Bunch of girls. Sandy's friends, mostly. It's by invitation of some sort. And he's sworn everyone to secrecy on it. Doesn't want to "add to his folks' pain," he says." There was a sternness in her eyes now. She kept shaking her head, like someone who'd been deceived by an online scam courtesy of a Nigerian prince and was now cursing herself for it. I told her I'd be sharing all this with the school, and speaking with Todd personally.

"I'd like to be there when you do."

"Hmmm. I bet. Not sure how that works. But, if I gave you my email address, could you summarize this whole thing? Your understanding of 'all things Todd?'"

She nodded her head slowly, then started to shake it as if kicking herself. She let out a big sigh, and closed her eyes for a bit. I took that as a good time to make my excuses. I wrote my email address on a receipt that someone had not taken, and promised her I'd be in touch.

***

Turning out of her store, I started to head towards school, then turned right at the first light. I had enough presence of mind to know that I was in a mood. A *fuck-that-yellow-light* mood. Not a state of mind in which to confront a teenager over what might be a huge lie.

Usually driving nowhere seems like a waste of time and gasoline, but this was almost cathartic. A veil had been lifted from some odd episodes this winter. There are no doubt some conditions that families do not share about their children, but often, when they're sending a child away for months at a time, they're pretty open about things. At a wedding once I ran into two nurses at different boarding schools, a couple of the most selective ones in the east. Both of them mentioned how many kids they have who take meds for this and that. This surprised me, but when I thought about it, it made sense. Perhaps a quarter of kids at those schools come from private day schools in New York and Boston, where some start in kindergarten. Their problems with attention become clear a few years later, but they're already in, and on track for other schools based on where they are, in spite of any maladies. Thus they still end up at some pretty good schools on a bunch of meds, or in the case of at least one president's son, dyslexia, and they slide on through. When things get hairy, a kid might take a break from school, like James Taylor did, checking into McLean Hospital during his senior year. Cancer, however, isn't something people keep quiet about. It prompts GoFundMe pages and people running 5K races for others, and if the family has piles of money, they don't let a kid wait at school to see if some treatment works.   I rolled back onto campus after 3 p.m. Thanks to Eric's sister, I'd had my fill of how well confrontations with a student without a third party on hand to witness it can issue can go, so I found Ralph. He was in his classroom breaking down the workings of a chemistry lab. I told him what I'd learned, and it was one of the few times that I've heard him swear. This might have been inspired by the fact that Todd Garmin is his advisee. He bit his lip, and waved a cautionary finger at me. "You better be right about this."

"Hey, I'm just going with what I know."

"Yeah but," he shook his head and took to rinsing out some beakers. "What is it with you? You just find these issues with kids from families you probably don't want to tee off. Why don't you pick on a scholarship kid for a change? It would make your life easier." His smile told all.

"I know, right? But I'm not picking on anyone. This is," I thought a second, then slipped into a rant on the larger concept of the school. "This is what we *do,* right? Get kids to seek truth, and *be* truthful. You don't want kids to leave your class thinking the world is flat, or that climate change is a hoax."

"No, but I got a few who think that this virus is a hoax. This probably comes from mom or dad. Weird: they can afford an expensive education for their kids, but can't think themselves into the twenty-first century. Too bad when people have more money than brains."

"Anyway, since Todd's your advisee, can you get him here so we can sort this all out?"

He let out an I'd-*rather-not-but-okay* sigh, and got tapping on his phone. "This will be a whole bucket of *fun*," he exhaled, and shook his head.

"Always admired how you text your advisees," I said.

"Yeah, well, they all tell me that email is *so* 2016."

"Maybe I'll give my advisees my phone number next year," I offered.

"If you *have* a next year here, 'way you're going. Speaking of which, you signed your letter yet?" He looked at me over his glasses.

"Not yet. Don't we have until the break?"

"Yeah, but it's not like what it says is going to change by Friday, right?"

He was right. He usually is. In less than a minute, he got a text back.

"He'll be here in ten minutes."

Looking out his window I could see the administration building. I was still seething over the bubble bath that Barclay and Scott concocted for Eric, but I didn't want anything *shared* with admins without me present, so I called Scott's cell. "Scott. Ben. Can you meet me in Ralph's classroom in five minutes?"

"What? No. Why?"

"I can't do this over the phone, but you need to be here."

"Ben, if this is about—"

"This is about something you've never heard of, but damn well better before some parents start calling."

Parents. The magic word. Administrators would sooner cut a finger off or sell a pet than so much as prompt parents to wrinkle their brows. Because they pay the school's bills, parent calls to change grades and excuse absences are usually treated as requests that admins are only too happy to agree to. The parent I was thinking of was the owner of One More Time; it didn't seem to matter that she was the parent of a child who didn't go here. The mere mention of the word got Scott to say he'd be over in ten minutes.

In something we couldn't have scripted, a few minutes later, Ralph and I heard some voices on the stairs outside his room. Todd and Scott. Ralph and I locked surprised glares. They both appeared at Ralph's door. Todd was in sweatpants, a Celtics hoodie and a hand-knitted ski hat. Behind him in a North Face parka, Scott ushered Todd in first.

"Ben - sorry, Mr. Minot." Scott caught himself, as if students don't know that teachers have first names. Scott made a sweeping gesture to Todd in the doorway. "After you, Mr. Garmin." He had no idea that Todd was the reason he'd been called here. Todd lurched in, eyeing us and the room warily. Scott unzipped his coat a bit, and held up a palm.

"If you folks have a meeting with Todd, can I pull rank and see what you wanted to talk to me about before you get to it? I've got a conference call in a bit."

"Actually," I raised a *stop* palm as Todd began to turn away, "could you both stay?" For two seconds they exchanged silent glances of uncertainty. "What I called you about involves Todd, so, maybe we could all sit."

Scott looked surprised for a few more seconds. Todd began to sit down mechanically, perhaps knowing this involved him, but not knowing what *this* was. His eyes were cast downward as he pulled out a stool at a lab table and slid onto it, looking like someone who knew that whatever was at hand was not good. He seemed convinced that making eye contact would make it worse. We sat around a science table as if about to play cards. I gave a kind of exhale one does before a twenty foot jump into a dark pond. Then I loosened my tie, perhaps feeling that I could afford a concession to informality, or perhaps because I've seen a lot of cop shows with interview scenes. As he's Todd's adviser, I asked Ralph to start us

Minot's Ledge

off. His *no drama* approach to everything and Morgan Freeman voice always suggest that whatever he's party to, calm will prevail.

"Todd," he began, "Mr. Minot has heard some things that need clarifying. They involve you, and honestly, on a couple of levels, we hope they're not true. But, they're of a nature such that Mr. Paone is here." Todd's eyes darted between us, showing no emotion. "Ben, you want to pick it up there?"

"Sure." I caught Scott's eye, and he didn't seem to be breathing. His palms were flat on the table, as if bracing for something. "Todd, a few days ago, I stopped by your room and asked you if everything was all right. Remember?" He nodded. "I'd run into some people, girls at basketball games, and off-campus, who seemed concerned with you. *About* you. Worried about your health. So when I asked you about this, you said all was good, yes?" He nodded slowly, and seemed to be bracing himself for a punch. "Can you remove your ski cap?" He slid it off and massaged the smooth, shiny top of his head. "I ran into someone today who told me something. But first, I want to get your side of things, okay?" He nodded. "Last fall, I remember being on duty when the soccer team shaved their heads." Here, I could almost see his face lose some color. He seemed to be holding his breath. "Obviously you've hung on to that look, and it's probably saved you a lot of time shampooing as a result." Lightening the mood a bit wouldn't hurt, especially since I didn't want Scott to see me conducting a Spanish Inquisition, which no one expects. "But...Ralph, you want to..." We didn't rehearse this, so he gave me a slight glare, a la *thanks for the spontaneous heads up*, then spoke.

"Mr. Minot has been told that you're continuing to keep your head shaved has involved informing some people that you are unwell." At this, Scott's eyebrows rose, and he turned to Todd.

"Hang on," Scott raised a palm to stop things. "Are we getting into HIPAA area?"

HIPAA is the policy regarding information on people's health, limiting what should be shared with others. Schools love confidentiality and keeping personal information in silos.

"I'm not sure we are, Scott," I said without looking at him, "as, maybe we'll see." Todd remained motionless, bracing himself for the next salvo. I faced him directly. "I've been told, by someone who's not part of the school, that she's been informed that you, have some form of cancer." He held my gaze without blinking. "Is this true?"

Just then, a ping was heard in the pocket of Todd's hoodie and he reached for his phone.

"Can I respond to this?" He looked at Ralph, who he probably thought of as his best friend in the room.

"I'm guessing it can wait," Ralph offered a hint of a smile that he meant to be reassuring.

"Whoa," Scott jumped in. "This is serious business. I'd like to get someone from Health Services to at least listen to this. I hadn't anticipated a discussion along these lines."

"That, ah, might not be necessary," I offered.

"Then, in that case," Scott pursed his lips, "if there is indeed an illness at the center of whatever all this is...Tell you what: let's do this." He leaned toward Todd with the most earnest of looks. "Todd, if anything along the lines of what Mr. Minot has said, about an illness, is true, please: just raise your hand a bit."

Todd didn't move.

"Did you hear me?"

Todd gave the slightest of nods. Nothing more. At this, Scott and Ralph sat back in their chairs.

"I'd like to put a finer point on things, if I may." I clasped hands under my chin and tipped my head in an indifferent way, as if I was asking a server at a restaurant whether the chicken on the menu was free-range. "Did you tell someone - anyone, maybe more than one person - that the reason for your bare head is chemotherapy? That you are getting that treatment as a result of having cancer?"

Nothing.

"Todd," Ralph gazed at him. "Got to talk to us, pal."

Looking over the edge of the table, I could see the young man's knee bouncing.

"Todd," Scott was now speaking as if addressing a six-year-old, "whatever your answers, you'll feel better once you—"

"It—started as…just a *joke!*" The dam broke. His palms opened, pleading eyes fixed on Ralph. "A bunch of us were watching something and saw some ad online for some hospital, St. Something, and someone said, "That kid looks like you." The kid in the ad. Then we were at this party. At some day student's house, and a girl asked me about my head being…this way. I *know*, I should have mentioned the whole soccer thing. But then, I remembered the cancer thing, from the ad, and…it just came out. As soon as I said it, I couldn't walk it back. I mean, admitting that I just lied to her would make me seem, like, you know, a jerk."

"Not like now." I couldn't resist. Scott shot me a reprimanding glare. "Scott," I returned the look. "I'm not wrong."

Ralph sighed and slumped a bit. "So: *after* the party?"

"She started texting me. Sending me links to stories about people who have cancer. Showing up at basketball games. I really started to like her. And her friends, they made signs for the games. One of them knitted me a hat."

Scott and I traded glances. Todd was resisting eye contact, picking lint off his hoodie.

"Did you post anything online about this?" I asked.

"I sort of created a blog. I kind of, you know, went with it."

Now Scott sighed, and shook his head. "So, you allowed others to believe that this was in fact a condition of yours?"

Todd nodded.

"Say it," I muttered. Todd looked at me, unnerved and confused. "Say, in a complete sentence, what you did."

He sighed, thought for a few seconds, and closed his eyes as he spoke. "I...allowed other people to believe that I was sick."

"I think you can do a little better than that, yes?" I wasn't going to stop squeezing until I heard bone crunch.

"What?" Todd twisted his face.

"That party. What you did there. And then with the blog. Spell it out." He wrinkled his brow. When he wouldn't budge, I nudged him. "*Today.*"

"Mr. Minot," Scott spoke up, and I raised a pausing finger to him without looking his way.

"Lay it out for us." Ralph added.

"I told someone," he blew out a deflating breath, "I had cancer."

"And," I let that hang there for a few seconds, "do you?"

He willed himself to shake his head.

"And?" Here I mimed typing and texting with my hands.

"And I pushed that story on my blog."

Perhaps a full half minute of silence passed. Eventually my eyes settled on Scott, who cleared his throat, and straightened up a bit to speak.

"Well. Disappointing. A pretty bad decision, Todd. You're going to have to come clean about this story, to everyone who has heard it."

"I think the term you're looking for is *lie.*" I offered.

"He's right," Ralph nodded. "This is not some embellishment, like you're on a team but told people you were the captain. It's a lie. Pure and simple."

"Not too pure," I muttered with a deadpan gaze that Todd couldn't meet.

"I didn't do it to...," Todd rolled his head and eyes toward the ceiling, not believing his current bind. "It's not like anyone did a GoFundMe thing and I made money from it."

Minot's Ledge

"Someone made you a hat." I pointed to the gray lump he was gripping with both hands. "Not that one maybe, but...money for the wool. Skill. Effort. Time."

"I think she likes me. She might have made it for me even if I..."

"And she might have pulled Santa's sleigh if she were a reindeer, but she isn't." My blood was up. "Hypotheticals are not a good play right now. They're better than lies though. Better than you saying you have cancer when you don't. That's a lie."

The only sound in the room was the clanging from an old radiator in the corner. I leaned forward, trying to melt his face with my glare. "Ever met my wife?" He winced at the non sequitur, then shook his head. "Yeah, I know you haven't. Know why? In 2001 I was teaching in southern Connecticut and during an annual doctor's visit, they found a spot on her lung. Never smoked a day in her life. Doesn't matter. Got a referral to a doctor in New York - some cancer specialist. She had a late morning appointment, so thought she'd look in on a friend in the financial district ahead of time. She had a classmate who worked at Cantor Fitzgerald, a company you probably never heard of. But maybe you've heard of the North Tower. There was also a South Tower, got it? So: Cantor lost everybody in that office that day. Any visitors there too. *Gone.* *There's* a story about cancer I really wish *wasn't* true. She could have been helping trophy wives in Stamford pick out window treatments for houses that were already perfect instead of killing time in the World Trade Center before her doctor's appointment - an appointment that might have told her she didn't have cancer at all. Maybe. I don't know. I don't want to know, you know? If it wasn't cancer, it just compounds the waste of her being there that day. So, Todd, you can see that I don't think a joke about cancer is funny. Probably a lot of people don't. I think it's sick. And it pisses me off and you piss me off."

Silence.

Eventually, Scott drew a deep breath and grimaced. "We'll need to look at this. Deeply. Todd, is there anything else that you have to say?" He shook his head. He was now tugging at the fingers of a glove, as if counting them again and again. "I'm going to ask that you go to your room, and wait to hear from Ral— Mr. Brady. We'll go from there. Do you understand?"

He nodded.

"What about his phone? His computer?" I asked. Todd looked up at me as if I'd suggested cutting his balls off, still counting the digits on the glove. "Most gloves have five fingers." I spat out. "He used these devices to spread a lie. Shouldn't they be confiscated?"

A pleading look for mercy went to Ralph and Scott, who both nodded slowly.

"But...I've got homework." Todd turned his head mechanically, seeking a sympathetic face.

"You got issues bigger than homework right now, pal." Ralph said.

"Please give your phone to Mr. Brady," Scott offered in a matter-of-fact way. "He'll accompany you to your room to collect your laptop. We will get in touch with you for the next step in this...matter."

One by one, the adults rose, and Todd reached out with his phone to Ralph, as though surrendering his passport in a foreign country with re-education camps. Ralph gestured toward the door and followed Todd out.

Scott texted someone briefly, exhaled audibly, and looked up at me. "Didn't see this coming. How did you stumble on it?"

I gave him the cliff notes version of my experiences at games, the groupies, and finally the thrift store episode.

"Wow. This is a new one." As he pulled on his parka and zipped it up, I thought of something else.

"Er, there's this too: if he created that blog, and sent any emails about this while on his school Gmail account, that's another wrinkle. Technically, the school is party to it. Making it possible."

He nodded and winced without looking up.

"Ben, I didn't know about your wife. I'm...sorry. Terrible."

I nodded. "It happened before I came here. No reason for you to know."

"Still. Sorry."

He patted me on the shoulder as we made for the door.

"I'll need you to write it all up. How you came to learn everything."

"Sure. You'll have it by dinner."

"Give yourself a break. Tomorrow morning is fine."

Outside, a gray March thaw was at work. We parted on a slushy walk. Passing a dorm on the way back to my house, I heard a room explode in howls, the kind that only five or six boys involved in a video game can produce. Their laughter was a nice sound.

Mar 17

Email from Mr. Zhang
> Dear Mr. Minot
> I'm sure that the abrupt conclusion of in-person classes at Griswold this spring has created a myriad challenge for everyone. It is impossible to know what meetings will be held once all are on campus again, so I am hopeful that you will find time to get the prefect recommendation for Eric done before the impending break. If you share it with me as a Google doc, that would be ideal. In the event that prefect selection occurs via online panel meetings, I'm sure your thoughts will have weight. I'm confident that the term ahead will pose challenges for teachers as well as students, but if all do their best, it should help dispense with frustration and lead to a good start for next year's school year. We should all be sanguine for matters to turn out optimally.
>
> *Cordially,*
> *Jianyu*
> *Jianyu Zhang*
> *President & CEO*
> *Sinotech Holding Company Ltd*
>
> *No.23, Wu Temple, Shatan N St, Falungong Dist, Beijing 100009, China (Houhai)*

Minot's Ledge

WHY DO SOME NON-NATIVE speakers of English try to sound like George Will? Clearly, even some adults insist on using Google Translate or some other such service to create a narrative which has syntax about as natural as an atomic bomb owner's manual. It does seem, however, that things have changed a bit. No doubt, given how money flows and to whom, Zhang is several gillion dollars richer than when I met him in the fall. His son's stock, however, would seem to have fallen. While he and I may have been the only ones aware of his cheating in September, Eric's dabbling with pyrotechnics is now known. Barclay and Scott may have squeezed some lemonade out of that lemon in the form of an upgrade to some building codes, courtesy of Dad, but the transgression is out there. Prefects are supposed to inspect rooms, not have fireworks hidden in them.

Having learned the hard way to never respond to emails after nine in the evening, I'll do so in the light of day.

Mar 18

GRADING THE END OF term papers this afternoon was a grind. Having online dictionaries has made some students think that they are as eloquent as William F. Buckley, Jr. with language. His name would mean nothing to them, nor would half the words he used in his writing. A junior hoping for a recommendation to take honors English won't settle for saying, "Her boyfriend wasn't thrilled with the dinner she prepared." A few clicks into a thesaurus, and when reading that paper, I get, "Her paramour responded to the Epicurean offering with aplomb." I put down my red pen and started tapping out or reply to Zhang.

> *Dear Mr. Zhang*
> *I've been made aware of your recent largesse toward Griswold in the form of building upgrades. Thank you. Fires, and anything that can prompt one, have been the bane of many schools with older buildings over time.*
>
> *No doubt you're aware that fireworks were found in Eric's room. Obviously this matter has been resolved administratively. Thankfully, a conflagration was obviated. On another level, in terms of endorsing Eric as a prefect, the presence of*

fireworks in his room colors that step. Given his involvement with these items which are not only against school rules but are also illegal to possess in the state of Massachusetts, I am honestly reluctant to convey to a residential life panel that I consider Eric an ideal candidate for prefect.

I'm sure that as a successful businessman, you have encountered individuals who are capable in various capacities, but who you might not recommend for responsibilities at other levels. Prior to the fireworks matter, I drafted a letter in support of Eric as a prefect. I'm afraid that his actions with these illegal devices prompt me to refrain from submitting it on his behalf. Nevertheless, he might well become a prefect without my thoughts as part of the mix. If not, with a clean slate next year, there's every reason to expect that he could apply for that position for his senior year. It is unusual for students to become prefects before senior year as it is, and ideally, this decision will not dash his hopes for grabbing this brass ring in the future. I hope that the logic of my reasoning is self-evident. Thank you again for your altruism toward Griswold. Such largesse is most magnanimous.

Warmly,
Ben Minot.

Two can play that game. Let him grab a thesaurus. Between offering the cause for my decision on Eric, framing the matter in a business-related context, and blowing smoke up his ass, I figured I'd covered lots of bases. As I mentioned that the letter wouldn't be forthcoming, I felt fine stretching the point that I'd already drafted it. (Alright, *inventing* the point.) I cc'd Barclay and Scott on this email and hoped that this would be the end of the matter.

For a second wind to help me dive back into grading papers, I stepped out for a coffee in the teachers' room. Just outside my door, I found Glenn Olson parked in a leather chair that is perhaps older than his parents.

"Glenn - hi. I didn't know you were here." He does have this habit of waiting quietly, and out of view. Like most kids, he's probably on his phone while waiting, but it's a bit weird.

"Hi Mr. Minot. I was wondering if you could look at my draft for tomorrow. Before I turn it in?"

In a Patagonia jacket that had seen better days and tousled red hair suggesting he had been standing on a runway at Logan, it was hard to blow him off. But timing is everything.

"Glenn, the paper is due tomorrow morning. Asking me about this a few days ago would have been a better idea."

"Yeah, I know," he winced. "I'm trying to make up homework in pre-calc, and it's kind of taking up a lot of my study hall time."

I willed myself to not default to an eye roll. "Fine." I gestured him into my room and to sit. "If your paper is on a Google doc, you want to share it with me?"

Glenn's paper was based on Steinbeck - an analytical look at three novels of his that we'd read, *East of Eden*, *Of Mice and Men*, and *The Grapes of Wrath*. Glenn can be very literal but doesn't always recognize patterns or themes as quickly as others. He always seems earnest, and fairly focused enough on doing his best. Thus, selling any Ritalin he is supposed to take for ADD or intentionally pasting a lifted passage into a paper as if it were his own are not in his DNA. We went over his paper together. He had the bones of an adequate essay. I suggested considering another word here and there and hinted that he offer specific examples from the books that suggest various themes. He tapped out notes based on what I said and asked about the length of the paper, which was supposed to be five to six double-spaced pages. His was currently just shy of four.

"You should aim for a couple more pages. Look at your notes from class, check the handout on Steinbeck I gave you, and see if you stumble on anything you haven't mentioned yet. And you annotated the texts, right?" He gave me a *pretty much* nod. "Go through all that. See what you come up with."

He scrolled down a few lines and tapped some more. "Look at your thesis, too. See if you can eek out an angle that's a little more novel. Remember: a thesis is something not everyone is going to agree with. Don't state the obvious - go out on a limb. Then back fill to defend it." All of this had been said in class and was on the handout when I assigned the project, but that doesn't mean everyone was listening or had read it.

"So, Mr. Minot. Tomorrow I've got a PT appointment at eleven in the morning. Right when class is. Can I share the paper with you or email it to you?"

"Will you be back before class is over?"

"I don't know. It's the first one. My knee is still healing from a hockey injury."

"Well, you need to hand in a hard copy. I assume you'll be back on campus for lunch. Print it out and bring it here as soon as you're back, okay?"

He nodded and started to pack up. As useful as Google Docs are, I'm pretty old school with papers, preferring to read hard copies on which I can write comments, ideally in red ink to build character. I also don't like staring at a screen all night to check student work. Students aren't the only one's blue light can keep awake.

After Glenn left and I finished grading the essays, I checked my email.

> *To: bminot@griswold.edu*
> *From: sears @griswold.edu*
>
> *Invitation to meeting with Barclay Sears. 4:30 p.m. Going?*

Barclay never lets on what such meetings to which one is invited are about. This is his prerogative I suppose, but it's also infuriating.

***

With no shortage of fresh hells - conversations with Bags tend to stay with me - I wasn't sure what Barclay Crowningshield Sears wanted to discuss, so I went for a run on the cross-country course to burn off my worry. Somehow, it didn't occur to me that the tracks would be all slush and mud. The gray ceiling and barren branches overhead provided a Gothic feel to the experience. As is the case with businesses, schools and by and large, absolutely every individual and society, we were now in uncharted territory in terms of what's next with the coronavirus. There's usually angst on the part of teachers that builds up at term's end, mostly over grades, and that's in *normal* times.

"Give me strength," Mary Carpenter once pleaded, to no one in particular in the Teachers' Lounge one day. "Could my directions be any easier?" We were sitting around a dark, oval table, wishing the coffee were better. "Look!" she held up a one-page handout for a paper she'd assigned. "Am I imagining it, or does this actually say, "Cite sources in MLA format?""

"Plain as day," Peter Burnham looked up from his magazine and nodded at her.

"Bags?" Mary held the sheet up toward Howard Bagwell, who was slouched in a chair across the table. Immersed in a crossword puzzle which he was doing in ink, he tugged at his John Bolton mustache, but didn't bother to look up.

"Mary, I have no doubt your rubric says MLA format. You're a school treasure, and not only because you agree with me about the lunacy of the Oxford comma." At this, he laid down his pen and looked up with *ennui*. "You surely must know, however, that there have been students admitted to the school who cannot *spell* MLA."

This prompted a few chuckles around the table, but in a corner of the room, a scowling Admissions assistant folded her copy of *The New Republic*, rose quietly and left the room.

"Not sure she's going to send you a Christmas card." Peter wagged a scolding finger at Bags.

"I'm crushed," he smiled. "Judas Priest. I saw her touring that kid from Plympton around campus in August. The hockey player from New Hampshire who we finally kicked out for bullying last month. She was gushing over him. And about him. The fact that he came from Plympton should have been a red flag."

"Nice arch in that town, though," I chimed in.

"Brooks Brothers outlet there too." Peter added.

"Ugh." Mary shook her head. "Why don't they just do what I *ask*? Or *ask* me to *clarify* what I'm asking of them. If I don't grade these papers on a curve…good Lord. Some of these juniors have asked me to write college recs for them, and they turn in *this stuff* to me?" She held up a stack of papers that especially disappointed her. "And here I am, worrying about how these grades will impact their averages, and what I write about them. And they can't bother to *cite their sources* correctly?"

"You're more worried about their grades than they are." Bags clicked his pen. "That's not healthy."

"But this girl," Mary pointed to the paper on top of her stack, "she's such a nice young woman. She wants to go to Vassar." She actually looked pained.

"It's good to want." Peter nodded.

I played this exchange through my head as I ran. Several kids had already left for break. Parents had booked flights midweek, so their children are skipping some finals and deadlines for assigned papers, the latter of which might be turned in via email or Google classroom. Or not. To allow your kid to blow off important parts of an expensive education in order to save a few hundred dollars on airfares seems dumb. Silver lining: such cases will allow me to paste in a boilerplate comment for them in terms of semester grades, making for a shorter task:

> *Josh left school without completing all of the requirements in this class, resulting in an incomplete grade.*

For years I've sweated about comments, sensing that I needed to put a shine on even the dimmest students' work. Somehow, maybe something to do with the running, it all boiled down to something pretty clear: if I sense that a child is unlikely to end up in Stockholm to collect one of Mr. Nobel's prizes, the parents of such a child have probably already figured that out. Thus, my comments shouldn't be breaking news. In some meetings, I will of course hear, "But Josh has always gotten all A's." To my credit, I've never responded to this with, "Josh has always had teachers who didn't challenge him and have instead preferred to pass him along while falsely fueling the idea that he is more than capable in this discipline." You have to pick your battles, but for some reason, I now felt willing to fight this one.

Cooling down at the end of my run, I chewed on all this after the endorphins settled, and it still made sense to me: candor could be more affirming than throwing more logs on the grade inflation blaze just to avoid an email full of umbrage. Perhaps my year away had made me leery of squeaky wheel parents. I can still be supportive and positive but might aim to be a bit less-saccharine in my comments this term. In addition to being disingenuous, saying that a student did wonderful work when she didn't sets the kid up for failure. She'll do mediocre work later on, and some teacher will call it what it is. She'll be flummoxed at this, since previously, she'd earned praise in spite of spelling errors, poor citations, and confusing empathy with sympathy. We're supposed to be a *college prep school*. Presumably one comes here expecting standards slightly more rigorous than PS 123. Not everyone is happy when they encounter these higher bars, and I'd hoped the run helped get worry about this out of my system.

Perhaps out of habit, I slipped on a tie for the meeting with Barclay. He was in open collared-dress shirt and four-panel trousers, aka *go to hell pants*. He gestured to a wing chair by a coffee table and took the other one of the pair.

"That a Nike tie?" He pointed to the yellow swoosh on a blue field around my neck.

"Nantucket."

" 'Course." He gestured to two armchairs flanking a coffee table. "I was there last summer for a memorial service. Griswold Alum. You probably heard about it, even though you were away. The whole matter was quite involved. Sad, really." Peter Burnham had provided blow-by-blow accounts of the episode last year via email and texts. A returning alum had a fall and cracked his head open in Chapel, all prompted by the actions of a student. It resulted in TV news vans being parked outside the school gates for a bit. Glad I wasn't here. Elbows on his knees, Barclay steepled his hands and leaned in.

"So, Ben. Todd Garmin."

"Todd Garmin," I repeated.

"He's made some bad choices."

I nodded.

"I'd go so far as to say some shameful choices. And the catalyst for them was his experience on the soccer team. That's when this head-shaving business got started." I nodded. "This calls for a consequence that will give him cause to reflect on his actions and how he might grow from them." He sat up straighter and raised an index finger for emphasis. "Todd will be suspended from participating in soccer - or any sport - in the fall. *That* will be quite meaningful to him. He will instead be required to devote two afternoons a week to volunteering at a local assisted living facility. Give him a *real* sense of what *serious health issues* are, and that they're not to be trivialized. Hopefully instill a little empathy in him."

With this, Barclay sat back, as if he'd just offered me a $10,000 raise and was expecting gratitude for it. I let his words sink in, and allowed a respectful silence to transpire so that he could realize I was chewing on his thoughts.

"And?"

"*And?*" Barclay looked a bit confused, as if I just asked for ketchup to smother my filet mignon. "Oh," he remembered, "and he'll be writing letters to anyone to whom he might have communicated the presence of a malady that he was not actually experiencing."

I wanted to walk through this discussion carefully. I let his words settle, and listened to the clicking of the Regulator clock behind his desk.

"I think the word you're looking for is *cancer*." I leaned forward in my chair. "And, there is no *might have*. I got it from a merchant here in town, and he had some interactions with a few other people on this matter. He admitted it all to Ralph, Scott and me. This ruse is out there. And that's what it is, a ruse. It's on a blog, that he probably created, or at least contributed to using the school's browser. But this is not a lightbulb joke. This is about cancer. Not a laughing matter."

"Agreed," Barclay nodded. "Absolutely. That's why we want to—"

"*Never mind*," a northern Jersey accent boomed in from his reception area. "I'll see myself in."

From outside his office, raised voices turned our heads toward the doorway. With the site of a somewhat stylish female at his threshold, Barclay froze for a second, then waved her in.

"Lynn. Hello. I didn't know you were…" The voice of a more civil female could be heard behind her. Barclay's secretary was trailing the woman, apologizing to her boss for the interruption.

Mackenzie Scott, aka Mrs. Scott Bezos, is no slouch. Now and again, however, behind a very successful man you might find a spa-pampered trophy wife. In this case, one who is perhaps a little more than twice her stepson's age. In a midnight blue bob cut, Ugg boots, jeggings under a Barbour coat and a Burberry scarf, Lynn Greenfield Lenox stood in the doorway, dangling a key chain, perhaps hoping I'd notice the make of the car key on it. Her black coffee eyes darted between us. Behind her, Barclay's septuagenarian A.A. pleaded helplessness.

"Mr. Sears. I tried to explain to her that—"

"Quite alright Barbara." He rose and patted down her concern. "We're good here." Barbara shot a parting glance at the barracuda before us and turned away. If looks could kill...

Months ago, a school magazine piece on accomplished businesswomen in our fold included coverage of the parent before us now. Lynn Greenfield Lenox was an administrative assistant in one of the Garmin companies when she caught the boss' eye. She was also studying fashion design at night, and he was impressed with her industriousness, among other things. In short order, she became the second Mrs. Garmin, but hung onto her name, perceiving "L.L." to be a future hook in commerce. As a result, not only did the first Mrs. Garmin make out pretty well via a prenup, but the younger, sportier model was still able to drop the joke that she has three towns in Massachusetts named for her: Lynn, Greenfield and Lenox. The article in the magazine noted a chain of upscale boutiques she had opened across Connecticut. It omitted, however, a detail in a *Vanity Fair* piece a year earlier - that the firm was largely funded by her husband. The school article made specific note of the new turf soccer pitch on the lower fields courtesy of the family.

"Lynn," Barclay flashed a smile and extended a hand. "How was Gstaad?"

"Cold," she huffed with contempt while pulling off black gloves finger by finger. "Place was full of..." She checked both our faces as if they would tell her how to finish that sentence. "It was crowded."

"I'm in a meeting right now. I wish you'd called as I could have—"

"I'm told you folks are planning to ruin my son's college prospects." Hands on hips, she cocked her head in an *is this true?* angle. For someone just back from Switzerland, she looked darn orange. Climate change, I guess.

"Actually, we were just discussing the matter. This is Ben Minot." He waved his arm my way.

"Hi. Oh. *You.*" Ms. Lenox's eyes widened with each syllable. Then she turned to Barclay. "Do you know what my son is *going through* right now? For trying to impress a girl? Are you *serious?*"

Barclay slid both hands into his pockets to help him produce a response. It sounded as though the consequences Todd would face had been made known to his parents already - already as in *before my meeting with Barclay*. It occurred to me that this may have been part of some negotiation with dad, but Lynn Greenfield Lenox was having none of it. A parent's blood was up because a child was getting slapped on the wrist for a fraud. The overarching reality was unspoken: the largesse of the family entitled her to barge into meetings and should allow her son to skate when he's in trouble. It also meant that she should not have to be polite to secretaries.

Not wanting to turn off Garmin revenue stream, Barclay massaged the matter as best he could. She commenced a rant that had him leaning back on his desk. Ms. Lenox didn't seem too annoyed at the whole matter not reflecting well on her son, but rather at the consequences of him having been found out. At the moment, it seemed to reflect poorly on the school that Barclay's secretary didn't have a taser in her desk.

"Lynn," Barclay pleaded, "I'm sure you can understand that for a local family, a merchant, to be under the impression, that Todd had an illness—"

"Cancer," I jumped in, looking her way with something stronger than mild disgust. Barclay shot me a flicker of contempt, then took a breath and continued.

"It could damage our relationship with the town. With local folks. And more than anything else, it's wrong."

"It was a, a..." she was looking about in frantic annoyance," a *thing* to get a *girl. Come on!*"

"That *thing* is a *real* thing." I glared at her. "Cancer alone kills over 130,000 people a year in this country, and lots of them don't even smoke. It's not currency to help a kid get girls."

"Lynn, he's right, of course." Barclay looked somewhat earnest. "We have to act here. The consequences of his actions will not scar Todd for life. Ideally, there's a lesson for him here. And if he keeps his nose clean next year, it won't appear on his transcript for college."

"*What?*" I whirled toward him, incredulous.

Ms. Lenox closed her eyes and shook her head. "Know what else won't be on his record? A fall sport. Todd *lives* for soccer."

"It's just one term," Barclay explained.

"So make that suspension from sports *next* term. Spring term." She tossed two palms skyward in a *problem solved!* sort of way.

"We have online classes next term, but no sports. No way around it. This virus has—"

"Fucked up the world. I know. Some of my stores' stock is stuck on container ships off San Diego. Goddamn Chinese. Al*ready* sent my business sideways this month. Why can't they eat like it's the twenty-first century 'stead of picking live eels out of some wet market for lunch. *Christ.*" At this, Barclay and I exchanged looks. I could see it in his eyes: *yes, Ben, that sounds like a bigoted remark, but please let it go for now.* "Back to Todd." She pulled a face. "It's not like he *stole* something or had drugs. *Come on.*"

"Hmmm." That did it. "Thing is," I waved a finger her way. "He ran a scam on some people. A scam involving something that does steal people. Like my wife." Her eyes widened, and she knew that more was coming. "And he did it, I'll bet, using the school's browser. At least using an aspect of a school activity - shaved heads for a soccer team - as part of it." I turned to Barclay. "Have you thought about this? Griswold is party to this...this..."

"Prank." she grunted with a *so what?* look.

"Prank. *Prank?*" I took a step toward her, which prompted Barclay to lean in a bit as well, as if I had more than words that I'd be using. "Pranks are funny. Why don't you take a tour of Dana Farber in Boston or Sloan-Kettering in New York and tell me how many people there are doubled over with laughter." Barclay moved towards us, and then I turned on him. "And what's this *not on his record* crap? He used school technology to perpetuate a fraud about having cancer. If everyone here is going to get a mulligan for such crap - and you *know* that everybody's going to know what happened to him, 'cuz he's going to brag about getting a pass on this - next year will be a disciplinary shit show." I don't think I've ever sworn in front of a parent, but she opened the door. "And don't forget that server in the dining hall. Remember that lady who lost her husband a couple of years ago even after all that chemo? I'm sure she'll be laughing her head off at the 'prank.' And the *Globe* will probably put it on the cartoon page."

With this Barclay shot me a glare. "We...handle matters here," he stabbed a finger at his desk. "I like to think that nobody's running to a newspaper about this." He cocked his head in a *'consider well your situation'* sort of way.

"Barclay, I wouldn't *have* to. You know there's no such thing as a secret at a school. It'll get out."

I was on empty and could think of nothing nice to say to either of them. The air seemed heavy, and I honestly didn't think I was going to hear anything there to my liking.

"I've got papers to grade." Hoping that Barbara would fill me in what was said next, I left the door open as I left. Heading back to my classroom, it occurred to me that Todd's mother actually has four towns in Massachusetts named for her: Lynn, Greenfield, Lenox, and Athol.

Mar 19

THE FOOD AT GRISWOLD is quite healthy, but who wants that? The exception to this being the pancakes that are always served on Wednesday mornings. I bring a small jug of Vermont maple syrup to the dining hall and camp out at a corner table. I try to appear as if I'm brooding so that nobody will sit down and strike up a conversation before my coffee kicks in.

I broke character this morning when I saw Jerome's sister stroll in and fetch herself some tea. When she saw me, I waved, and she nodded. You can balance what I know about fashion on the head of a pin, but I'm pretty sure that the winter white business suit she had on was designed by someone whose name would impress people who know about such things. Her clothing and carriage are not those of a high school bio teacher and have a way of putting me on edge. I sensed she'd been up for hours and was on a mission. Following small talk, she explained that she was there to pick up Jerome.

"He's done with finals, so hopefully he's packed. I told him to meet me here at 7:30."

"Getting to breakfast wanes as the year rolls on," I told her.

"Oh I get it," she nodded. I'd forgotten she'd been at school as well.

"Is he packing just clothes, or everything?"

"Everything?" She cocked her head.

"His room. I know there was talk of him being at another school. Next year."

"Yeah. We scrapped that plan." She waved a hand for emphasis. "My mother is pretty swamped by all things corona. She wouldn't mind if he went to a day school in D.C., or where my sister and I went, but three schools in three years…" She shook her head. " 'Sides, he derived a certain amount of *schadenfreude* from learning about the fate of those two boys who were with him in Cambridge that day in the fall."

"Oh yeah…" I allowed a knowing smile, recalling the incident.

In late February, a freshman girl asked her roommate what a good price was to charge for oral sex. Once the roommate pulled her jaw off the floor, she went to her advisor. Her roommate who was looking for a price range was asked who inquired as to this charge, and once assured that she had nothing to fear in terms of her involvement in the matter, she gave up two names. They were the same two boys who were with Jerome when things got hairy at Coop. Only three people know what truly went on that day, but last month, two of them got on the school's radar again. A day later, they were gone from campus.

"Holy Milton Academy, Batman!" Peter chuckled at lunch after word of the matter got out. A similar matter was actually transacted at that school a few years back, prompting the moniker 'Mouthful Academy.'

"Do you believe in karma?" Jerome's sister smiled.

"I'd sure like some proof that I should," I managed.

"Oh? Who is deserving—" and before she could finish the sentence her phone went off. Jerome had overslept. She rolled her eyes, smiled and was off.

Heading to my room, I scanned the quad. The sun was still low enough that it hadn't begun to work on the slick paths underfoot.

The black ice would be gone before lunch. Some of the white clapboard and Georgian brick buildings around me had weathered well over a hundred winters. Somehow though, this morning they seemed weakened. In some invisible way, deflated. Not physically, but as if they stood for less than sometime previously. It was as though I was looking at a museum that had recently had to repatriate some of its prized paintings and Egyptian finds, yet the structure that had housed them remained. One building, the Admissions office, reminded me of a small Cape I'd stayed in one summer in Connecticut. I was teaching at a summer program and sharing the place with a fellow from Culver Academy. He had this adage about such institutions: "A good school should be hard to get *into*, but easy to get *out* of." High standards, and rules that if you break a few, you're gone. Whether it was walking past the Admissions Office or events of late, I started turning his phrase over in my mind again and again. I wanted us to be such a school. I think that Griswold *was* at one time Then a series of events and circumstances slowly grew the gulf between some schools and others. Wealthy alumni and parents gave huge gifts to their old schools, beautifying campuses with new science buildings and athletic complexes that attracted other well-to-do families, who piled on more money. Then there were the numbers.

With smaller families these days, there have been fewer kids applying to schools everywhere. Thus, even the best schools are taking the B students they might not have a generation ago, and the back-up schools are left with the C students, and so on. This has left some schools like airplanes after 9/11: if you can buy the ticket, you can get on board, but once aboard and the doors are closed, you stay there. Unlike airlines though, lesser schools aren't worried about kids leaving C4 under a seat; they just like keeping the kids - the paying customers - on board, apparently regardless of conduct.

Collecting papers at the start of my 11 AM block, I read the first two sentences of each one as bellwethers of what was or was not to follow. Some were double spaced, some were not. Many followed directions for the introductory paragraph. Some clearly found the word count limit optional.

"Sorry, Mr. Minot," they explain sometimes, "I had to go over the word limit. I just couldn't say what I had to say in two thousand words." This is usually offered in a matter of fact way, a 'la *I'm sure you understand that my thoughts are so interesting that I require more space for them.* I smile as they hand them over with this explanation. When I return them, among my comments is usually some iteration of, "the total word count of the Declaration of Independence is 1,337. If Thomas Jefferson only needed that many words to found this country…" Invariably, the response is a rolling of the eyes. This is followed by a frequent question: "Okay - so where is my grade?" They flip through the pages. I write letter grades in a corner on the back of the first page, or bury them in comments: *Well said, Jenna. You truly seem to get what Langston Hughes is about. Using some specific passages to illustrate your point would be even better, and the B+ you earned for this might have been even higher, but nice work!* For students concerned mostly with grades, as opposed to learning and feedback to grow on, this can be maddening. Many are all about the letter grade and comments are viewed as cannon fodder that take time to read. Few of them realize that comments *explain* grades. Orange may be the new black, but grade-wise, C+ is the new F. My theory is that we have t-ball to thank for this. Everybody scores, everybody gets a trophy. Sorry, that's not how high school English works. Unlike Lake Wobegon, not all children are above average.

The last class before vacation can be a Sisyphean task for teachers trying to cover something. It's like asking people in a movie theater to stay in their seats for the credits after the film is over. After papers were collected, I handed out a one-page biography of Ernest Hemingway, and mentioned the title of his work, *Death in the Afternoon*. Asking them to speculate in a hundred words or less what that story might be about, it occurred to me that it is a vague enough title that I could get fourteen different answers from my fourteen students. They were to type this into a Google doc that they would share with me, the length of it being short enough at a hundred words that I would print them out later. I doubted anyone would leap to think it was about bullfighting, thus if someone did, I'd guess they'd stopped off at Google *en route* to their G-doc.

When seniors finished their Hemingway responses, they could go, so with fifty minutes left in the period, my room was empty. Counting the papers I collected at the start of class, I was one short. This always sends me into a panic: *how could I have lost a paper in the space of twenty minutes inside my own classroom?* Then I checked attendance and remembered that Glenn Olson had physical therapy this block, and said he'd bring his paper by during lunch. Exhale. Suddenly with the time to kill, I broke character and decided to put it to good use, diving back into my term-end comments. Usually, I wouldn't have minded being interrupted, but as I was actually being productive, of course there was a knock at the door.

"Ben," Scott poked his head in, and scanned the room as if to be sure that I was alone. "A word?"

He closed the door behind him, to which I made a request.

"Leave it ajar will you? A student is dropping off a paper in a bit."

He unzipped his parka to reveal a foulard tie over a white oxford shirt. Except for the day of student arrivals and Trustees' Weekends, this was a bit dressy for him. Silently he moved to a table near my desk and pulled out a chair to sit.

"We need to talk." Now what? "Got a call from Mr. Zhang. I… he's got two kids here and he's grateful for all we're doing for them. One of them is in your dorm, yes?"

I nodded. Scott thinned his lips, clearly not wanting to continue, tapping a pen on a yellow legal pad. He pressed on.

"He's made an allegation, Ben. About you. In the dorm. It involves his daughter. Before I get into it, I want to hear from you. It goes back to the fall. You know what he's referring to?"

At that moment, an image flashed through my head: Ralph getting stopped by police in town his first month here. He hadn't done anything wrong, but in Griswold, driving while black was enough to get him pulled over. Owing to the birth lottery and genetics, I've never had that experience, but suddenly had a slight sense of what it might feel like when those blue lights flash in the rearview mirror.

I leaned forward at my desk, and considered how I should walk through the next few minutes. I chose my words carefully. "Mr. Zhang and I had a conversation in the fall, and I crossed paths with his son, Eric, in Mary's class when I subbed for her, and not in a good way. This is well before the fireworks matter. But," I sat back, "this is your meeting Scott. I'm all ears."

With this, he pulled out a laptop and tapped at it until he found a document which appeared to have a narrative on it.

"This is an email I received from him this morning. I should add that he cc'd Barclay on it. Actually, it was sent to Barclay, and I was cc'd on it. He cleared his throat.

> *Dear Barclay.*
>
> *I hope this finds you well. I feel the need to convey to you a matter which distresses me on several levels, but as a parent and someone with an interest in Griswold School, it is essential that I share it with you.*
>
> *Last fall, while on duty in a female dormitory, Ben Minot entered my daughter's room without what she found to be adequate warning. Without going into detail, she was not in a state of dress that teenage girls prefer to be in when adult males are encountered. I suspect that Mr. Minot has not mentioned this matter to you, but obviously my daughter has mentioned it to me. Although this occurred in the fall, it was only recently that*

she had the courage to share it with me. Needless to say I was distressed to learn of this matter and wanted to bring it to your attention promptly.

I am familiar with the concept of in loco parentis at boarding schools, and sadly do not feel as though this policy was honored by Mr. Minot at that time. As someone with two children at Griswold and an interest in the school, I am hopeful that you will look into this episode. I look forward to learning how you respond to this matter, and to seeing the plans for the updated building systems we have spoken of.

*Cordially,
Jianyu
Jianyu Zhang
President & CEO
Sinotech Holding Company Ltd
No.23, Wu Temple, Shatan N St, Falungong Dist, Beijing 100009, China (Houhai)*

    The only noise that I recall once Scott was done reading this was a high-pitched ringing in my ears. It was as if an ominous sound from one's car engine, one that you haven't heard for months, was now pounding its way through the auto's hood - on a country road during a snowy night when there is no cell phone service.

    Scott tipped his head and offered up a hand. "Okay. As I said, I want to hear what you have to say."

    I took a deep breath. "For starters, yes, obviously I do duty in his daughter's dorm. Check the dorm log for that night I was on. It's all there. The fire in the microwave and the subsequent alarm, and me having to enter her room when she didn't answer the door. Maybe she didn't like it, but frankly, I didn't either. It was part of my job. The alarm was going off, so I had to clear the building. But that was the end of it. Until Trustees' Weekend in October. That's when Mr. Zhang spoke to me. Actually, he just dropped in, unannounced. I was meeting with some student, and he just showed up. I knew who he was, and the student left the room. The discussion focused on how earlier, I'd covered a class for Mary, and caught his son cheating on a quiz. Gotta hand it to him. He had crib notes inside a water bottle on his desk. Talk about Smart Water. But he knew that I'd caught him. Didn't like it one bit. Knew I'd report it. It was a Thursday, and Mary's class, so I figured I'd speak with her before I wrote it up since she may have some policy about it, or at least ought to be in the loop. I didn't see her or email her about it before Eric's father showed up the next day. He starts explaining away his son's actions, then pulls out the whole dorm thing, which hadn't been a thing until he didn't like that I caught his son cheating." I leaned in. "He made a not-too-subtle point about how pressing the matter on Eric might cause the dorm matter to be raised, and to be misinterpreted. The message was clear. *Forget my son's cheating, or this other matter will be raised and twisted so as to make you appear to be a creep.* A Peeping Tom."

Scott was scribbling frantically, nodding a bit, and furling his brow and vigorously. When his pen stopped, he looked up at me. "And…why am I just hearing about this now, five, six months later?"

"Why? *Why?* I just told you. This guy is smooth. He didn't get to become a gillionaire playing by the rules. He's bringing it up now because of what I wrote about his son being a prefect. He wanted me to write a rec for him. I didn't want to, but I like having health insurance, y'know? Then I found fireworks in his room, so now I'm not going to recommend him for it. Told the father so in an email. Not the kind of email he enjoyed, I'm sure, so he brings up this dorm thing, which is actually nothing."

"Okay. Still though, why not come to me? Or Barclay. I mean this is serious on a number of levels, Ben."

"Yeah. No kidding. And I'm serious about keeping my job. And this guy knows just what levers to pull."

"Are you sure about all this?"

" 'Course I'm sure. For crying out loud, Scott. I'm also sure that his eyes are gray 'cuz this place is always blowing smoke up his butt. His son has fireworks in his room, so he writes a check and it goes away. The school wants his money? Fine, but that doesn't mean his kid deserves to be a prefect, but me telling him so? That triggered all this." He gazed at me, tapping his pen. "I'm not wrong."

Scott exhaled and started tapping this pen slower and emphatically. "Thing is Ben, if you had documented any of this…but, now, it's just that he has this narrative. And he's a parent."

"He's an *uber* parent. A trustee whose birthday is probably on Barclay's Google Calendar."

Scott held up a palm. "Ben - forget his money. He's a par—"

"Forget it? Really? *Really?* Did you just *hear* yourself?"

"Ben," he went on, "if you'd told someone. You know how it is these days. St. George's, St…Paul's. The stuff at those schools involving teachers made front page news. It's like red meat for the media. They love it when places like this have a scandal. I'm not saying that this is one, but all this news elsewhere, it spooks every school. So now they circle the wagons and have to be extra careful. Can't have even an appearance of—"

"There was nothing that even *appeared*…to be…*anything*." I stabbed a finger in the direction of Eric's dorm. "Here's what there was: the kid's a cheat. His sister is a liar, or at least an embellisher, and dad sat here and spun this whole web so that his kid wouldn't get in trouble for his water bottle stunt." This was offered in what mother would call my outside voice.

"There's no reason to —"

"There's *every* reason to do whatever just violated your delicate sensibilities. C'mon Scott."

"But." he tapped his pen emphatically. "It. Would. Help. If. You. Had,…" With each word he bounced his black roller on the yellow pad. Then he stopped, poising it over the paper, as if searching for the next word, but tapping in the same cadence continued, in a different tone. It was the only noise breaking the silence. We both eyed his motionless pen, then each other. The tapping stopped, and a hinge in need of oil was heard. We looked toward the door, through which Glenn Olson stepped.

"Hey Mr. Minot." He pulled a paper out of a backpack. "Got my essay." His red hair in a tussle, a hoodie and down vest open, he looked like he'd hurried here from his PT appointment. It's a miracle more of our kids don't come down with pneumonia in the winter. The snow that was promised after lunch had started early, and was glistening on his reddened face.

"Th-a-a-a-a-n-k you Glenn," I rose to meet him halfway. "You have a good break, okay?"

As I turned away, he stood still.

"Thanks for the help with it. And…if it matters, I heard the thing that day…here…with Eric's dad."

I paused for a second, to think about whether I'd heard him correctly, then turned back to him.

"What? I'm sorry…*what did you say?*"

"That day when Eric's dad came by. I was here. You were going over some paper with me, like you did for this one, and he showed up. I got a text when I left and sat down outside to respond to it." He tilted his head toward the door. "I texted back, and was waiting for an answer. That chair outside there. It's really great. You could sleep in it. And it was really quiet. In the hallway." Scott was like a statue, chin on his palm, eyeing him. "I wasn't, like, trying to hear stuff," Glenn's facial expression grew defensive. "Like I said, it was real quiet. You couldn't like…*not* hear."

"S-s-s-o-o-o-o-o," I looked away from him and at Scott, "as perhaps the discussion that's been going on here has been a bit more…passionate, for want of a better term, would it be fair to say that you've also heard some of that too?"

He nodded. "I wanted to give you my paper, but I didn't want to interrupt."

"Eavesdropping," Scott cleared his throat, "is not a hobby I'd recommend, Glenn."

"Like I said, I was just, like, here. It's quiet here. Half the school is, like, gone already. Everybody who's still here is at lunch." He started to backpedal toward the door, which was the last thing I wanted.

"It's okay, Glenn," I raised what I hoped was a calming palm. "This is important." I took a deep breath. "It sounds like, you actually remember my conversation with Mr. Zhang. Is that correct?"

"Y-y-y-e-e-a-a-a-h. Maybe because I saw some movie with something like it around then. It had that woman from "Friends." My roommate loves her. "The Rail" or something. He watched it, like, all weekend. It was, like, weird. But, like I said - he loves her. And it sorta reminded me of what, like, Eric's father was saying to Mr. Minot."

Jennifer Aniston. I love her too, although we've never met. The movie is "Derailed." She's in on a blackmail plot that involves squeezing someone to do something. I watched it on a flight to Houston years ago. Wow. I'd never been a fan of parents giving their kids here their streaming passwords - until that moment.

"When you say 'weird,' Glenn, what do you mean?" Scott crossed his arms and legs.

"It sounded like Mr. Minot caught Eric. Mr. Zhang sort of, like, changed the subject. To something in the dorm. I mean, I know a kid in that class. Other kids could see what Eric was..." I turned to look at Scott, who started tapping his pen again.

"Is there a reason that," Scott thinned his lips, "you didn't say anything about this at the time Glenn?"

"Hey," he held up two palms defensively, "This is a teacher thing. And some other kid's parent. I didn't know what I...and like, you're getting on my case now for, like, hearing stuff. And--"

"You hear stuff because you seem to lurk outside doors…" Scott winced.

"Yes," I jumped in, "Thank Christ."

"And what?" Scott asked.

"What?" Glen was a bit unnerved.

"You didn't finish that sentence, about others knowing what Eric was doing."

With this, Glenn looked away for a second, then skyward, then twisted his mouth the way people do when saying something they don't want to utter. "It's…kind of like a thing. Now, anyway. So, some kids when they have tests, they like… He's not the only one who, like, does it. *Not me. Really.*" With that he shot me a pleading look. "You *know* that *right*, Mr. Minot? I don't have a water bottle in your class. You *know* that, *right?*"

For a second, I conjured up the image of Glenn at his desk. Maybe a NY Jets ski cap, but no, no water bottles. I nodded to reassure him.

"How is it you remember all this?" Scott asked.

"The water bottle thing." Glenn shrugged. "It sort of became, like a thing after that. Kids were talking about it in the dorm that night. And hearing a teacher discuss it, like, the next day, I kind of wondered if…y'know, there'd be some new rule about no water bottles in class. And I remembered the fire thing. A whole girls' dorm, like, standing around outside during study hall. We thought we'd be having a drill next, then when, like, the trucks came, we realized it wasn't a drill. And…this kid on my floor – he knows Eric's sister, and heard her talking about it, and saying that she was going to…play it up, sort of."

The three of us were silent. Outside in the distance, shouts of *woo - hoo*! and *done*! were muffled by the windows, suggesting that a final exam had just been let out. Glenn turned slightly and ventured a thumb toward the door. "Can I go?"

I waved his paper in my hand. "Fine with me. Have a great break. Make sure you have the zoom code for my class, okay? And...thank you, Glenn." He nodded once, and looked at Scott.

"Yes, Glenn," Scott nodded, almost begrudgingly. "Thank you for...your perspective." He forced the kind of smile one offers when told that you can't substitute one vegetable for another on a restaurant order. Glenn disappeared into the hallway and I took a chair.

Scott shook his head. "Wow," exhaling and rolling his pen between two fingers and his yellow pad. "I'm...sorry that I had to be so thorough in trying to understand the big picture, Ben."

"Hmmm," I looked out the window behind my desk. "It's good to be *thorough*, but you were doubting my version of things. Doubting *me*." Then I looked at him with my best Liam Neeson stare. "How long have we known each other? I mean, how many times have I lied to you?" I like rhetorical questions. "I'd just like to know something: why would you immediately embrace something a parent says. I'm like...compared to him, the shit on your shoes."

"Ben," he exhaled, "it's not you. And I *did* ask for your version, right? You know the story. Those schools I mentioned. All the scandals: Exeter, Brooks...Because of those creeps, when someone just hints that a teacher is casting any eye towa—"

"Which. I. Didn't. Do." I let the words wash over him. "I was trying to clear the dorm - not for a fire drill, *but an actual fire*, in the microwave, anyway. For Chrissake. Next time I'll just get out the marshmallows."

He let out a sigh of exasperation. "Ben, there's just an increased sensitivity. And we had to follow up on what Zhang said."

"Okay, I get that, but *now*, are you going to follow up on what Glenn said? On what I said that he backed up? I mean, until he spoke up, it sounded like, 'Well, Mr. Zhang said it - it must be true.'"

"I know," he nodded. "It's gotten so we're all scared. A friend of mine at Loomis, which had some nasty stuff come to light there says that even before the facts came out, 'You're accused, yo—'"

"I know, you lose. So when did the Constitution stop applying to us?"

"I know, right? Probably sometime after the former Milton Academy teacher got extradited from Thailand. I mean, the media looks at this stuff the way Sylvester looks at Tweety Pie. So we get proactive and hope we don't turn up on the front page of the *Globe* some morning."

I digested all he said, which sadly had some truth in it. "Okay, but good luck getting teachers to coach a team of the opposite sex or to hold office hours anywhere other than the dining hall during first lunch. I gotta say, Scott, sure, this coronavirus thing sucks, but after the past week - Garmin, this Zhang crap - being remote looks pretty good to me."

At this he nodded ruefully. "I'll write this all up for Barclay," He turned to reach for his coat. "He won't like it, but, nobody should. He might want to hear things from Glenn, but since we heard it, that should do it." He stood and pulled on his coat. "I wouldn't want to be in business with him - Zhang."

"Huh," I reached over to slip Glenn's paper onto my desk. "We already are."

He absorbed this while zipping up his parka and I returned to behind my desk, as if to resume grading.

"Going to lunch?" He slung his pack over a shoulder.

"Not just yet." I forced a hint of a smile. Sometimes you want nothing more than to eat alone.

***

I'd planned to finish grading after lunch, but instead found myself checking the websites of other schools. Seems like everybody is looking for an English teacher, so it might be a good time to cast about, and see if I could scare up some interviews. No place is perfect, though, and Griswold doesn't have the monopoly on kids or parents with defective moral compasses. You have to wonder about schools that have a lot of positions posted - are they lousy places to teach, or are there just a lot of older people on the faculty looking to retire? I've liked to think that our kids are different from kids at public schools, either with their smarts or something else; maturity, the ability to live away from home, something. But most of them were public school kids at one time. It's just arrogant to think that they *are* different.

By four, the snow was still coming down, and I figured I'd move my car so they could plow. Most students had left the dorms by then, save the international ones who have flights tomorrow. In the failing gray light through the flakes, I spotted Fred Tallyrand on the same path I was taking, coming from the library.

"Ben," he waved, trying not to slip on the snow-ice mix underfoot. "Check your email tonight. We're pushing back the deadline for when grades and comments are due. It's now a week from today." As he neared me, he seemed to be wincing in pain.

"You alright Fred?"

"My glasses. I can't wear them in this snow, but I'm blind without them." His face sort of mirrored the sky above; bleak and unremarkable. He looked like a career reference librarian, pale as a result of being cloistered inside for years, who doesn't love his work, but can't retire.

"Guess no outdoor curling for you tonight, eh?" I loathe small talk, but one should seem social.

"No, but we do need someone to drive a van full of students to Logan at five. Interested?"

"In this stuff?" I tossed my head skyward. "Think I'd rather keep grading." This was not true, but nor was I in a mood to be some kids' Uber. "Besides, their flights might be canceled, but comments won't be."

He smiled and nodded. The student activities director sends out email blasts looking for drivers for such runs. If nobody bites, she has to do it. As so many kids now spend weekends in their rooms playing video games rather than signing up for the outings and the things she schedules on campus, her job seems like it's got as much security as that of a lifeguard on a barrier island beach - something that eventually won't exist.

Fred looked up at the snow, then cocked his head to one side, pointing to my woolen Rooster neckwear. "I thought you were going to leave those on the tie rack, after our discussion in the fall."

"Well, I was wearing paisley that day, and said I'd not wear anything like that again this year. And I haven't."

At this, he pulled a face, as if I'd just said that in spite of appearances, it was not in fact snowing all about us. "You mentioned how being literal has merit, or is a thing that matters, to students. So, I was being literal. No paisley since then. I do, however, have a few others."

Here he flashed me a *you-know-better* smirk, but with all that was ahead of us, he had other things to think about. Or so I thought.

"Just, out of curiosity: will you be wearing ties when you teach online in a few weeks?"

Along with how I'll run class discussions on zoom, I hadn't thought about it.

"Is there any reason I shouldn't?"

"I suppose…there isn't." He broke into a slight grin. We both sensed that this would be a good point to part. "Have a good break, Ben."

***

At home now, I just checked the news, and it sounds like not much is going out of Logan. From the lights on in the dorms across the way, I'm guessing no driver was ultimately needed. I started a fire when I got home, just wanting to kick back in front of it with a drink, but goldfish and bourbon do not a dinner make. My unsigned letter for next year was due in Barclay's box by five, but it remains on a sofa end table. Countless teachers go from one school to another each year, and a new school would mean new everything. Coming back to the same place after a year away has been another matter. Just enough things here have changed just enough for it to seem alien in some small ways, and some not so small. It feels like getting a coat back from the dry cleaner that you know has been nicely scrubbed and pressed, but there are still a few spots that just won't come out.

Educators are manic about changing things. In the 1960s, schools taught reading with phonics. Then someone decided that whole language learning was better. Schools and districts went back and forth over which approach was best. One had to sprinkle any discussion of reading with terms like *fluency, context clues* and *scaffolding* in order to sound competent as an educator. Then in the late 1980s, a few bright folks came up with a program that made their company north of $100 million in the first twelve months. Last year, an online version was downloaded over 500,000 times - it's called "Hooked On Phonics." Some people can't leave well enough alone.

I'm not sure if it's just Griswold or teaching in general that's changed. Good parents have long supported their kids, but terms like *helicopter* and *snowplow* parents weren't around a generation ago, and are met with eye rolls and examples when the terms come up; everybody knows a few. Coaches put unathletic kids in starting line-ups rather than hear from parents about how little playing time their children are getting. With the likes of the Zhangs and the Garmins in our midst, hard to know what's ahead. I don't recall any classes on dealing with the likes of *them* in grad school, but schools need families like them, because a school is a business, no matter what anybody says. The new turf fields and gluten-free lunch choices don't just fall from the sky. We call ourselves non-profit, but *genuine* non-profits are like four leaf clovers, yet charities and universities still enjoy that umbrella. Last year, Yale's endowment was more than the GDP of Iceland. Thinking in terms of how some students and parents can be, there might be more prima donnas in New Haven than there are in Reykjavik.

If the paths are shoveled tomorrow, maybe I'll sign my letter and put it in Barclay's box. Not a very calculating way to make a career move, but perhaps I'll be more contemplative in the light of day without the help of this Kentucky product in my glass.

There are no school vehicles plowing the paths or parking lots. From my window, I can still make out the lights in a few faculty houses in spite of the storm. School years and students come and go. I still get emails from kids I had a decade ago, yet have to fumble for the names of some recent graduates when I see them two years later back on campus. No doubt my name and those of other teachers wash out of the minds of countless new grads, perhaps with the help of all the pitchers of beer that are drained in those freshman years at college.

An image under a lamp post at the end of my walkway tonight seems to capture things. Out of the night, big flakes fall into the light's orbit. They swirl around in the glow a bit. Then, just as quickly, they fade into the darkness. Come the morning, they'll be part of a pristine, unspoiled scene for a while. It won't last, but I'll enjoy it while it does. By late spring, all traces of it will be gone. Then, next year, snow will come again, just as students will. There's something to be said for a part of life that is, if not perfect, at least predictable.

Acknowledgments

COMPLETING A BOOK IS nothing if not an exercise in humility. For every accolade one might receive for a 'finished' work, there is a question, suggestion or silence from an individual at a reading which can give an author pause; I don't remember putting *that* dialogue in there...Ultimately, such nudges serve to produce a work that is better than it might have otherwise been. Some people in particular have been both most gracious - and gentle - with their ideas when my own were off the mark. Doug and Sally Cook, accomplished and entertaining authors in their own right, continue to be keen editors who don't miss a thing. Were either of them to become an auditor with the IRS, our nation's federal deficit would soon vanish owing to the "missed" tax payments and corrections they would surely discover.

    Caswell Nilsen is a veteran of several independent schools, and as a summer colleague at Northfield Mount Hermon, he's offered some sage observations about such institutions that have hopefully occurred to administrators as well. A former Poet Laureate of Hampshire, England, Brian Evans-Jones has the gift of thoughtful and gentle suggestion; would that all teachers could do this. I'm thankful that he forsook the old Hampshire for the New one. Jay Gnadadoss and I taught summers at Phillips Academy, and I've treasured his friendship ever since. He once hosted me at Woodbury Forrest School, a visit that inspired a thread in this tale.

Richard Arlington Martin Allen has an eye for detail and flair with technology that was indispensable in this presentation. His ideas were sound, and his talent most appreciated. Page Powell's proofreading underscored the folly of my typing in the wee hours. Eternal thanks, P.

Finally, my wife Holly knows the world of this tale as an alumna and housemother at some of the schools mentioned in this work. She continues to be a paragon of patience as I cloister myself away to write, either in the Crows' Nest or elsewhere. Her support in the face of this anti-social insistence, including a solitary spell in Newport in February of all months, is more than gracious. To her, my enduring love and gratitude.

About the Author

DAVID STORY ALLEN HAS attended and taught at independent schools in the United States as well as in East Asia, including some of the actual schools that appear in this book. With degrees from Syracuse, the University of New Hampshire and Harvard, his novel *Off Tom Nevers*, set at a New England boarding school, was published in 2017. He recently completed a nonfiction book on two murders that occurred years ago in New Hampshire, where he currently teaches and sails.

Minot's Ledge

BACK AT HIS BOARDING school after a year-long sabbatical, English teacher Benjamin C. Minot runs afoul of one of the institution's major donors. Over the course of his tenure, Ben, a notoriously hard marker who has earned the moniker, 'Benjamin C. Minus,' has seen the realities of education morph, with schools now run like businesses where grades and discipline are minefields with parents. The early academic year includes confronting racial profiling, dealing with plagiarism and a whiff of blackmail involving his future. As a strange, new virus emerges, forcing administrators to decide whether to keep the school in session, a teacher weighs whether to keep the school out of the newspapers.

Made in the USA
Middletown, DE
05 May 2024

53855553R00181